Dispossessed

S.A. Khan

BLUEROSE PUBLISHERS
India | U.K.

Copyright © S.A. Khan 2024

All rights reserved by author. No part of this publication may be reproduced, stored in a retrieval system or transmitted in any form or by any means, electronic, mechanical, photocopying, recording or otherwise, without the prior permission of the author. Although every precaution has been taken to verify the accuracy of the information contained herein, the publisher assumes no responsibility for any errors or omissions. No liability is assumed for damages that may result from the use of information contained within.

BlueRose Publishers takes no responsibility for any damages, losses, or liabilities that may arise from the use or misuse of the information, products, or services provided in this publication.

For permissions requests or inquiries regarding this publication, please contact:

BLUEROSE PUBLISHERS
www.BlueRoseONE.com
info@bluerosepublishers.com
+91 8882 898 898
+4407342408967

ISBN: 978-93-6452-756-9

Cover design: Shivani
Typesetting: Sagar

First Edition: July 2024

Disclaimer

While every effort has been made to ensure the accuracy of the material in this book, the author and publisher cannot guarantee error-free content. Therefore, they disclaim any liability for losses, damages, or disruptions caused by errors or omissions, regardless of the cause.

All characters depicted in this book are purely fictional, and their actions, thoughts, and expressions do not reflect the author's beliefs, convictions, or intentions. Any opinions expressed by characters within the narrative are solely for the purpose of storytelling and should not be interpreted as conveying a message or endorsing any particular viewpoint.

The places and institutions mentioned in this book are either entirely fictional or used to fulfill the story's demands. They should not be construed as disrespecting any real-life institutions.

In the event of any defect in printing or binding, the publisher's liability is limited to the replacement of the defective copy with another available copy of this work.

Preface

In the silent depths of our hearts, stories take shape, formed from the intricate patterns of life's experiences, bound together by the strands of memory.

Step Inside: A Firsthand Journey:

This book is written in captivating first-person American English, inviting you to step directly into the protagonist's shoes. Through this immersive narrative style, you'll experience the character's emotions firsthand, witness their observations and thought processes, and gain insight into their unique approach to life.

The Unseen Struggles:

Journey into the hidden recesses of hardship and heartache, where the resilient spirits confront the tangled webs of societal norms. Amidst the backdrop of their struggles, interconnected tales of forbidden love and tragic loss unfold, illuminating the resilience of the human spirit in the face of adversity.

The Veil of Religion:

Religion: The ancient fabric that intertwines belief and fear holds sway over our existence. Its echoes resonate through centuries, reverberating within the sacred spaces of temples, mosques, cathedrals, and synagogues. But what if we dared to lift the veil? What if we glimpsed the unvarnished truth beneath the rituals?

Faithful followers staunchly protect their beliefs, using sacred scriptures as powerful weapons in their defense. Is God truly an omnipotent puppeteer, pulling our strings from celestial heights? Brace yourself for a tale celebrating our differences and underscoring our shared humanity.

For My Guiding Lights:

This book is a testament to my wife's unwavering love. Her patience has been my anchor throughout the years, and her love has been a constant source of strength. I dedicate this book to her with the deepest gratitude for being my rock.

To my daughters, sons-in-law, and grandchildren, whose laughter and triumphs are like a life-giving elixir. Their vibrant presence fuels my desire to see the world unfold, and their encouragement is the spark that keeps igniting the fire within me to write another tale.

Contents

Chapter One 1
    Rajesh Gupta
    A Wish in a Basket

Chapter Two 14
    Angelina Daniel
    A Name, not a Lineage

Chapter Three 26
    Mahendra Reddy
    A Journey of Resilience and Success

Chapter Four 54
    Rukhsana Jahangir
    Life is a Toss

Chapter Five 113
    Samuel Thomas
    Love's Melody

Chapter Six 144
    Aarti Anya
    Betrayal & Loss

Chapter Seven 186
    Mahendra Reddy
    Unrequited Love

Chapter Eight 197
    Angelina Daniel
    Heart of Cold Stone

Chapter Nine 225

> Samuel Thomas
> **Love Across the Divide**

Chapter Ten 245

> Rukhsana Jahangir
> **Reclaiming a Stolen Breath**

Chapter Eleven 278

> Mahendra Reddy
> **Can Scars Ever Truly Heal?**

Chapter Twelve 284

> Angelina Daniel
> **Whispers of Redemption**

Chapter One

Rajesh Gupta

A Wish in a Basket

I, Rajesh Gupta, am a successful businessperson dealing in commodity goods domestically and internationally; my business operation was primarily focused on exporting pulses and rice under our brand name or in bulk packs. At least every alternate week, I had to travel in or outside the country to sort out the marketing and procurement issues or to meet with existing or potential customers. On this chilly morning in December, I arrived from Frankfurt. Even though I slept on the flight all the way in the comfort of business class, I felt sluggish and looked forward to a hot shower and a couple of hours' rest.

Despite being the only child of a wealthy family, my upbringing was in a straitjacket. My mother, a politician at heart and a strict disciplinarian, would invoke my father's dictate whenever I challenged her decisions or refused to adhere to them, proclaiming she had no power to overturn them. When I complained to Dad, he always advised me to adhere to Mom's instructions. I had no choice but to follow the upsetting instructions, like requiring me to wake up early on Saturdays and Sundays for karate classes, swim for at least an hour, and receive tennis lessons from professional coaches in the late afternoon. Every day after school, I would have four different teachers come in one after the other to teach me my prime subjects, with just a fifteen-minute break in between. My mom was shelling out a lot of money for these tutors, and she made it clear that if I didn't get top grades, there would be consequences. Visiting friends was allowed occasionally, with vexing conditions attached. I didn't get a moment of relaxation until I finished school.

Because of Mom, even Dad had to live a structured and disciplined life akin to hers. She ensured all of us slept well, woke up on time, never missed the morning walk, and ate heart-healthy and nutritious food. She never allowed Dad to keep alcohol in the house; however, Dad was permitted to bring a bottle of wine on the weekends, or when we went out for dinner, he was allowed to have a couple of wine glasses.

When I joined the college to earn my commerce degree, I convinced Mom to allow me to go to college in the car, minus the chauffeur. Initially, she refused, but she agreed with a promise to act and behave well. She firmly told me, "Don't you dare to think of getting involved with anyone and must never forget that you would only marry the girl I chose for you."

The car Mom bought for me wasn't expensive but good enough to impress the girls. Since I started going to college, Dad has been filling my pockets without informing Mom, and I found several girlfriends with benefits, happy to enjoy bites and the backseat.

After graduation, I expressed my aspiration to pursue an MBA in the USA, but Mom asked me to enroll at a local university instead. Reluctantly, I complied with her decision and completed my master's degree with good grades; otherwise, Mom would have roasted me alive.

Upon completion of my education, I joined Dad's business, and Mom got busy hunting for the right girl for me to wed. I was about to complete my two years of working life when I got engaged to Ridhi Gupta, a beautiful girl from a wealthy family who was finishing up her postgraduate degree in economics. She was the sole inheritor of her family's wealth following her unmarried brother's demise in a car accident during his Canadian vacation. Our matrimony seems more like a corporate collaboration than a romantic alliance. During our courtship, I observed that she was highly organized, more interested in investment and how to multiply her wealth, and not at all a housewife like my mom. Everything was okay with her, albeit she lacked any capacity for romance; she never allowed me to exceed a few kisses and instead found tremendous joy in discussing financial matters. Whenever we met, she spoke of the world economy and investment opportunities for high returns or about her studies. She ate food to keep her body engine running and never had more than a couple of glasses of wine, whereas I was opposite to her. After completing her postgraduate studies, she joined her dad's business, informing me that we wouldn't merge the two firms, as she wanted to run her dad's empire independently, and I agreed. My father's calm demeanor was a gift I inherited, and I admired how he wholeheartedly supported my mother's endeavors, never clipping her wings. Naturally, I aspired to continue this legacy in my own life.

We eventually got married and had two sons, just under two years. However, after our second child, she refused to have any more, citing concerns about her physical appearance and her unaffordable extended absence from work. I was depressed for several months as I wanted a girl, and even Mom and Dad wanted her to have a third child in the hopes of having a granddaughter. Despite attempts to persuade her, her resolute character made it difficult to sway her opinion or compel her to conform to our wishes.

Her father's health had been deteriorating since the loss of his son. Faced with constant challenges, she lamented the poor skills of her existing staff. The dilemma arose as her father opposed firing them. Instead of letting go of fatigued staff members, I suggested she relocate them to positions where routine work is required, hire a team of young and dynamic brains, adopt a decisive leadership approach, and demonstrate strength and compassion. With her steadfast dedication to business development, she cultivated a team of exceptional minds, and through my continuous support, she effectively retained control over her enterprises. Soon, through her tireless efforts, she singularly achieved the extraordinary milestone of turning the business into a billion-dollar company. My business was also experiencing growth, though it was still far from matching the scale of her hugely diversified enterprises.

She was a loving wife and caring mother. Despite having a team of nannies and caregivers, she made sure to spend enough time with our children. At least once or twice a week, she would take them out for some fresh air and indulge them with their favorite food. She became my weakness as she looked after me so well that I did not have to move a finger, my clothes, my inners, my food, and exhausted my physical needs, so I didn't have to fool around. She once told me whatever I did before marriage wasn't her concern, but now, if I dared to play around, she would ensure that my tool became ineffective. Though it was meant to be funny, I couldn't shake off the seriousness of her tone. Anyhow, I wouldn't dream of hurting my caring and understanding wife, and even otherwise, I was so wrapped up managing my business's expansion that there wasn't even a spare moment to consider playing around.

Tragically, in the fifth year of my marriage, my parents were involved in a fatal car accident. Their vehicle collided with a speeding truck while returning from a marriage reception held at a distant farmhouse situated along a single-track road. 'When it rains, it pours,' just as we were still reeling from the loss of my parents, another tragedy struck.

Ridhi's father passed away due to organ failure. With Ridhi's mother left alone and almost bedridden, we brought her to our house. Overwhelmed by grief from the loss of her son and then her husband, Ridhi's mother stopped eating, gradually wasting away until she joined them in death just a few months later.

My house was on the city's periphery, in an affluent neighborhood where only the wealthiest families could afford to own a property.

In the midst of my wandering thoughts, I encountered an incredible sight. Barely 100 meters from my house, lying on the footpath, was a shining baby carry cot. I instructed the driver to stop the vehicle and check the cot to see whether or not a baby was inside. He returned and said, "Sir, there is a baby in it, and most likely alive since I noticed the abdominal movement indicative of respiration."

I got out of the car to look and noticed a gorgeous infant with golden hair, who looked like a Caucasian, swaddled in a pricey blanket. A sticky note named 'Rukhsaar Daniel' was affixed to the blanket, indicating that she was a girl. It was evident from the umbilical cord that she must have been born just a few hours ago, and upon lifting the nappy, it was confirmed that it was a girl. Unfortunately, there was no one in the vicinity, and I feared that if I did not take her to a place where she could be nourished and cared for, she wouldn't survive beyond a few hours. So, first, I captured several photos of her using my pocket camera, which I carried during my travels. Subsequently, I contacted the area assistant commissioner of police and notified him that she would perish unless I took her to a place where she could be fed and looked after. The officer agreed, saying, "If anyone reports a missing baby, I'll contact you." I then called my wife and informed her I would come late; I found a newborn baby girl, and she must be handed over to a care center, or else she wouldn't survive.

A few years ago, I learned that one of the city's most prominent convent schools also had a small orphanage. Only newborns who had been abandoned were accepted into this institution. During the colonial era, the school was established to cater specifically to British subjects and was situated on sprawling land. Additionally, on the same premises, an orphanage was constructed to house the children of British army men and women who could not raise them for various reasons. Following the country's independence, the local clergy assumed control of the facility's administration and successfully maintained its upkeep.

After arriving at the school, I was guided to a separate building on the far left of the expansive school grounds. At the entrance of the orphanage, a welcoming nun listened to the reason for my visit. Then she led me to the office of the orphanage's administrator, Ms. Lisa Fernandes, an elderly nun in charge. She greeted me with a broad smile, and after hearing me patiently, she asked the name of the assistant commissioner. She then called someone and asked whether there was an officer by the name I had given her and disconnected the line upon hearing the response. Next, she took out an address book, and after finding what she was looking for, she dialed another number and asked the person who answered the call to connect with the assistant commissioner to whom I had informed about the baby. Finally, after conversing with him briefly and getting a reaffirmation of my statement, she ended the call.

She rose from the chair and thoroughly checked the baby and the cot without telling me what she sought. She returned to her desk, pressed her desk call bell, and asked the attendant to send Ms. Joseph. A few minutes later, a young nun entered the office and got instructions from Lisa to take the baby and feed her, as she must be hungry and dehydrated.

After a while, she addressed me and said, "Sir, the police officer you had mentioned confirmed that you're a respectable businessperson, and you did find the girl on the road leading to your house. The officer's statement was enough for us to take the child into our custody; however, you need to sign a document confirming your statement and that we're authorized to hand over the baby to the police if they receive a complaint of stealing her."

I agreed and expressed my gratefulness to her for accepting the baby. She paused momentarily and said, "You must give your written approval to our terms before we can admit the baby into our facility. Firstly, children in our care are baptized to follow the Christian faith. Secondly, all children are placed with loving families before they reach the age of ten, and we maintain the confidentiality of the adoptive families' identities and whereabouts. In the event that the child does not find a family before completing their schooling, we encourage them to either seek employment within the school or find a job of their choice. However, since I assumed responsibility, this situation has never arisen."

"Given her mixed Muslim and Christian heritage, I don't see any problem with your stipulation that she be christened. Next, I'll adopt her before she reaches your threshold age of ten years. To guarantee my commitment, I want to become her Godfather, and I'll give a substantial donation to provide you confidence in my commitment," I stated firmly.

"That's wonderful, and I have no issues making you her Godfather and accepting your donation to confirm your adoption of the baby in the coming years," said Lisa.

"I would like to donate a substantial amount in exchange for special care for the baby. Is that possible?" I questioned.

"We take great pride in providing the highest quality care for all the children under our watchful eye, which cannot be improved further with our existing resources. So, I must refuse to accept your request for special treatment; let me tell you that we maintain a strict policy of not providing preferential treatment to any child in exchange for compensation. I want you to know that we are operating near full capacity but still accommodating the baby you brought." With a slight raise in her voice and a touch of sarcasm, she continued her ramblings, "As you are someone who is well-off and has shown an interest in becoming the child's godfather, it might be more suitable for you to provide her with accommodation in your house."

"You're right; I have significant financial means and wanted to ensure the baby receives the best care possible. The thought crossed my mind to have her stay with us, but I had a feeling my wife wouldn't be willing to accommodate the idea. Moreover, I'm hesitant to assign the responsibility on any of our domestic help. I learned about your orphanage a few years back and wanted to include your institution in my Diwali donations, but it slipped from my memory. Regardless, let's leave the past behind. Please inform me of the amount required to improve the facility so that every child receives the finest care and education, allowing them to become valuable members of society and the nation," I said earnestly.

After hearing me out, she composed herself, paused briefly, and said, "Sir, rather than specifying our requirements, I prefer that you contribute whatever amount you feel at ease with giving. However, allow me to be candid; we needed money to renovate the building's interiors, buy new furniture, fittings, and furnishings, and increase the number of caregivers."

When I told Lisa I wanted to see the inside of the children's accommodation, she immediately agreed and asked a nun to give me a building tour. I observed that the orphanage was segregated into four sections: the initial one for newborns, the second for children aged 3 to 5, and separate halls for boys and girls aged six and above. The building was sprawling and sturdy, made primarily of stone and timber, but only one-third was currently occupied.

Everything inside appeared to be in dire need of repair or replacement. I was informed that the orphanage was home to 49 boys and girls; however, girls were the majority. The staff responsible for their care included two cooks, two cleaners, and five nuns. Lisa correctly stated that the support staff scarcely met the facility's requirements.

Before departing, I signed multiple documents and obtained the institution's bank details to deposit my bequest.

I had no idea, but the moment I set my eyes on the baby, I immediately felt a profound, heartwarming love for her, perhaps because I had always wanted a daughter. I knew my wife too well; she wouldn't look after the baby and would not allow me to bring her home, even to entrust her to a nanny's care. Attempting to persuade or charm her into accepting the idea was futile; she was unyielding as a stone, and expecting any flexibility from her was a mere daydream.

I reached my office late in the afternoon. First, I transferred five million rupees to the orphanage's bank account. Following that, I got in touch with my wife, encouraging her to transfer a substantial sum to the Christian orphanage where I had admitted the newborn girl I found this morning. Understanding the pressing need for enhancements at the orphanage, she, without any hesitation, agreed to match the amount I had donated, a figure that held little significance for her. Next, I called all my close business associates, and nearly everyone consented to donate whatever they could. By the following evening, slightly more than twenty million rupees had been deposited into the orphanage's bank account.

Before I could call Lisa to inform her of the transferred funds, she called and thanked me for the generous donations, which would be more than enough for refurbishing and procuring furniture and furnishings. Additionally, I need not be concerned about the infant's welfare, as she had been entrusted to the care of one of their most skilled caregivers.

In a gathering attended by a few orphanage officials, Rukhsaar Daniel was rechristened as Angelina Daniel, and I gladly accepted the responsibility of being her Godfather.

Time began to flow at its own pace. Days morphed into weeks, weeks stretched into months, and months progressed into years. When Angie was three years old, I sold my business to a corporate entity that had grown weary of my undercutting tactics, which had caused them to struggle to maintain their market share and profitability. The sales money received was 160 crores; out of this amount, I invested 120 crores to buy shares of my wife's company. With the remaining forty crores, I carefully deliberated, consulting with my wife, and finally made the decision to start a construction company. We saw the immense potential in the city's expansion and the increasing property prices. The decision proved to be wise, as by the second year, I not only recovered all our expenses but also generated a modest profit. Things started picking up for my business in the following years, bringing in nice profits. During one of my visits to Angie, who was then eight years old, she posed a question that pierced my heart. She asked me, "Papa, why don't you take me to your home? All my schoolmates live with their parents while I reside in an orphanage." I struggled to respond for a few moments before finally saying, "Honey, once you grow up, I'll tell you everything you want to know." But she never asked me that question again. However, a few months later, I learned from Lisa that Angie had asked her why her Papa never took her to his house, and she had to answer her.

During a courtesy visit to Lisa when Angie was twelve years old, she shared that Angie was brilliant in her studies, consistently ranked at the top of her class, and only spoke when necessary; otherwise, she was always busy with her studies. Unfortunately, the orphanage doesn't have any children her age; the others are much younger, leaving her without a suitable companion. Additionally, Angie was known for her selflessness as she would give anyone who asked her anything she had: the word 'NO' wasn't in her vocabulary. Although Angie had an enviable wardrobe full of high-end clothes, courtesy of her Godfather, she never seemed to put much effort into dressing well. For Lisa, this was the only flaw she could see in her personality.

Year after year, my business soared as I built villas in gated communities for the affluent. I adhered to the principle of exceeding customer expectations in delivery time and the quality of deliverables, fueling remarkable growth.

My wife's great-grandfather, a UK-educated landlord, established a bicycle production venture with assistance from a British Engineer employed by The Raleigh Bicycle Company, a renowned UK-based firm founded in 1888 in Nottingham. Over time, the business expanded under the leadership of her grandpa and father, branching out into the production of truck, car, and two-wheeler tires. My wife then took over and expanded the business further, collaborating with Japanese manufacturers to produce small to medium-sized pickup trucks and tractors. Recently, she established a massive unit to manufacture cars under the license of a well-known Japanese brand. Our sons, who have completed their MBAs, have joined her. The older son oversees the African continent from Cape Town-South Africa, while the younger son is stationed in Hong Kong to manage the Asian countries. Under her leadership, her company went public; she retained seventy-six percent of the stock while offering only twenty-four percent to institutions, corporate entities, and the public.

I was interested in having one of our sons join my business, but both declined, and I completely understand their rationale. On the one hand, there is a massive multi-billion-dollar empire; on the other, there is a teeny-weeny construction company. It would be injudicious for anyone, even a fool, to make such an imprudent choice. I anticipated this scenario a long ago and was preparing Angie to assume control of my business. She's currently pursuing her M.Tech in Construction Engineering and Management from IIT, New Delhi, and is expected to join me in half a year. God tremendously blessed me with an amazing child endowed with intelligence, compassion, and a caring nature. I am confident that when the time comes for me to pass, she will be the one by my side, providing me with the needed comfort to pass peacefully.

Chapter Two

Angelina Daniel

A Name, not a Lineage

The other kids at the orphanage looked up to me with envy because my wealthy Godfather bought me clothes, fashion accessories, and the latest electronics, regardless of whether I needed them.

Since my days in secondary school, a deeply ingrained notion persisted in my mind: I was born with a disadvantage. Unlike my fellow students, I lacked a place to call home, a mother or father to share stories about the school activities or tell friends what their mothers cooked for them, where they spent their weekends, the movies they watched in theatres, and how their fathers pampered them. Unfortunately, my misfortune extended beyond these absences, as most of my fellow girls in the orphanage were adopted by European or American families before they turned ten, presumably relishing the comforts of their foster homes.

From eighth grade onward, apprehension about my future gripped me when I found out that my Godfather had signed my adoption papers, planning to take custody of me after I completed my school education. I once mustered the courage to inquire why he couldn't bring me to his home like the other children at school. His response was cryptic, promising to reveal everything when I reached adulthood. Several months later, I received a call from Lisa Ma'am, who was checking up on my studies. Seizing the opportunity, I asked her why my Papa hadn't taken me to his house like the other kids. In response, she patiently elucidated the concept of an orphan, shared the story of how my Godfather found me, and explained that he was a prosperous businessman and compassionate person. She urged me to take pride in being adopted by such an extraordinary person, reassuring me that he would warmly embrace me into a new and loving home once I had finished my schooling. I had a constant fear looming over me, the fear of what if something happened to him or if he didn't take me into his home, I would spend the rest of my life in this dismal dungeon, condemned to sweeping classrooms and cleaning toilets. The mere thought of spending the rest of my life within the school premises sent shivers down my spine, leaving me drenched in cold sweat. Nonetheless, I had no choice but to face whatever was my destiny and remain focused on my studies.

When I was in the tenth grade or, say, my final year in the orphanage, my class teacher recognized my exceptional aptitude in all the math subjects. She advised me to pursue engineering, acknowledging my natural gift.

During the same year, I gathered the courage to confide in my Godfather and said to him, "Papa, your adoption has caused me great discomfort and stress. I understand that you cannot make me a member of your family and take me to your house. However, I am clueless about what awaits me once I complete my schooling. All the girls and boys younger than me have been adopted by Europeans and Americans and must be living in the comforts of their new abodes. In contrast, I'm living in a precarious situation, not knowing what I'll do once I finish my schooling. Papa, I want to make it clear that my concerns are not rooted in ingratitude. I genuinely appreciate your generosity and the way you have cared for me, akin to that of a biological father. However, I have come to a point where my future seems uncertain. If I don't take the reins and plan my path forward while I still have time on my side, I fear I will be condemned to a life of unhappiness and hardship."

With a surprised look and a smile teasing his lips, Papa said, "It's such a joy to witness my baby has matured, considering her path ahead. Tomorrow, take a break from school and join me so we can brainstorm and devise strategies to ensure a secure future for you."

"Papa, I apologize if I unintentionally hurt your feelings. Lately, I've been experiencing terrifying nightmares, and it's been causing anxiety attacks and making it difficult for me to concentrate on my studies even when I'm awake," I explained sincerely.

"Honey, you should have informed me earlier. Although I may not be your biological father, please never question my love for you. Remember, your Papa is always here for you, ready to provide both time and resources," Papa said.

Papa's comforting words struck a chord, and tears welled up in my eyes. In a choked voice, I managed to express, "Thank you, Papa. When should I expect you to come and pick me up?"

"Around ten, and bye for now," Papa said, came to my settee, took me in his arms for a couple of minutes, rubbed my back, kissed my forehead, and left the reception room of our building. I noticed his moist eyes.

The next day, as promised, Papa picked me up at ten, took me to his bank, opened a bank account in my name, deposited fifty lakhs into it, and gave me a debit card. From there, he took me to his three-story office building, which had a brass metal signboard of Rajesh Builders, a beautiful reception area, and a plumpish lady behind the reception counter who welcomed us with a big grin.

Papa stopped at the reception and addressed the receptionist, "Nikitha, meet my daughter, Angie; whenever she visits, kindly escort her directly to my office, regardless of whether I'm with visitors or in a staff meeting."

Nikitha and I shook hands and exchanged pleasantries, and then Papa guided me to the back of the reception to an elevator that took us to the third floor. Lift opened in a long open hall with small cubicles where men and women worked on their computers. At the end of the corridor were several small and large glass cabins occupied by probably senior executives, and at the far end, two rooms made of concrete walls adorned with teak doors. One of the rooms had a Meeting Room brass plate, while the other had a Managing Director plate. Papa walked ahead, approached the MD room, opened it, and gestured for me to enter. Stepping inside, I found myself in a spacious room featuring a large desk and a high-back leather chair. In front of the desk were four leather sofas arranged with accompanying coffee tables, a large glass-top table in the middle, and on it a fresh assorted flower bouquet. Papa took hold of my hand, guided me toward his chair, and asked me to sit on it. Despite my reluctance and protests, he insisted, pushing me into the chair until I slumped on to it.

Papa sat on the sofa facing me and said, "This is your office and your business; study hard and make yourself worthy of running this company. We're among the top ten builders in the city and construct gated communities, high-end luxury villas, and apartments. At any given time, we have a minimum of ten and a maximum of fifteen sites in various stages of construction. We have earned a reputation in the market for delivering projects ahead of committed time and giving more than what was promised on paper. Our annual turnover for the last fiscal year was a little over three hundred crores, with a net profit of fourteen percent.

"Soon, I'll buy in your name a lavishly furnished villa in one of our upcoming compounds. I'll make sure you have a car at your disposal to get around. Plus, I'll hire a dedicated team of housemaids to take care of everything, with two of them to stay with you around the clock. In addition, every month, one lakh rupees will be deposited into your account to cover your personal expenses.

"In a while, our company lawyer will come and brief you on what I have done for you to ensure that you receive a reasonable income as long as you're alive. Honey, your fears are not unfounded, and if I were in your position, I would also think about my future, particularly when I didn't provide you with any financial security instruments. However, I thought about it several years ago and took a life insurance policy of twenty crores and made you a sole beneficiary. In case of my death due to any cause before the age of sixty-five, you would receive this sum, and if I cross the set age limit, you will get a lumpsum amount that would also be significant. The lawyer's office has got the policy document and my WILL," before Papa could finish his oration, there was a knock on the door.

A smartly dressed man, probably in his late forties or early fifties, entered the room, and Papa gestured for him to sit beside his sofa.

"Angie, this is Amit Kumar, our chief accountant; he'll brief you about our company's future plans," Papa said. Amit cleared his throat and slowly said, "Hello, Angie; as your dad informed you, I look after the finances of the company. Yesterday, your dad instructed me to convert our sole proprietorship company into a limited liability company (LLC). This change in structure means the business will have at least two directors/owners. Once you turn 16 years old, you will become a Director and a forty-nine percent stakeholder in the company. When you come on board as director, you will receive a monthly salary equal to your father's, along with the same perquisites he currently enjoys. These benefits include but are not limited to a company car, an accommodation allowance, worldwide medical insurance cover, four weeks annual paid leave, and a company credit card for customer entertainment expenses."

I stared at him blankly, unsure of how to respond. I couldn't express my gratitude to Amit since he was doing his job and thanking Dad in front of him felt awkward.

"Any questions?" Amit asked.

"I may not have in-depth knowledge about the legal aspects of company formation, but I do know that Papa's biological children are the legal heirs of his business and could potentially challenge this decision in court, deeming the partnership formation illegal. Therefore, excluding me from being a partner or even an employee would be best," I said earnestly.

Papa cut in, saying, "Angie, you've hit the nail on the head. The biological heirs might have a rightful stake in the business, but their immense wealth makes the prospect of a business generating merely a few crores a year unappealing. I'll fill you in on my wife's business shortly, and rest assured, there's no need to fret over such matters. Our corporate lawyer will be joining us soon to clarify everything."

"Papa, I respectfully decline to join the company. I couldn't bear the weight of feeling like I've unfairly taken someone else's share of wealth," I stated firmly, though softly.

After a brief pause, Papa excused the accountant and turned to me, saying, "While I may be your foster father, my love for you surpasses compared to my two biological sons. Besides, they have already joined my wife's business, which is a massive multibillion-dollar empire. They would never waste their valuable time dragging you into court over a business with little significance. To provide more insight into my family dynamics, I offered one of my sons the opportunity to join my business. Still, both declined and chose to work for their mother's corporate enterprise instead. So, please don't feel guilty that you have unjustly taken away anyone's wealth. It's your Papa's self-acquired business, and you have every right to become a partner in it and eventually become the owner of this company. Allow me to share my family business, which I sold."

He explained the scale of their business, noting, "We had ten massive warehouses equipped with a variety of loading and offloading equipment and numerous trucks. The assets were valued at nearly 80 crores." He further shared that he obtained an equivalent amount, 80 crores, as goodwill. He then established this company with forty crores and invested the rest in his wife's company, which has grown significantly. That investment also belongs to me, as his wife and children have signed the WILL in confirmation that he's free to assign the shares to his foster daughter.

I silently listened to Papa's words with a stone face; his words failing to sink in could be why I didn't feel elated or dismayed. I wasn't a person of hunger for anything; I just wanted to continue my studies and find a job to make two ends meet. My nightmares and anxiety attacks originated from the uncertainty of whether I could continue my studies and become an engineer or remain on the school premises to do odd jobs. With the fifty lakhs in my bank account, I hope to continue my studies, secure my dream engineering degree, and even secure a postgraduate degree from here or abroad.

Papa broke the silence and said, "Angie, I have a request for you. I believe it would be beneficial if you aim to secure a Construction Engineering and Management degree from any IIT. This qualification will greatly assist you in running this business. Over the past few years, I have faced tremendous pressure from my top executives to expand our operations both here and across major cities. I have consistently resisted this pressure, as I didn't want to overwhelm myself with excessive work and stress that could harm my well-being. However, once you're on board, I will invest substantial money, allowing you to expand or diversify the business according to your preferences."

"Papa, I have aimed to secure a degree in engineering and will go according to your wish; however, I don't want to join you because I don't believe your children would easily relinquish a few crores that could fill their coffers annually. Please, Papa, I implore you to keep me away from your business and allow me to study as much as I desire to earn a respectable livelihood," I pleaded earnestly.

As I was speaking, the intercom bell chimed. After I concluded my statement, Papa walked over to the table, picked up the phone, listened to the caller, and said, "Please, send him in." A bald man with an average height and build, appearing to be in his early fifties, entered the room within a few minutes. He wore a neatly pressed light, beige-colored suit with a dark blue checkered tie. My father introduced him as Jatin Parikh, the general practice lawyer handling all personal and corporate compliance issues. After exchanging pleasantries briefly, my father requested the lawyer to provide me with a comprehensive overview of his WILL and the company's formation and to address any queries I had.

Parikh turned to me and said, "Angie, it's important for you to know that nearly five years ago, your father made a definitive WILL, naming you as the sole heir to his business and properties. This inheritance includes the substantial real estate he acquired from his parents and the shares he held in his wife's company. As of today, your dad has no debts, and there is no possibility of him incurring any in the future because the company has a comprehensive insurance policy that covers any losses resulting from poor workmanship or accidental dismemberment or deaths of workers during the onsite execution of projects. This ensures the company's financial security in such unfortunate events. In addition to what was stipulated in the WILL, he bolstered further security for you by obtaining a Life Insurance Policy worth twenty crore rupees, with you as the designated beneficiary.

"His WILL was countersigned and accepted by your dad's wife and his two biological sons, which means that it cannot be legally challenged, regardless of whether your dad is alive or not. Your Dad has initiated the process of converting his sole proprietorship company to a limited liability company, making you a forty-nine percent partner in the company. You will become the company's sole owner in case of his death. If you have any questions, feel free to ask me."

"Papa, why are you doing this? It's unjust to your family. They may have been coerced into signing, and I fear they'll come to regret it, perhaps even resorting to harming me. If you could support my college education, that would mean the world to me, and I would be eternally grateful. I beg you to rescind the WILL and grant me the chance to live a peaceful life," I pleaded, tears streaming down my cheeks as I struggled with the pain deep within.

Papa beckoned me to come and sit by his side, and as I obliged, he embraced me tenderly, gently wiping away the tears on my cheeks with a paper tissue. "Angie, you cannot comprehend the immense wealth that my wife possesses. Compared to hers, my own riches are meager crumbs on her plate. My sons willingly signed the WILL without any pressure or coercion. In fact, they were delighted to have a foster sister and glad that I am leaving my modest wealth to you. Please, do not burden yourself with guilt over taking away their inheritance or causing them any injustice.

"I brought you here today to show you my office so that in the future, if there is ever a situation that prevents me from visiting you, you may call any of my executives or come here to find out where I am. The other objective was to introduce you to my lawyer to explain to you my WILL and the partnership in the company once you turn sixteen. I thought you were too young to comprehend the WILL or business partnership and that I should wait for you to complete your school education and then enlighten you. However, from our conversation yesterday, I understood that you have grown up and are worried about your future, which is giving you anxiety attacks and nightmares. Now, you must have learned that you can educate yourself as much as you want, and as an adult, even without working, you can live a comfortable life as long as you're alive," Papa said. His words flowed into my ears like a soothing balm, relieving me from the burden of insecurity and unease. My goal in life was never to rely on Papa's wealth but rather to become an engineer, ensuring I earned a respectable livelihood. When the time is right, I will inform Papa that I wish to live life on my own terms, without the need for the money that rightfully belongs to his sons, the legitimate heirs. Since that moment, time has flown by, and now I am in the final year of my master's program in Construction Engineering and Management at IIT, New Delhi. When I began my advanced studies here, nearly every male student in my class and even some seniors proposed marriage to me. However, I politely declined their proposals, informing them I was already betrothed. Long ago, I made the decision that I couldn't hide my past, and even if I were to marry a virtuous person, eventually, one day, he or his family would use my past to humiliate and hurt me. It is better for me to remain single and find happiness in my work, travel across the world, and please myself with whatever worldly possessions can give me pleasure.

Chapter Three

Mahendra Reddy

A Journey of Resilience and Success

Twelve years ago, I, Mahendra Reddy, opened my eyes in a village orphanage far away from Hyderabad City. The orphanage was established by a philanthropic couple from the same village, who unfortunately could not conceive a child of their own. They transformed their ancestral agricultural land into a haven for abandoned babies. On a gloomy, rain-soaked night, a mysterious car materialized out of the darkness and dumped me in a cradle placed outside the orphanage. This battered wooden haven, a designated dumping ground for unwanted children, was my first home.

For better or worse, I somehow managed to survive that fateful night, eluding the grips of frigid temperatures, thirst, and starvation. The compassionate couple, known for their early-rising habits, discovered me and promptly provided care, ensuring I was cleaned and nourished. They named me Mahendra even though nothing was great about me and graciously bestowed their surname upon me since they belonged to the Reddy community. When I was nine years old, the boys and girls at the orphanage started teasing me, saying I must have been fathered by a film hero, given my fair complexion and distinct features that set me apart from others. I was notably the tallest among all the boys of my age.

The orphanage premises stood a capacious residence comprising two large halls segregated for the girls' and boys' dormitories. Additionally, there were six rooms: one for the care of toddlers, another was a playroom for kids of 3-5 years, one room was the residence of owners, two rooms were for the women caregivers, and the remaining one large room was kept vacant for visitors. The kitchen was adjacent to the main building, boasting a spacious cooking area and several steel chairs and tables in a corner for dining. A buffalo pen at the far end of the six-acre backyard accommodated about five impressive animals adjacent to a sizable poultry enclosure. Additionally, there were four rooms allocated for the families who managed the agricultural tasks and cared for the buffalos and hens. The remaining expanse of land was devoted primarily to cultivating vegetables and rice.

Almost every weekend, an NGO based in Hyderabad would send a group of five to ten young boys and girls to our orphanage. They would arrive loaded with books, toys, cookies, and chocolates and stay with us for the entire weekend. Their purpose for visiting was to play with us and assist with subjects we struggled with. Their effortless conversations in English with each other intrigued me, igniting a strong desire to speak the elite language with equal fluency.

Through our village schoolteacher, we all managed to learn a few English words to read, but without understanding their meaning. While every child in the orphanage eagerly looked forward to the weekend for the treats it brought, my excitement came from a different source. I anxiously awaited the weekend because it gave me the opportunity to observe them conversing in English.

The young girls and boys seemed to be coming for a joyful picnic. They eagerly joined in activities like milking the buffalos, picking fresh vegetables, collecting eggs from the poultry enclosure, and assisting the cook in preparing mouthwatering chicken biryani and curries. Although they were expected to teach us, their youthfulness prompted them to enjoy most of their weekend, and neither we nor the supervising couple ever requested them to educate us in any subject.

For reasons I couldn't quite explain, I discovered a profound love for cooking, alongside my fervent ambition to master the English language. While other children engaged in various games during the evenings, I spent my time in the kitchen, assisting the cook with dinner preparations. I enthusiastically chopped vegetables and onions, ground spices, and skillfully prepared chapatis and rice. Thanks to my cook Guru, who valued my services and supported my enthusiasm by teaching me how to cook. By the time I turned twelve, I had become skilled in whipping up delectable vegetarian and non-vegetarian curries, effortlessly managing the intricacies of cooking rice, and smoothly mastering the art of rolling chapatis. Nowadays, my passion is dedicated to further enhancing my culinary skills, specifically in the precision of preparing pulao, biryani, and a variety of sweet dishes.

I never neglected my other passion for becoming proficient in English. Apart from English course books, I used to bring old English newspapers from school and read them without thoroughly understanding even twenty percent of the contents. Since I was nine, I began constructing small sentences, although speaking posed a challenge. Despite the difficulties, I persisted in my efforts. One day, a visiting boy asked me about my strengths and weaknesses in various subjects. I poured my heart out and expressed my desire to master English, speak fluently like him, and write like a newspaper columnist. Curious, he inquired about my reading and writing abilities. I confessed that while I could read, I struggled to comprehend hardly twenty percent of the text, and my writing was limited to simple few-word sentences that could have grammatical errors. Speaking was particularly tough, with only a few words at my disposal.

He reassured me not to worry and promised to send a few books with the next group arriving the following week, which would greatly aid my language learning. As promised, the following week, I received a package containing the following books:

- The Blue Book of Grammar and Punctuation, by J. Straus, L. Kaufman, and T. Stern
- Merriam-Webster Dictionary.
- The Quick and Easy Way to Effective Speaking by Dale Carnegie.
- Word Power Made Easy by Norman Lewis.
- Speak English Like a Star: Learning English was Never So Easy by Yogesh Vermani.

I dedicated nearly four months to thoroughly studying the entire Grammar book, assiduously memorizing the foundational concepts until constructing a sentence without a grammatical error became effortless for me. Afterward, I began dedicating myself to improving my spoken English by utilizing the three books on spoken English. Upon returning from school, I would seek out a secluded spot and audibly recite the book's contents, tirelessly practicing the steps of speaking. My distinctive behavior aroused speculation among those at the orphanage, as they observed my reluctance to mingle or engage in play, leaving them wondering about the cause of my isolation. Instead, I spent my time either in the kitchen or in a corner, earnestly speaking aloud to myself.

I incessantly educated myself to the point where I could speak and comprehend the Lingua Franca with remarkable proficiency. This accomplishment astonished the visiting boys and girls, who wondered how well I had educated myself. I frequently requested feedback on my language and diction, but they consistently assured me that no correction was necessary. Instead, they urged me to increase my vocabulary as much as possible, stressing that effective communication relies heavily on using well-chosen words. I took their advice to heart and devoted the following year to precisely this endeavor.

As I approached the age of fourteen and attained a height of five feet and eight inches, surpassing all the other boys, I realized it was time to bid farewell to the orphanage. Moreover, per the orphanage's rules, once we turned sixteen, we had to take some travel and subsistence money and say goodbye, or we were sent to Hyderabad NGO, which assisted us in securing a suitable job and a place to reside. The NGO primarily arranged positions for boys as waiters in moderately priced restaurants or salesmen in retail stores. At the same time, girls were typically offered roles as domestic help or saleswomen, but they don't accept anyone less than sixteen years old.

The prospect of waiting another two years and continuing to study mundane subjects like history and geography was disheartening. One day, I made a firm decision: no more waiting. I resolved to seize control of my destiny, venture into the city, secure any job as a temporary respite, and subsequently explore opportunities that had the potential for growth and provided a means to make a respectable living.

Opting not to contact my ailing Godfather, who was confined to his bedroom due to illness, I sought assistance from Sujata Ma'am, the wife of the orphanage owner and the Amma of all the children. I expressed my desire to leave the orphanage, and she looked at me for a while and said, "Since you're not sixteen yet, I can't send you to the NGO. Are you willing to venture out on your own, find a job, and settle down?"

I replied, "Yes, Amma. I may not be sixteen, but I appear mature, and apart from Telugu and Hindi, I can speak English fluently. With these strengths, I am confident that I can secure employment that would provide me with at least two meals a day and a place to stay."

She acknowledged, "You're correct, and I have no doubt that you would have no trouble finding a job as a salesperson or some other similar job. However, I do have concerns due to your age."

Considering her almost agreement but needing further persuasion, I politely responded, "Amma, I humbly request your permission to venture forth with your blessings. Not only have I experienced physical growth, but I have also cultivated a mature mindset that enables me to confidently confront any challenges that come my way to ensure my survival."

Her gaze fixed upon me with intensity, and after a moment of contemplation, she replied, "Very well, I bestow upon you my blessings and offer you two thousand rupees. If you encounter any hurdles in securing a suitable job, do not hesitate to return; this place will always be your home. Remember, you will forever be my baby, and even if you succeed in achieving your aims, visit us whenever you can."

"I thank you, Amma, from the depth of my heart and promise to visit you whenever I find time," I said earnestly.

The following day, I boarded the morning bus bound for Hyderabad, carrying my meager possessions of a few books, two pairs of jeans and T-shirts gifted to me by a girl who had visited a couple of months ago, and two thousand rupees. Upon reaching Hyderabad at noon, hunger gnawed at my stomach, prompting me to wander towards a moderately crowded street, hoping to find a street food vendor to satiate my appetite. Fortune smiled upon me as I stumbled upon an elderly man peddling samosas (Rissole) from his four-wheeled pushcart. I purchased two samosas from him, which were yummy, and noticing the absence of customers, I took the opportunity to share my story. I told him that I had journeyed from a small village in search of employment and asked if he knew of a place where I could find a frugal home to sleep and wash. Curious about the kind of work I sought, he inquired, to which I replied that I was open to any job, but I had some cooking knowledge and would prefer to work as a cook's assistant. He proposed an arrangement: if I could assist him for a few hours each morning in preparing the samosas, he would offer me a place to sleep in his home. Agreeing to his proposition, he requested that I wait until he concluded his tasks, which he anticipated would be around six in the evening. Rather than idly observing his sales, I suggested that he handle the cash collection and allow me to serve the samosas to the customers.

As expected, Ganesh Sir, the Samosa vendor, managed to sell all his stock by six o'clock. While we were walking towards his home, he shared his story with me and said, "I've been involved in the Samosa business since I was ten. It was a family business, and I used to assist my father and elder brother with the preparation and frying at home. When I turned fifteen, my father bought me a pushcart and asked me to venture out on my own while my elder brother stayed with him. My older brother limped as a consequence of a polio-virus infection. I welcomed my father's decision as it broke the monotony of being at home, and I had no friends available during the day to kill the time.

"My father gave me explicit instructions: I must pay him the cost of samosa preparation from the sales proceeds and save the remainder for my wedding and the purchase or rental of a house. Our home has only two rooms, and I cannot have one after my marriage.

"Within the next five years, I saved an excellent amount and fortunately found a 150-yard piece of land a developer was selling at a throwaway price in a desolate area, away from the city and now three kilometers away from where I sell my samosa. Thirty-five years ago, it was an undesirable location, far from the city, and only appealing to lower- middle-class individuals with dreams of owning a home. I found a builder to construct a two-bedroom house made of reinforced concrete. The prices back then were so reasonable that I managed to acquire a brand-new home using my savings and still had enough money left over for my marriage.

"While my house was under construction, fate introduced me to the love of my life: an elegant young girl who would occasionally visit in the evenings to purchase a few pieces of Samosa. On one such day, with no other customers in sight, I seized the opportunity to inquire about her and her family. She revealed her name as Nalini and shared that she resided in a rented two-room flat at the back of the street. Nalini had two younger brothers; her father was a driver, ferrying passengers across India. Although she had completed the 10th grade and was eager to continue her studies, her parents refused since they wanted to save money for her brothers' education. Following that, I shared with her the story of my upbringing and the inception of my business venture, which began when I was just fifteen. Additionally, I informed her that I had managed to save enough within a few years to acquire a 150- square-yard plot and erect a two-bedroom RCC house. Moreover, I have saved up sufficient funds for my impending marriage, which will take place once I find a wife of my choosing. Regrettably, our discussion was curtailed by an unexpected surge of customers.

"During Nalini's next visit, I gathered the strength to propose to her to marry me. She accepted joyfully but requested that my parents seek her hand in marriage. Our marriage transpired, and Nalini bestowed upon me the honor of being a father to two daughters. She refused to have more children, even though I wanted a son. Citing health constraints from undergoing two C-section deliveries and a deep commitment to educating our daughters,' she aimed to prevent a recurrence of the difficulties she had faced. From an early age, both my daughters exhibited intelligence and ambition, opting to carve out their own professional paths rather than conforming to the traditional role of a housewife dependent on a spouse's income. Upon completing their school education, my eldest daughter pursued her aspiration of becoming a medical nurse, securing admission to a renowned nursing college in Kerala. Inspired by her older sister, the younger daughter followed suit, and now both are accomplished nurses working in government hospitals.

"When they were in college, we decided to keep them within proximity; I purchased two newly built houses identical to ours, just half a kilometer away from my own residence.

"Today, both of my daughters are married and have families of their own. They visit us almost daily, serving as a source of great joy. Though I don't have a son, I couldn't be happier, as both my daughters have proven to be invaluable to us, surpassing even the expectations one might have for sons. Additionally, they earn higher incomes than their husbands, holding positions in government hospitals during the day and co-managing a clinic in the evenings, where they provide care for patients with minor illnesses or injuries."

The remainder of the walk was spent in silence. The house was in a locality with small lanes and single-story houses, probably built on 50 to 80 square yards. Evidently, residents must be fighting to keep themselves above the water. The house we entered had a gate and looked much larger when compared with the neighboring houses. To the utmost left, under a tin shade, there lay a large steel table with two commercial stoves. Two rooms and a toilet were visible when we sat on the plastic chairs placed on the verandah.

I asked Ganesh Sir, "Can I call you Uncle?"

"Please do that. Nalini will come in a while; generally, she goes to the market to fetch groceries at this time," Uncle said and excused himself to freshen up.

Upon entering the house, I felt apprehensive about making it my abode. Uncle suggested I stay and assist with the cooking, but my presence would inconvenience both of us. Furthermore, residing there would limit my freedom of movement. It would be preferable to find my own place where I could come and go as I please.

A few minutes later, Uncle came back, and I shared, "Uncle, staying here might be troublesome for both of us. I'll likely have to travel across the city for job hunting and may come home at odd hours, which could cause considerable bother. Please let me know if you know of any nearby place where I could sleep. I'll be happy to come and assist you with cooking every morning around ten or as needed.

"You might be right. My wife is quite particular about her daily routines and prefers not to be disturbed during her rest or sleep. Luckily, I know of a boys' hostel just a short walk away from here. If they have an available bed, you can stay there and pay a weekly or monthly charge for as long as you need. Let's wait for my wife to return, enjoy a cup of tea, and then I'll accompany you to the hostel," Uncle suggested kindly, and I expressed my gratitude. Initially driven by emotion, Uncle showed generosity in making the offer. However, later, he must have begun to have second thoughts, which could be the reason why he accepted my suggestion without any attempt to convince me to stay.

I found a new dwelling, a tiny room filled with ten people, ten wooden beds, and ten plastic cabinets. The house consisted of two rooms and ample open space. You had the option of sleeping on the verandah or in the open area on a makeshift wooden bed tied with plastic ropes for a slightly less charge. Compared to this wretched place, my orphanage was a palace. The entire premises reeked and lacked hygiene, but I remained confident that this was just a temporary setback rather than a permanent situation.

The following morning at nine o'clock, I had a disappointing breakfast of poorly made Idly and Sambar at a nearby restaurant before heading to Uncle Ganesh's house. I spent an hour and a half there and took charge of frying all their Samosas. Nalini Auntie expressed great satisfaction and appreciation for my assistance and skill. As I was leaving, I asked if I could come around eight in the morning to assist her with kneading the dough or preparing the Samosa and its filling. Nalini auntie gladly accepted my offer and replied, "Eight is when we have breakfast, so join us, and then we can all work together." I promised to be on time and left.

Because the hostel toilets were overcrowded in the morning, I had to give up my usual routine of showering first thing and instead went to Uncle's house. Around eleven, I left the house, stopped by the hostel to freshen up, and then headed to the same restaurant for lunch, where I had eaten an inexpensive breakfast. After lunch, I planned to explore the city to find a suitable job.

At approximately 12:30, I entered the bustling restaurant. It was packed with customers; most of them were standing outside and devouring their meals. The restaurant offered generous platters comprising rice, lentil curry, vegetable curry, mango pickle, and fried macaroni, all for a mere fifty rupees. I purchased a plate and quickly realized that the dishes were good to eat, only for being inexpensive. I was confident that I could make significantly tastier dishes using the same ingredients. I decided to approach the owner and offer my services to prepare, at the very least, the lentil and vegetable curries in exchange for reasonable compensation. My goal was to work here for a while and establish a reputation as a skilled cook, enabling me to secure a job at a better establishment with a substantial paycheck.

I waited patiently for over an hour to avoid the chaos of the lunchtime rush. Finally, I approached the portly man seated at the cash counter and politely asked, "Excuse me, sir. I would like to speak with the owner of this eatery. Could you kindly inform me where I could find him?"

"I'm the owner; tell me what you want to talk about," he growled.

"Sir, I'm a cook, and from the age of seven, I worked under a highly acclaimed cook in my village. I just had your lunch platter and was disappointed with the preparation. I'm confident I could prepare much better curries using the same ingredients that your cook is using," I said confidently.

"I don't have a cook. I prepare all the dishes with the assistance of two helpers, and due to my limited ability to stand for extended periods, I don't give the time needed to ensure the curries are tasty. My clientele looks for gratifying and budget-friendly meals, valuing practicality rather than gourmet and tantalizing dishes. However, if you possess the skill to prepare delicious dishes using the same ingredients I use, I would consider hiring you. You know I'm over sixty, and day by day, my ability to even spend a few hours in the kitchen is becoming a challenging task." stated the proprietor in his deep baritone voice.

"Sir, you hire me only if you're satisfied that my dishes taste much better, and it will help increase your customer base," I stated with confidence.

"Tell me about yourself, like your name, age, village name, when you came here, where you're staying, and can you read and write," the owner asked.

I revealed all the details to him, ending with the fact that, although I hadn't taken my 10th-grade exams, I was fluent in Telugu, Hindi, and English, both spoken and written, while cleverly avoiding mentioning my age out of fear of losing the job due to being underage. The owner, Narayan Rao, introduced himself, boasting of his impressive 28-year tenure overseeing the restaurant. Before that, he had honed his skills as an assistant cook in a similar eatery. He then called one of his kitchen helpers and asked me to go with him and prepare two or three vegetable curries and a lentil curry. I took a little over an hour to prepare the curries and served them to the owner. He was delighted with the preparations and asked the two helpers to taste them and give their opinions, and both of them confirmed that the dishes were delectable.

To my surprise, Narayan Sir offered me a salary beyond my wildest expectations and asked me to start the next day. Later, I discovered that he desperately needed a cook and had been reaching out to multiple cooks every day to work in his kitchen. Unfortunately, no one thus far has shown interest in working for him, and it's completely understandable. The kitchen was afflicted with stubborn oil stains that seemed impossible to remove, while the neglected utensils conveyed a sense of abandonment over an extended period. Moreover, the overall condition of the place was highly unsanitary and unhygienic, posing a significant health risk.

On my first day, nervousness engulfed me as I had never prepared curries for such a large number of people before. However, I relied on the training imparted by my Guru and dove into my work. Fortunately, two skilled helpers excelled at chopping vegetables and grinding spices, which eased some of my concerns. I started cooking at 10:30 a.m., meticulously crafting each dish with the utmost care and finished the preparations just before lunchtime.

I tasted the preparations repeatedly, ensuring they were flavorful and free from excesses. Our lunchtime lasted from 12:30 to 3:30. Much to my delight, numerous customers expressed their satisfaction with the delicious curries, conveying their happiness to Narayan Saab.

As time passed, days transformed into weeks, and weeks evolved into months. Before I knew it, I found myself approaching the end of my second year, having entered my seventeenth year of existence. Along with this growth, I had also reached a height of five feet and eleven inches. Throughout this duration, I honed my skills in the art of Samosa making. Each day, from eight to ten in the morning, I assisted Uncle and gradually became an expert in the craft. Not only did they generously feed me breakfast, but they also compensated me with a small amount for my services. I kept almost ninety percent of my savings in Nalini Auntie's bank account and used only ten percent for my essentials.

I had a strong desire to move out, eagerly awaiting my eighteenth birthday so I could secure a job at a prestigious upscale fine-dining restaurant. An unfortunate event occurred just as I entered my third year of service there. Narayan Sir suffered a Hemiplegia attack, which left the entire left side of his body paralyzed and even caused damage to his brain. Fortunately, the brain damage was not extensive, but he ended up confined to his bed. A friend of Narayan Sir told us about it. As a result of his illness, the eatery was closed. No one had access to the keys, and even if we managed to open it, we were uncertain how to keep it running smoothly. However, on the fourth day morning, a glimmer of hope emerged. Mrs. Joyti Narayan, the owner's wife, came to the eatery accompanied by a young man who was seemingly in his early twenties. All the restaurant staff were sitting outside of the restaurant for someone to come and either terminate their services or open it to run. She looked at all of us and said to me, "Are you Mahendra?"

I nodded in agreement, and she entrusted me with the keys to the restaurant, instructing me to open it.

Once we entered the restaurant, she asked other staff to clean the place, asked me to sit opposite her, and stated, "You must have been informed about your uncle's health, which has left him bedridden. Closing the restaurant isn't an option, and I'm reaching out to you to manage it. Mahendra, your uncle has praised you in the past, highlighting your outstanding culinary abilities and proficiency in three languages. With these skills, I'm confident that overseeing the restaurant and keeping track of sales and purchases will be effortless for you."

I replied, "Of course, Ma'am. However, I would need your approval to hire an assistant to handle the cash counter, keep a record of suppliers' deliveries, and do a few other tasks."

She authorized me to employ a young man and gave me a mobile phone, with the directive to always carry it with me. Before departing, she mentioned she would stay in contact and consider a salary raise within a month, depending on how well I performed. With no suitable candidate in sight, I pushed myself relentlessly, driven by the pressing need to get the job done.

Mrs. Joyti Narayan called me every morning and evening to inquire about the sales and purchases and to find out about any challenges I encountered. After twenty days, she requested that I visit her residence after closing the restaurant to discuss a business proposition, and her son would pick me up from the restaurant at ten. Consequently, I arrived at Narayan Sir's house at 10:30 PM.

It was an independent two-story villa. Mrs. Narayan's son guided me to the living room, which was furnished aesthetically with comfortable sofas.

Mrs. Narayan came in a while and initiated the conversation, saying, "After careful consideration, we have decided that for us to run the business is impractical. My son will depart in two weeks to the US to do MS, your uncle may take an extensive recovery period, and I have a business to run. And in addition, I have to give a lot of time to your uncle. Considering this scenario, we have resolved to sell both the business and the building to you at a mutually agreed-upon price and with flexible payment terms. So please tell us, are you interested in buying the property and the business?"

She deftly sidestepped, telling me that she had failed to find any buyers. Many potential buyers have visited the restaurant over the last twenty days. Still, it appears that none of them have made any reasonable offer or shown interest in acquiring the business. This was understandable, given that I had just calculated that even working nonstop for seven days a week would hardly bring in thirty to forty thousand a month, making the business unappealing from an investor's standpoint.

After a few moments of consideration, I responded, "I am willing to purchase the property and the business if you can negotiate a fair sales price and offer favorable payment terms."

"We need twenty lakhs for the property and five lakhs for business goodwill. For payment terms, you tell us whether you have any money to pay upfront and how many months you need to pay the balance," Mrs. Narayan said.

"Ma'am, I must tell you, your expectations are excessively high. You know well that the restaurant is in an area primarily inhabited by lower-middle-class folks who typically aim to spend as little as possible. Making a good profit from the restaurant is as tough as trying to squeeze water from a stone. Plus, the building that's much like a run-down house sitting on a small plot of land probably wouldn't sell for more than ten lakhs. If we were to be liberal, the entire value of business could be, at best, twelve lakhs. The chances of finding a desperate buyer are low, but even if you did, it would be difficult to fetch more than fifteen lakhs," I calmly stated my observations.

"Twelve lakhs is far too low, and I must emphasize that we are offering you favorable payment terms. The maximum I can consider is twenty lakhs, to be paid over 36 monthly installments. If this proposition is acceptable, we can proceed with transferring the property to your name immediately. However, you will need to mortgage the property with us, and upon the completion of the agreed payment, we will release all the documents," Mrs. Narayan stated firmly.

"Ma'am, I must express my gratitude for considering the monthly installments option, but even then, the amount is still beyond what I can afford. The business isn't generating sufficient profits to cover such installments. The most I can offer is fifteen lakhs, with three lakhs I'll pay upfront and the remaining balance in 36 monthly installments," I stated with conviction.

"I'm sorry, but I must decline your offer. Nevertheless, please allow us some time to confer internally. I will convey our definitive decision to you within the next three days," Ma'am replied.

Her son dropped me to my boys' hostel, and while dozing off, it struck me that I should seize this opportunity to start my own business. If they insist on twenty lakhs, I must agree to that on the condition that they accept a payment plan of sixty monthly installments instead of thirty-six. The potential for business growth was immense, but despite my numerous suggestions, Narayan Sir never approved any of them. He was a satisfied person, and perhaps his contentment was also fueled by the knowledge that his son had no interest in running the restaurant.

Mrs. Narayan took five days, instead of the promised three, to finally reach out and inform me that they had agreed to accept my offer. During these five days, two more potential buyers visited the property, and it became evident to me that she was still fishing, hoping for a better offer. However, when those attempts didn't yield better results, she eventually accepted my offer.

Within the next ten days, I handed over her three lakhs check to finalize the deal, and the property was officially registered in my name. As per our agreement, we also signed a mortgage document outlining the process for me to pay the remaining amount.

The next morning, as I was enjoying my breakfast, I addressed Uncle, "Uncle, considering you're approaching sixty, it would be best for you to give your body rest. Standing for eight to ten hours daily isn't good for your health."

Before I could finish what I wanted to convey, Uncle interjected and responded, "I understand, Mahendra. It is becoming more taxing and exhaustive each day. However, if I stay home, I will get bored and fall sick. So, I don't really have a choice."

"Uncle, if you don't mind, could you please tell me how much you earn in a month?" I questioned.

"Typically, I earn around six to eight hundred rupees per day," Uncle replied. "If the vegetable prices are lower, then I make more, but six hundred rupees is the minimum on an average day."

"Uncle, I'd like to discuss the restaurant situation with you. As you're aware, juggling both the kitchen and the cash counter has become quite demanding for me. Therefore, I have made the decision to hire a trustworthy and reliable person to handle the cash counter. If you are interested in taking up this position, I am willing to offer you a monthly salary of twenty thousand rupees.

"Auntie, I want you to continue your excellent work of making the samosas. I will supply all the necessary ingredients, and you will be responsible for preparing the filling and assembling the samosas. I will personally fry them at the restaurant to ensure that our customers receive freshly made, hot, and delicious samosas. I am prepared to offer you a monthly salary of ten thousand rupees for your services.

"Please inform me of your decision within the next two to three days, as I am in a rush to have a cashier as soon as possible," I stated.

Uncle and Auntie exchanged glances; Auntie spoke up, saying, "I have been urging your uncle to retire for the past two years. We have enough to sustain ourselves without relying on regular income, and our daughters are also willing to contribute whatever they can to support us. So, from my side, it's a resounding yes, and you need to let us know when we should begin."

I looked at Uncle, and he immediately grasped that I was awaiting his response. He expressed, "Mahendra, how could I ever go against your Auntie's wishes? Just inform us when we should start, and we will be ready."

"Starting today, please excuse me as I have numerous tasks to handle at the restaurant. Auntie, when the samosas are ready, please send them along with Uncle," I said, leaving them to celebrate this joyful moment. It was a win-win for all of us.

The samosa business experienced an astonishing surge within a few weeks, and within three months, we were selling a staggering one thousand plus pieces each day. To support Auntie in managing the increasing demand, I provided her with two girls to assist in the preparation, and I doubled her salary from ten thousand to twenty thousand rupees per month. To enhance our menu, I introduced non- veg platters for both lunch and dinner, offering customers a choice between one piece of fried fish or a two-piece chicken curry. I added a delightful paneer palak option in the veg platter for an extra charge.

Our non-veg platters became our best-selling items, particularly in the evening, when people lined up to get their parcel of preferred platters. Most days, our non-veg stock was entirely sold out by nine o'clock, even though we closed at ten.

The financial outcomes were extraordinary. My monthly net profits surged past two lakhs in just half a year, even with a significant rise in overhead expenses. Business flourished, and the tireless effort and commitment from my team and me yielded impressive rewards.

In under two years, I acquired the adjacent house, demolished it, and constructed a two-story building. The upper floor was for my accommodation, and the lower floor had two large halls: one for food storage and the other for pre-preparing spices, vegetables, and non-veg items.

I am in my twenties now, and apart from my real estate assets, my bank balance was nearing thirty lakhs, with an average monthly addition of over three lakhs. As each day passed, my cooking time was reduced to tasting the dishes because most of my time was consumed in managing suppliers and accounts. It felt insufficient despite putting in 12 to 14 hours of strenuous work. Still, I was thinking of expanding the business and opening outlets in similar or middle-class neighborhoods.

One night, while lying in bed, it struck me that I had never visited the orphanage, even though I had promised Amma that I would visit her when possible. It was a terrible oversight on my part, which must be rectified immediately. The following day, I went shopping and purchased various gift items. I bought a gold chain with a pendant of Goddess Lakshmi for Amma, along with four expensive sarees and shawls. I also bought gold chains for my Godfather, my cook-guru, and several pairs of dhotis and shirts. Additionally, I bought plenty of treats for the boys and girls at the orphanage.

The following day, at the crack of dawn, I took a taxi to travel to my village, where I spent the first fourteen years of my life. As I arrived, I noticed that not much had changed since my departure, apart from a few newly constructed RCC houses and concrete roads. The orphanage stood just as I had left it, although all my former colleagues had moved on, and the younger ones had now entered their teenage years.

Despite her advanced age, my Amma remained vibrant and bursting with vigor. She greeted me with delight, embracing me tightly. Amid our reunion, she delivered the unfortunate news that her husband and my Godfather had passed away four years ago. Next, I met with my Guru, who taught me how to cook and was pleased to see me and receive the gifts.

Most of the children were at school, so I sat with my Amma and discussed various subjects. She informed me that she had transferred property ownership to the NGO that has long supported the orphanage so they could run the facility in case of her demise.

During our conversation, she abruptly rose from her chair, said she would return in a few minutes, and left the hall. After a brief absence, she reappeared and addressed me, saying, "When you left, I was filled with regret due to my advanced age. There was something I should have given you before you left, but I forgot. Here is the chain we found on you when you were left in our care."

She handed me a little gold chain with a pendant depicting the crucifixion of Jesus Christ. I looked at Amma inquisitively, and she said, "Your parents must be Christians, which is why they put the chain on you so we could raise you as a Christian. Unfortunately, we didn't have the facility to make you practice Christianity, so we raised you as a Hindu. It's your choice now whether to continue practicing Hinduism or convert to Christianity."

With my head bowed, I deliberated for a few moments before slowly responding, "Amma, what difference would it make to my disposition if I converted to Christianity, and why should I follow my parents' religion when they abandoned me to die? No, Amma, I'm content with my faith, and there was no need to be considerate or feel guilty about disgracing the parents who failed to control their hormonal upsurge. When the fruit of their love manifested, they distanced themselves from their responsibilities. Amma, whenever I walked past a school in the morning, my heart ached as I watched parents escorting their children, holding their hands, ensuring they entered the school, and giving them kisses to comfort and assure them of their presence. Coming out of the mess they created for me was not an easy task; fortunately, I remained focused and disciplined and attempted to create a place for myself in society, but I don't believe any girl from a decent family would marry me if she knew I was raised in an orphanage. However, I don't complain because I've seen that life is unfair for many, particularly those born in poor households, where there is nothing but hunger, humiliation, and destitution.

"In my daily interactions with people of diverse faiths, I've observed a spectrum of characters, ranging from unpleasant individuals to those possessing admirable virtues. The idea that any religion can transform a fundamentally flawed person into a paragon of virtue is a fallacy; individual intrinsic nature dictates actions and defines character, with religion serving as a moral guide rather than a transformative force.

"Most religions advocate moral rectitude, compassion, and righteousness, urging adherence to specific rules for spiritual enlightenment and a place in paradise. However, the reality persists that no religion can alter an individual's nature. A person with a malicious disposition may fervently follow a faith's tenets, yet their actions betray the essence of that religion. Those who vocally profess their religious piety frequently resort to the most unethical behaviors when in need of money or power, driven by their insatiable greed for worldly possessions, or when they risk losing any of their ill-gotten gains. They may also resort to deceit to shield themselves or their loved ones from the repercussions of their punishing actions.

"On the flip side, inherently good-natured individuals don't need religion to show kindness, empathy, and altruism. While their religion can provide a framework for expressing values, it's not the driving force behind their goodness. So, the belief that any religion can make someone perfect is off the mark."

"Nevertheless, I'm content to embrace the faith of my foster parents. They've imparted valuable lessons on leading a peaceful and fulfilling life, emphasizing the significance of extending assistance to fellow human beings, regardless of their religion, caste, or creed."

"You're an adult capable of leading your own life, but returning the chain we found on you was imperative. However, as your foster mother, I feel obligated to advise you that holding onto grudges or dwelling in unhappiness, believing that life has treated you unfairly, will only invite negativity that can erode your beautiful personality.

"Forget judging folks on their mixed messages. We all preach one thing and do another sometimes, faith or no faith. It's just human. You focus on your own path, your own north star. Be the change you want to see, live your truth with integrity, and let others figure out their own mess. Peace and contentment come from walking your own walk, not policing everyone else's," Amma sombrely expressed in her usual relaxed and smiling face. Amma was educated and went to college but didn't complete her degree because her parents decided to marry her.

"Amma, I'm not the person who passes judgment on everything that I see, but it's vital to remember that there are never any exceptions to the rule that wrong is always wrong.

Irrespective of the situation, societal pressures, or the stance of one's family, abandoning a child is an utterly callous deed. Moreover, I must emphasize that I did not come into this world in the midst of a war-torn or genocidal rage; I was born out of my parents' raw sexual passion. While I hold no grudges against my parents, I cannot endorse their actions, condone their wickedness, or follow their religion," I calmly expressed.

Amma sensed my resolute stance, deftly diverted the conversation, and suggested, "If you have an address and contact number, kindly jot it down in my personal diary. Who knows, perhaps I might sojourn and spend a few days or even months with you."

In genuine earnestness, I stated, "It would truly be an honor to have my Amma stay with me, whether for a short duration or indefinitely. I pledge to cherish and support you for as long as I live." Following this declaration, I offered Amma a check worth one lakh rupees. However, she resolutely refused, asserting that she possessed more than enough and did not need my hard-earned money.

When I tried to thrust the check into her hand, she pulled her hand and said, "Thank you for your generosity, but I'll have to decline. You've truly brought joy to my day. May God bless you, and may a young lady grace you with a kiss," Amma chuckled warmly.

Amma passed me her diary, and I swiftly noted down my address and phone numbers. As we continued discussing my endeavors, we shared a meal together. Finally, I said my goodbyes, promising to visit her as frequently as I could, but it never happened, as within two months of our meeting, she passed away from an attack of acute pneumonia.

I'm now twenty-seven and the owner of five eateries in low-income localities and four fine-dining restaurants in upscale areas, all built on purchased properties. I converted my residence into an office, hired accountants, purchasers, and computer programmers, computerized all the restaurants' billing, and made it online. I earned more than sixty lakhs monthly in pretax profit and spent most of the earnings on purchasing new properties in upscale areas to open new fine-dining restaurants.

Currently, I am renting a luxurious residence in a towering apartment building. I bought an expensive four-wheeler vehicle but had no friends or a social circle. With my twelve to fourteen hours of arduous labor each day, I had no time to even think about having friends. By the time I retire for the day, I'm so worn out that I can't muster the energy for much more than a good night's sleep.

My new task was to purchase a palatial pad in the city's heart because the building society was pressuring me to bring my family. While renting the apartment, I informed them that my wife was studying abroad and would be back within a year.

Chapter Four

Rukhsana Jahangir

Life is a Toss

I, Rukhsana Jahangir, was born into an affluent family of high achievers. My grandfather migrated from Afghanistan to the Princely State of Hyderabad, ruled by Asaf Jah VII, also known as Mir Osman Ali Khan, son of Sir Mir Mahboob Ali Khan Siddiqi Bayafandi, who was the 7th and last Nizam of Hyderabad. He ruled Hyderabad State between 1911 and 1948.

As per my mother's account, my grandfather was born into a well-off trader in Kabul, Afghanistan. Tragedy struck when he was a mere seven years old, and his mother passed away during the birth of her third child. However, his father never ceased to love him or his two younger sisters, even after marrying another woman who gave birth to four sons and three daughters. He received his education from top-notch tutors, a privilege that wealth afforded. By the age of fifteen, he gained remarkable knowledge in various subjects; however, his amazing prowess in mathematics astounded even his instructors, and his proficiency in Persian added another feather to his cap.

By the time he reached the age of twenty-five, he and his two sisters were all married with children; he was blessed with one son and effectively managed his father's primary horse breeding and trading business. A significant turn occurred when his father approached him, handed him a bag containing gold coins, a few diamonds, and precious gemstones, and asked him to relocate to Hyderabad and establish a new life there due to concerns that his stepbrothers were plotting to kill him.

His father arranged for the family to accompany a caravan of merchants who regularly took dry fruits and returned with Indian spices. They arrived at the destination without any untoward happening. Rented a small house in the city's heart.

While searching for suitable employment, he encountered a member of the Royal Guard who, for a small charge, agreed to take him to the Nizam's weekly public audience so that he could ask for a job. As the guard had promised, he was presented directly to the Nizam.

It seems he informed the Nizam how he had come to the region as a tourist but became so enamored with the place that he decided to settle if he could secure a job. When Ruler questioned him about the specific kind of employment he desired, he stated his academic achievements and proudly announced his proficiency in accounting and flair in Persian. Mastering mental calculations, he could effortlessly execute divisions and subtractions involving five-digit figures. In addition, he had the remarkable ability to add ten or more five-digit numbers without the need for written aid. Last but not least, he could skillfully maintain account books and generate perfect profit and loss statements. Initially skeptical, the King summoned a senior officer from the treasury department to verify the man's claims. Amazingly, he effortlessly demonstrated his extraordinary skills to the officer, leaving no doubt about his abilities.

Impressed by his talent, the treasury officer privately recommended to the King that the man be given a senior position in their department, as they were in dire need of someone of his caliber. The King agreed and made an offer for a high-ranking position in the treasury department, which he thankfully accepted. The Head of the Treasury Department sanctioned him a large piece of land and gave him a loan to build his residential accommodation a little away from the city, where only a few elites resided.

Grandpa was blessed with another son when he was in Hyderabad, with a fourteen-year gap from his first child. After their studies at a distinguished convent school, both sons were sent to England to pursue higher education. Upon his return, the elder son secured employment in the government of the British Empire. My father, the younger son, returned after earning a civil engineering degree just when the country secured independence. He established his construction business and began by tearing down the family's ancestral house, replacing it with a sleek, contemporary home to highlight his craftsmanship and innovation. This strategic move proved instrumental in attracting high- profile clientele seeking to replace their outdated residences with modern ones. Swiftly, he earned acclaim as the premier builder catering to elite clients, paving the path to fame and wealth.

My father married and became a parent first to my brother and then to me, with a nine-year gap between us. Regrettably, he married late and suffered a heart attack early, at the young age of 46. My brother was in his third year of pursuing an electrical and electronics engineering degree, proving incapable of running his dad's business.

Fortunately, Dad found two college buddies who were happy to take a thirty percent stake in the company and become working partners. Although Dad maintained a daily presence at the office, he limited his workload to a bare minimum and parted most of his day-to-day responsibilities with his two partners.

Bro continued his studies and pursued his goals, obtaining a master's degree in Electronics Engineering. While searching for a suitable job, he took the UPSC exam and not only passed on his first attempt but also secured sixth position. Consequently, he was offered a prestigious IFS post, which he enthusiastically accepted, leading to his posting in Tokyo, Japan.

Due to the impressive stature of both my parents, my brother and I gained considerable height. At our zenith, I stood at a height of five feet eight inches, while my brother exceeded me and reached six feet. Our distinct features and pale skin texture never failed to attract attention wherever we went. My brother's aura had a charm that made him irresistible to the ladies. Perhaps this charm led to his marriage to a Japanese female business executive within two years of his posting.

According to my brother, his wife was beautiful and educated. She was the only child of a prosperous family and worked for an organization that gathered data on the socioeconomic and political conditions of almost every country worldwide. This information was provided to governments and multinational firms seeking to establish operations in those countries. Their paths crossed at an event organized by her company for various consulates, and my brother's charisma hooked her.

Soon after, she began calling my brother to share updates on various countries, and it wasn't long before the true motive emerged with a dinner invitation. Enthralled by her intelligence and beauty, he decided to marry her after just two months of courtship. Bro was transferred to another country after three years of employment, and instead of relocating to the country where he was to report, he quit and decided to settle in Japan. Bro and his wife established their own company to work in the same field his wife worked: data collection on countries' health for investment. They added a few more lines, such as the new products that would enter the market, what products would take a back seat, which new manufacturer has the potential to grow and why, and so on. Within a year, his venture became profitable, with enormous growth potential.

With a whirlwind of international travels, my brother and his wife presented to governments, leading corporations, and investors, amassing significant wealth. What began with modest funding in a tiny corner of their flat has transformed into a thriving business employing over 100 people, housed in a spacious office in a prime commercial building downtown.

Mom used to shout at my brother for not calling her daily, but he barely managed to speak with her once a week for a few minutes. And since he started his business, he didn't come to see us.

I took my electrical engineering degree from a prestigious college and applied for a master's degree in electrical engineering and computer science at the Massachusetts Institute of Technology (MIT). Luckily, I got admission. I had to seek Bro's assistance to gain permission for my further studies in the US, given that both Mom and Dad strongly opposed me and insisted on me getting married and no more education, as they have plenty to make my future financially secure.

My brother deftly convinced our parents, allowing me to say tearful goodbyes before I took to the skies to chase my dream. Even though Dad had the financial means, my brother was resolute in taking on the entire burden of my education costs. He paid for my tuition and boarding fees and supplemented me with a generous monthly allowance, reassuring our parents that it wouldn't strain his finances in the least.

During the second semester, I met with Daniel, a senior. He was slender, standing about six feet or maybe an inch less, a Caucasian blond with golden hair and blue eyes. I was in the canteen, taking a coffee break before heading to the library; he approached me, holding a coffee cup in his hand, and courteously said, "Excuse me, would you mind if I join you?"

I asked with a hint of disapproval, "What makes you want to sit here when there are so many empty tables around?"

"May I have a few minutes of your time to explain why I am asking permission to share the table with you?" Daniel said pleadingly.

"You have time till I finish my coffee; since it's hot, you would get three to four minutes," I said indignantly.

"My name is Daniel Theo, and I'm doing the same postgraduation course you're doing, senior to you being in my third semester. Please accept my words with no intention of offense. To begin with, I must confess that I've been observing you over the past couple of months. There's an exceptional quality about you that distinguishes you from all the other girls I've met or interacted with. I must clarify that I'm not alluding to your physical attractiveness, which seems to be a topic of discussion among male students. Instead, what captured my attention was the unique aura you exude and the unwavering discipline you follow: starting your day with jogging, never missing a lecture, investing hours at the library each afternoon, and consistently striving to be one of the top achievers in your class. I deeply admire your traits, and your exceptional looks are a bonus to your personality. In conclusion, I am genuinely looking forward to exploring the possibility of nurturing a friendship with you and investigating the potential to develop our bond into a lasting and meaningful relationship," Daniel expressed, maintaining a composed manner.

Though this wasn't the first time a boy expressed such compliments, quite a few attempted to lure me with their praises when I arrived here, and I brushed them off. I didn't want to distract myself from my studies, and next, a fellow student meant it would take a long time for him to settle down and earn decent money to shoulder the family responsibilities. This made me decide I should go for a readymade boy, a well-educated businessman, or an executive earning a decent amount and who has no potential to become a parasite on my wealth. However, nothing quite matched this smarty-pant's eloquent remarks. It took a while before I collected myself and deliberately took a few sips from my still-warm coffee to calm down and allow Daniel's unexpected onslaught of praises to sink in. Once I got control over the increased heartbeat, I responded with a poised demeanor, "Daniel, I'm grateful for your kind words about my traits and looks. However, I'm currently unable to invest time in any relationship. I must complete the course on my first attempt and go back to my ailing parents, who need me beside them. I believe it's better for either of us to remain focused on our studies; hence, I ask for your understanding and wish you the best in finding the friend or partner you're seeking at an appropriate time and place," I said with a big grin. I stood up from my seat, signaling my departure.

"Please allow me a few moments more to finish sharing my thoughts. Considering that this might be our last interaction, please comprehend that my intention is not to make any unwarranted advances or to jump on your bones; just a brief conversation," Daniel's voice carried a profound state of mental distress.

I pondered whether this handsome hunk was genuinely captivated by my looks or whatever he had seen in me, or was he fabricating stories to get into my pants? Then I thought, let's settle this matter permanently; give him the opportunity to explain and then decisively close this chapter. I am resolute in my stance to avoid investing my time in any frivolous flirtations. My foremost objective is to earn my degree and return home to avoid causing distress to my elderly parents, who must be counting the days of my return.

"Since I believe this will be our last conversation, take your sweet time to say whatever you want. However, remember, I've no plans to settle down in this country, even if I find the person of my dreams in you. So, please spare me from telling me how infatuated you are with me or your concocted stories of my looks or whatever that you haven't seen in any other girl on this campus or elsewhere. I unequivocally refuse to become entangled in the deceptive narrative you're trying to weave to serve your ulterior motives," I asserted with determination.

Daniel looked at me with an agape mouth; probably, he wasn't expecting such sharp and disheartening comments from me. Anyhow, he didn't lose his cool. He first cleared his throat and calmly and politely said, "Thanks for your gesture of allowing me a few moments to express my thoughts. I was born and raised in this country. I studied in a private school, thanks to my rich parents, who are chemical engineers with doctorates and work for a pharmaceutical company as senior scientists. They are based in Los Angeles and have been happily married for over twenty-five years.

"I wanted to be like my parents, a scientist, but in a different subject, and to be precise, I have a keen interest in designing Computer Memory and Storage Chips that would be much faster and have mammoth storage capacity. A lot of work has been done in developing the existing chips, and a lot of work is in progress to develop faster versions, but there is a dearth of young scientists. Since I'm passionate about working in this field, I chose to be a new entrant, but not before I got my doctorate.

"Everyone, including my parents, speculated about my sexual orientation when I was young due to my unexplained aversion to female company. I never challenged these assumptions and instead focused on my academics. However, upon seeing you, my intellect and heart have reached the conclusion that you are the girl I've been waiting for. You possess every quality I admire in a partner, and I'm committed to building something deeper than a passing fling to fulfill my masculine desires. I have loaded pockets to enjoy casual pleasures, and even if I had no money, many girls on this campus would strive to please me. There's no rush for an answer right now. Take as much time as you need to weigh it carefully. Once you've thought it through, please tell me if you're leaning towards saying no or if you're interested in exploring the possibility."

Even if I downplay the significance of my skill in reading facial expressions, I must acknowledge his words as something deeper than transient infatuation, a genuine affection, to be precise.

My mind ceased to function, leaving me dumbfounded. Instead, my heart was asking me to grab this handsome man's hand and flee to a deserted island where I could spend eternity in his embrace. Setting aside his demeanor and intelligence, his fastidious self-care is apparent through his well-pressed clothes, neatly trimmed nails, flawlessly styled hair, and clean visage capable of eliciting any girl to go weak in her knees. His choice of attire was impeccable; he wore a light blue checkered shirt tucked neatly into sky-blue denim trousers and fashionable sneakers. The scent he wore was almost intoxicating in its allure.

I was allowing my foolish impulses to take control; forming judgments based on knee-jerk reactions is imprudent. My liberal upbringing and time spent in the United States have substantially broadened my perspective on marriage. I am now convinced that dating before making a commitment is sensible.

This approach enables meaningful conversations on various topics, facilitating a genuine understanding of a person's preferences and aversions. It's also essential to gauge the temperament threshold, and if he has a short fuse or is violent, then it is better to stay away.

A lifelong companionship isn't constructed merely upon looks, education, riches, or etiquette. There must be depth to an individual that goes beyond their external allure, ensuring your happiness and contentment throughout your life.

Even if I put aside the fact that Daniel and I don't share the same religious beliefs, pursuing a romantic connection with him presents another major non-negotiable obstacle. I cannot remain in this country and abandon my aging parents to the care of servants or an old age home. Daniel undoubtedly must have a desire to work in this country, and his motivation might not be necessarily monetary or driven by his parents. Rather, it could be linked to the research he aims to undertake, which is most effectively pursued exclusively in the US. Considering this single factor, it's evident that embarking on a romantic journey with Daniel would be ill-advised. Even if he were the epitome of an ideal partner, the reality remains that a foreseeable shared future is absent. Given this circumstance, I must respectfully decline his proposal for courtship.

"Daniel, I really appreciate your comments, which are possibly genuine. However, I could see hurdles that I could not overcome, even if I wanted to, so it's better we don't embark on an expedition that would only bring despair and pain to either of us. Please understand that I'm not alluding to our divergent theological convictions or my state of commitment.

Let me affirm that neither the dissimilarity in our theological beliefs is a matter of concern for me, nor am I committed to anyone. My parents hold liberal views. My older brother married a Japanese girl and settled in Japan with my folks' consent. If I decide to marry someone I truly care for, they won't raise any objections, as my happiness is of utmost importance to them. You have to excuse me for a personal reason; I must say no to exploring the possibility of a permanent relationship," I conveyed calmly and evenly, devoid of emotion.

Daniel gazed at me with a dispassionate expression. After a few moments of contemplation, he inquired, "I came to know through one of your professors that you possess exceptional academic abilities and an analytical mind. He believes you have a promising future in the realm of scientific innovations, provided you continue your studies and obtain a doctorate. I'm curious as to why you intend to cease studying after earning your master's degree. Why not earn a Ph.D., contribute to humanity, and bring both you and your family honor?"

"To begin with, I have no desire to spend an additional four to five years in this country. Furthermore, even with a Ph.D., my intention to depart this country will remain unchanged, and the challenges I face today will likely persist. Thus, what tangible impact would it truly have with my doctorate except for a personality development exercise, not beneficial to me or anyone else?" I was crisp and challenging as I spoke.

"Ms. Jahangir: I assume your worldly knowledge must be better than mine. Nonetheless, it's important to note that the obstacles that appear overwhelming at this moment could suddenly disappear, and the pledges you're resolute in honoring may become inconsequential. What I'm requesting is that you continue your studies and pursue a doctorate; during this time, the obstacles or personal reasons that you believe you would be unable to overcome even if you wanted to may not exist in their entirety. It would make me happy if you went back to your country with a Ph.D. certification, regardless of whether we date or not or if we find we're not compatible to go the extra mile and tie the knot," Daniel's expression broke something inside me. I felt I should give his suggestion a thought but not date him.

"Daniel, your encouragement towards pursuing a doctorate means a lot to me. However, the reality is that my parents may not be supportive of this undertaking. Convincing them for my master's degree was a considerable struggle, but with my passion and my brother's influence, I managed to obtain their approval. The idea of seeking approval for a prolonged stay of four to five years for a doctorate seems like a daunting uphill battle. Nonetheless, I've not taken your suggestion lightly and plan to discuss it at an opportune moment to gauge their reaction.

"Is there anything else, Daniel, or can I leave?" I asked politely and smiled while asking for his permission to leave.

"Yes, I'd like to ask you a huge favor; since you come here every day at this time, have a snack and a cup of coffee before heading to the library. Can I join you when you're here? We could spend a few minutes together and update each other on how we are faring on personal and educational fronts. If you are disinclined to engage in conversation, I understand; allow me to sit with you and have my coffee without conversing," Daniel asked so politely that it melted my heart, but he was contagious. Togetherness with him is like asking for trouble. Rukh Babe, avoid his company or be prepared to deal with issues that could complicate life and make my folks very unhappy.

"Daniel, have you considered that it might be better for both of our lives if we avoided each other? We cannot have a platonic relationship; our frequent interactions might inadvertently lead to emotions that could impede our studies and cause pain. Please do not pressure me to agree to your request," I stated with conviction.

"Understood, Ms. Jahangir. However, I must express that my life would be incomplete without you. I wanted to hold your hand and travel with you through the trials of this ephemeral existence. I yearned to savor every worldly pleasure and explore the globe with you by my side. It will be challenging to live without you beside me, and rest assured, no other girl could ever take your place within my heart. In all likelihood, I will die a premature death as the thought of life minus your presence would become a constant pain, making it a meaningless journey that I would prefer to be over; the earlier, the better. Please accept my best wishes for a fulfilling life and remember me as nothing more than an idiosyncratic who you dismissed," Daniel stated with profound pain in his voice and quickly rose and left, leaving me without the chance to respond.

Daniel's poetic allusions to my personality created such a disturbance in my life that I avoided the canteen for my evening coffee for several days out of fear of running into him. Considering our limited familiarity, it's baffling that he's telling untimely demise unless I'm part of his life. What nonsense! It's heartwarming to know someone is pining for me; he can continue doing so without any worries from my end.

However, from my point of view, the idea of love without the experience of dating seems like a fleeting attraction, prone to fading when familiarity transforms into contempt. Even if you believe and practice the principle of taking well-thought-out risks and truly getting to know each other before committing to keeping the reservoir of affection full, many people will discover they've landed in a dry well.

In the US society, most of the youth are uninclined to marry without undergoing the process of dating or cohabitation. And here's a young man embellished with a multitude of appealing qualities: attractiveness, exceptional education, financial stability, and parents who exemplify a long-standing, unshakeable marital bond that no sane girl would be willing to let go of this golden opportunity. This bounty fall is making me think, is it bait he's putting forward to lure me into his trap?

Ever since our meeting, I've spent countless hours contemplating these aspects but failed to grasp the motivations that drove his intense attraction toward me. Nothing seemed to add up; why would a good-looking, educated individual of Caucasian descent, financially well-off, and hailing from a decent family see me as his life partner? It's hard to believe that his perception of my looks and traits alone could account for this; there might be a hidden motive or some other factor at play.

Conflicting emotions stirred within me. On the one hand, there was the looming fear of falling into a trap, while on the other, the potential regret of possibly missing out on an exceptional opportunity to enjoy life alongside an educated, cultured person with an excellent family background.

One afternoon, as I was heading to the library, I pondered: Why have I been so cowardly as to avoid confronting him? I need to strongly discourage his unwelcome advances if we ever cross paths again, whether it be in the cafeteria or elsewhere. Why venture into a domain that seems destined to bring about hurt, especially when I'm aware that seeking the happiness I desire from my future partner will, in all probability, end in pain and despair?

I veered in the direction of the canteen, a sense of relief washing over me for summoning the courage to confront him should he approach. Upon entering, I saw him seated at the table of our first encounter. Engrossed in a book, a coffee mug adorned the table before him, exuding an air of sophistication. Picking up my coffee and cheese sandwich, I deliberated for a few minutes and decided to join him, hoping to purge his influence from my life forever.

Heading toward his table, I confidently seated myself across from him, skirting the formality of seeking permission and shedding any pretense of politeness. I quipped with a touch of sarcasm, "Did you eagerly await my arrival, or were you deep in thought about the misfortune that spared me from getting caught in your intricate web?"

Daniel's expression changed to one of surprise, and he exclaimed, "Indeed, I anticipated a reprimand for taking a seat at a table that you had once occupied. I beg your pardon for such impoliteness, which is unbecoming of a person of decency and refined manners. In any case, I appreciate that you graced the table. Could I have the audacity to enquire about your whereabouts over the past several days or the reason for the change in your routine, having a bite and coffee prior to your library visit?"

"I've intentionally kept my distance in recent days to steer clear of potential interactions with you and to spare myself from hearing your woeful love story and other irrelevant details. However, today, I've decided not to let your presence interfere with my coffee routine. I feel it's necessary to advise you to back off, as I won't hesitate to report your behavior as stalking, if necessary," I asserted calmly, maintaining a composed tone.

"Ma'am, today you're gracing my table. I admit, once I approached you and allowed some foolish notions to escape my mind. The canteen supervisor can vouch that I am a regular visitor here, always alone, seeking solace over coffee and snacks. I neither disrupt others nor allow anyone to occupy my space. Interestingly, it seems you share this solitude, a trait we both possess. So, what if we shed this label and convene here daily, engaging in discussions about life's highs and lows? Rest assured, I won't resurrect my earlier, naive goal of expressing how desperately I yearned for your presence in my life. In hindsight, my earnest desire to be with you for life, sincere as it was, seemed to oversimplify matters. I hadn't fully appreciated the complexities that life inevitably brings," Daniel concluded his remarks in a soothing tone, the volume set at a gentle cadence.

His words and demeanor continued to captivate me, and I yearned for his discourse to persist without interruption. It felt as though my mind was emitting waves of euphoric hormones while my heart experienced an elevated rhythm.

He possesses an almost supernatural ability to captivate anyone and bend them to his will. I also found myself falling under his influence. After all, we're only talking for about fifteen minutes; why should I be overly particular? Meeting with him seems like a worthwhile endeavor. As someone who's my senior, I could glean a few insights into subjects where I currently face challenges.

He gazed at me with hopeful anticipation, clearly seeking a positive reply. I paused briefly before speaking up, "Daniel, I'd rather not invest my time in discussions about trivial matters, political dynamics, socioeconomic trends, or the insensitivity of others manifested through inhumane actions; essentially, anything that might divert my focus from my studies. I have my entire life to keep abreast of global or humanitarian issues, but this time, I strictly want to devote myself to my studies. Nonetheless, I will certainly mull over your proposal. If I decided to spend my fifteen-minute coffee break with you, we would discuss our academic pursuits only."

Daniel's face lit up, and he grinned wide. "Certainly, that's completely fine with me. And to be clear, if you choose not to join me, don't stress about it, and please don't interpret my being in the canteen as stalking. Just like you, I'll be here, relishing my coffee and adhering to my usual routine."

"Alright, Daniel. I'll make a move. But don't get your hopes up about sharing a coffee with me," I playfully taunted, a grin on my face.

"Allow me to stay optimistic. I believe that by this time tomorrow, we'll be engaged in discussions about our studies and our favorite subjects," Daniel replied, his enthusiasm mirrored in the gleam of his eyes.

With a goodbye, I left for the library. Later, Daniel's cheerful visage materialized in my thoughts as I laid my head on the pillow at night. I'm inclined to believe in his authenticity, and the prospect of a friendship with him seems delightful. Nevertheless, the risk of this pleasure evolving into anguish looms large, considering the potential for our camaraderie to develop into a romantic entanglement; he's not likely to relocate to Hyderabad, and I have no intention of remaining here. Trusting in a mere platonic bond between two adults of opposite genders is farcical. Dany Baby has made no secret of his fondness for me, and within two meetings, his powerful charisma has completely drawn me in, setting the stage for a potential disaster. I must maintain a distance from him to ensure my happiness and remain focused on my academic pursuits. That's the rational dictation of my mind. Yet, my foolish heart urged me to trust my capabilities of maintaining a friendship without succumbing to a romantic liaison. This inner conflict raged on, eventually fading into my subconscious as I drifted into a profound slumber.

As I made my way to the Canteen the following day, I resolved not to meet with Daniel. However, not to my surprise, he was seated at the same table with two coffee mugs and two plates of sandwiches. I casually strolled up to him and took a seat opposite, teasingly asking, "Is this your way of enticing me to join you?"

"No, Ma'am. I noticed your coffee sessions typically last a maximum of fifteen minutes, and I thought if you choose to sit with me, I shouldn't allow you to waste the valuable time you would spend fetching the drink," Dany said with an air of innocence. It's becoming apparent that this man is poised to cause me great anguish, as I can already envision myself falling irrevocably for him.

For some inexplicable reason, I uttered the words I hadn't planned on: "Okay, Daniel, I'll join you at your table whenever I come to the canteen for my coffee. But mark my words; the instant you steer the conversation toward your fabricated tale about my appearance or traits, I'll get up and part ways for good."

"Of course, Ma'am. As a starting point, would it be all right if I address you as Rukhs? Your full name might prove a bit of a tongue-twister for me," Dany said with a smile.

"Feel free to use whatever name comes easily to you. And as for me, addressing you as Daniel seems a tad too formal. How about I go with 'Dany'?" I suggested playfully.

"Dany coming from your lips is a delightful sound, no pun intended," he replied, his smile carrying a hint of mischief.

As we both held our coffee cups, taking delicate sips, I asked Dany, "Tell me, were your parents strict disciplinarians who instilled in you an unwavering focus and discipline in your studies and personal life? Did they leave no room for leisure activities, or did they wield a stick to shape you into the person you are today?"

"My parents have always practiced a very disciplined lifestyle. They get up early, jog together, and put in long hours at work five days a week, on average, clocking in at 10-12 hours a day. Occasionally, they spend a few hours at the lab on weekends and holidays. They don't make much time for things like going out to dinner with friends or having guests over, but they took time to take me out for lunch or dinner on the weekends. The only people who were ever invited to our house were close relatives, and even then, it was only on Sundays for brunch or tea.

"Regarding my upbringing, my parents consistently encouraged me to participate in sports, socialize with friends, and enjoy the popular leisure activities prevalent among the other kids in our neighborhood. They felt compelled to do so because they observed that I was content in my own company. In addition to my weekly allowance, my mother would even secretly slip extra money into my pockets to ensure I never shied away from where I wanted to go or shop for what I wanted.

"Nevertheless, what genuinely interested me from childhood was emulating my parents routines, going to bed early, joining them for a jog, showering, having my breakfast, and leaving for school. On the weekend holidays, I'd prefer to spend my afternoon watching an action thriller or shopping for essentials. I stopped spending time with male classmates or neighborhood guys as they were only interested in booze and girls. Moreover, I did venture into dating when I was fourteen years old, but it didn't take long for me to realize that the girls I met weren't the right fit, and the timing wasn't ideal either. So, I made the conscious decision to put dating on hold until I finished my studies and felt prepared to settle down," Dany expressed the comments in a smooth flow, reflecting honesty and sincerity that impressed me.

"I must commend your lifelong commitment to self-discipline; I've always believed that discipline is the stepping stone to success," I whispered in response to his statement.

Dany, intrigued by my perspective, asked, "Tell me a bit about your upbringing. Did your parents keep you in a straitjacket, or was discipline something innate in you?"

"I was an incredibly spoiled child. My father doted on me, my brother treated me like his own daughter due to the age gap of nine years, and my mom never asked me to do anything except feed me the sweet dishes and chocolates I liked the most. Up until the tenth grade, I was overweight, lazy, and solely interested in indulging my cravings. No one ever told me that I was overweight or that it was unhealthy to be so fat, and it could be because I was excellent in my studies.

"It wasn't until I entered college that things took a turn. While chatting with a friend one day, I overheard a conversation between a few boys standing nearby.

"One of the boys asked who would wed this triple X lump of fat, and another guy responded that it would have to be a man with a weighing scale in his hand, searching for the fattest girl in the town, and they laughed aloud. The cruel laughter reverberated like a heartless chorus. I stood there, wounded and aflame with heartache, my girlfriend's chatter fading into the background. My heart bled profusely, and the nerves in my brain felt as if they were on the brink of splintering.

"That evening, I cried for two hours. My parents tried to console me, but when their efforts failed, they scolded me and left. My brother called me from Japan. My parents must have informed him about my wailing, and he told me that crying wouldn't change anything. If I didn't want people to call me fat, I needed to act. We had a vast backyard and front lawn, and he suggested I start jogging for an hour in the morning and evening, completely cut down on my sugar intake, and take light and early dinners. No late-night gorging. He also asked me to use his gym, which was a few steps away from my bedroom, and do exercises like push-ups, crunches, and squats, promising I'd become as fit as a fiddle within a year. He really supported me in my fitness journey, and within four months, I built up the stamina to jog for an hour twice a day. I told my mom not to serve me sweets or sugary drinks. Just as my brother had predicted, I lost 18 kilos in one year and another 16 kilos the following year. I went from 90 kilos to 56 kilos. My laziness vanished, and I became more energetic and active. The discipline I developed in my exercise routine spilled over into every aspect of my life. I now weigh 58 kilos; a two-kilo increase is mainly due to Canteen food, limited time for jogging, and no exercise," I concluded, rising from my chair. "That's enough personal talk for today. From tomorrow, let's focus solely on our studies. Goodbye for now." I said and walked towards the library.

As the days went by, our daily meetings became an indispensable part of my routine, an unmissable fixture in my day. This urbane gentleman exerted a magnetic pull on me, drawing me closer to him with each passing day. As I yearned for a more relaxed and extended time together, I found myself eagerly anticipating the moment when he would finally ask me out for lunch, dinner, or a movie. He had never mentioned the subject since our coffee dates began nearly four months ago. I suspected he was apprehensive, fearing that if he violated my initial terms for our meeting, I would refuse even a coffee meeting.

I couldn't quite express my desire to spend some leisurely time with him. Still, the impulse grew so compelling that I mustered the courage to ask, under the pretext that I needed to pick up a few essentials, whether he would accompany me to the recently opened shopping mall over the weekend. Without hesitation, he agreed and offered to pick me up from the hostel entrance around five o'clock in the evening.

The night before our shopping mall date, I had barely slept. My mind was racing with thoughts of what to wear, how much makeup to apply, which heels to choose, and whether I should take him for dinner afterward or grab a bite at the mall's food court. This date was exciting for me, as I had never been on one in Hyderabad or here.

The first three years of my degree course in Hyderabad were lost in shaping up my body, shedding flab, and achieving a svelte appearance. The final year, in contrast, seemed to have sped by in a whirlwind, driven by the intense pressure to secure top grades in preparation for my postgraduate studies at a prestigious US university. Therefore, my excitement is entirely justified, and the anticipation of how this experience would unfold added to my feelings of both nervousness and exhilaration.

The following day, I dedicated my morning to the task of choosing the perfect outfit for the evening ahead. While coming here, my mother thoughtfully packed a selection of formal dresses suitable for evening gatherings. Among them were three elegant floor-length ball gowns and four exquisite Indian Anarkali suits. These Anarkali suits were meticulously crafted from flowing silk fabric and adorned with intricate embroidery, sequins, and various embellishments, making them appropriate for daytime wear as well.

Observing numerous Indian women confidently strolling through the streets and shopping malls in traditional attire, I felt assured that wearing an Anarkali suit wouldn't make me stand out but rather blend in, albeit garnering some attention, especially from male onlookers. Given that Dany had primarily observed me in jeans and tops, I believed it was the perfect time to introduce him to my Indian heritage.

I commenced my preparations at three in the afternoon. It began with a soothing herbal beauty bath, followed by applying a gentle daytime makeup look, and finally, getting dressed. I opted for a lovely light green Anarkali outfit. After the final touches and before going down, I looked in the mirrors; I wasn't entirely sure if I was a stunner, but I was confident that my poise would captivate many.

Dany was waiting beside a gleaming snow-white Range Rover at the hostel's entrance. He looked dapper in formal beige trousers and a neatly tucked light yellow full-sleeved shirt, accentuated by his Walnut Burgundy suede leather Oxford shoes.

He graciously opened the passenger door and assisted me into the car. As we began our journey, he inquired, "Are you certain we're going to the Shopping Mall?"

"Why this question?" I asked, a hint of surprise evident in my voice.

"Just a heads-up, I hope this doesn't come off the wrong way. You look absolutely stunning, but I worry about the evil eye of young girls and men. Envy can be pretty strong, and I don't want it casting a shadow over you," Dany commented, his smile warm and genuine.

"I had no idea you were so skilled in the art of flirtation! Are you attempting to achieve any hidden motives with such adulation?" I questioned, genuinely intrigued.

Dany spoke sincerely, "I'm not trying to butter you up or anything. I genuinely believe you look absolutely captivating, especially in your Indian attire. It really brings out your elegance and grace. I hope everything goes well for you."

"As much as I appreciate your flattering words about my beauty and grace, I'm not sure I buy into all of it. Let's skip the superstitions about the evil eye, okay?" I said with a playful grin.

"Let's hope we come out laughing and enjoy a lovely dinner in a restaurant of your choice," Dany stated with a big grin.

"No, we won't be dining out. If we feel hungry after shopping, we can grab a snack from the food court and return, as I must devote a solid three to four hours wrestling with my course books," I stated firmly. Despite my desire for a cozy meal with him, accepting the offer on our first date would be unwise.

"Rukhs, you cannot refuse to have dinner with me; I accepted your asking without a fuss, and it's your turn to reciprocate," Dany pleaded.

"I'm dead serious; dedicating three to four nerve-wracking hours to my course materials is a sacrifice I can hardly make," I persisted, expecting a more enticing counteroffer from him. He didn't respond as we entered the mall parking area.

The newly built mall was incredibly spacious, and it housed almost all well-known brands and much more. First, I bought a couple of silk tops, and as I approached the cashier to pay for them with the credit card that I got from my bro, Dany hurried over, eager to settle the bill. I looked him square in the eye, a stern gaze, and reprimanded him, saying, "If you pay even a single cent, I'll leave all my shopping in your car."

"Thanks, Rukhs, for spoiling my chance to enjoy spending some money," Dany said, his voice tinged with disappointment. His initial excitement faded quickly, overshadowed by the weight of my critical words, leaving a palpable silence between us.

I ignored his comments, and we walked out. I continued my shopping spree: scarves, hair and makeup accessories, and so on. While passing a perfume store, I decided to check out if I could get glued to a new fragrance. While entering the store, I asked Dany whether I could buy him a perfume of my choice, and surprisingly, he said yes to my offer. I bought him a Christian Dior Fahrenheit, and he was pleased with my choice.

It was almost two hours since we entered the mall, and he didn't complain or look tired, but I was uncomfortable because of the leather sandals I wore. So, I said to Dany, "If you're hungry, we could eat something here or else drop me at the hostel."

"Rukhs, I'm very hungry, but I don't want to eat anything here, and after dropping you off, I will find an eatery for my grub," Dany said in a depressing tone.

"You sound very upset. Is it because I refused your dinner invitation?" I said with a smiling face.

"Yes, Ma'am, I'm unhappy. I know you're excellent in your studies, and if you miss one evening, it won't affect you; you could easily catch up with the few hours you sacrificed," Dany said in an unhappy tone.

"Okay, Dany. I've enjoyed the shopping tremendously, and right now, the best way to bring a smile to your mopey face is to have a bite with you. If you want to feed me lamb or chicken, take me to an Indian restaurant, or else take me to a place where I could get seafood. Now cheer up, please," I said smilingly.

Dany's face glowed with happiness, and he asked me, "Rukhs, give me your hand."

I gave him my right hand, and he took it in his two hands, kissed the back of my palm exactly at the thenar eminence area, and said, "Thank you, Rukhs. I'm very pleased, and now I'm feeling famished. Please suggest a decent Indian restaurant, as I have heard a lot about Indian food but have never had the opportunity to enjoy it."

I suggested that we go to the 'The Maharaja' restaurant, which is around two miles from the campus. I have been there a few times; it has an excellent ambiance, and the food wasn't out of this world but perfect for my taste buds.

Dany appreciated the restaurant's decor and felt even more satisfied when he noticed several Caucasian diners. He asked me to place the order but with mild spices. I ordered Tandoori Chicken Wings and Onion fritters for the starter and, for the main course, 'Butter Chicken, Rogan Josh lamb curry, and Hyderabadi Biryani with flat bread Nan.'

The food was delicious, with very mild spices, and with every bite, Dany was proclaiming that whatever he heard was much conservative and, in fact, it was much more than just delectable.

The following week, while sipping coffee at the canteen, Dany informed me that on Saturday, his parents were coming for the weekend to celebrate his birthday, and I had to join him at his apartment for the celebrations. No one will be there except his parents, just four of us. I wanted to meet with his parents but had no idea why; I accepted the invitation.

On Saturday morning, I went to a shopping mall and bought a Creed Aventus Eau de Parfum and an assorted flower bouquet. Dany picked me up from the hostel at seven, and on our way, he informed me that his parents met when they were doing their doctorate and decided to marry instead of wasting time on dating, which they did. I was born within a year after they secured their doctorates; I don't have any siblings since one child was enough for them. They joined a newly founded Biotechnology Company established by a large pharma company primarily aimed to research and develop new drugs, medical devices, diagnostic test equipment, and other products that can improve human health. The company lured them with an offer of 7% each company share plus fantastic salary and perks. The company has grown tremendously and currently produces medicines and equipment that are hardly in competition. They are loaded with money but live a very simple life, traveling by economy class, wearing cotton clothes and sneakers, and driving more than seven-year-old cars. Their affluence is evident solely in the state-of-the-art Grady-White Freedom 336 yacht and the opulent seaside residence. Both are crazy about scuba diving, fishing, or spending time together eating freshly caught fish in the ocean.

"Do you also accompany them and love fishing and diving," I inquired.

"They taught me all the skills when I was hardly ten years old, but I'm passionate about windsurfing. However, since I joined MIT, I haven't been anywhere near the ocean," Dany replied.

Dany's two-bedroom rented apartment was furnished with basic necessities and had an open living room and kitchen hall.

Dany informed me that his parents would be back shortly since they had gone to collect the birthday cake.

Meeting Dany's parents was a pleasure. They were so down-to-earth and unassuming that you would never guess that they were wealthy and accomplished scientists. Both looked like they were in their mid or late thirties, though they were in their fifties, were slim and tanned, and moved with grace and ease. I believe they were also gifted conversationalists, as they talked to me as if I were an old acquaintance. They asked me about the well-being of my father, mother, brother, and his Japanese wife, my future plans, and so on. Dany babe is updating them about me and my family, which is good to know.

Dinner was from Maharaja, and I believe Dany brought all the dishes that were on the menu. It was the first time their parents tasted Indian food, and they loved it and cursed themselves for not going to an Indian eatery before.

After dinner and the cake cutting, Dany and his dad decided to go for a walk to settle the excessive eating. I also wanted to go with them since I didn't want to sleep with a bloated tummy, but Martha Theo, Dany's mom, was unwilling to let me go and wanted me to give her company.

She prepared green tea with a dash of lemon and honey, and after a few sips, she cleared her throat and addressed me, "You know, Rukhs, I was dying to meet with you. Dany is madly in love with you and has told me everything you ever said to him. From childhood, he never showed any interest in girls; his passion was his course books or movies, mostly thrillers. When he was fourteen, he dated a few girls, but I do not know what transpired; he decided not to date any girl until he completed his education and established himself. We thought his sexual orientation was different, which he was hiding from us. I was pleasantly surprised and unhappy when he informed me that he had found his dream girl, but it looked like he couldn't marry her. She's an Indian and has no plans to stay here after her master's, and I cannot relocate as I have to do my doctorate and work here.

"Tell me, Rukhs, why do you need to go back? It seems you're a brilliant student, so why do you want to stop after the master's, do your doctorate, and settle down in this country? If you need any assistance, regardless of whether political clout or financial, we can provide everything; you have to name it."

After a few moments of pause, I gathered my response, "Can I call you Auntie, or do you prefer Martha?"

"I love to hear Auntie from you; I was the only child of my parents and never had any first cousins with children who could call me Auntie," Martha said, reflecting lots of love in her tone.

"Auntie, my parents are old; has many ailments. Dad had a bypass surgery performed at a US hospital a few years back.

I have one elder brother, who's nine years older than me, and he married a Japanese girl and settled in Japan. He and his wife established a company that is doing very well. It's impossible for him to return to India. I came here with the promise that I'd do my master's and return, and even if they allowed me to stay here, I wouldn't, as I want to be their walking stick when they become frail and need someone to give them life support care. Moneywise, we're sound; my father obtained a civil engineering degree from a prestigious UK University and opened his own construction company, which did very well. However, after the heart attack, he almost stopped working and partly sold his company to two civil engineers who also worked as partners. When he was running his company, he bought lots of barren and fertile land and commercial buildings and invested wisely in major Indian corporate houses. All his investments must be giving him good dividends. I do not know how much wealth he has, but I know he has a lot because our lifestyle is only affordable to super-rich people. I'm studying because I believe that regardless of your plentiful money, you must still work and never sit idle, as that could destroy you physically and mentally. This was why I chose to get my postgraduate degree here: when I return, I could either find a decent job in a prestigious organization or establish my own venture."

"Rukhs, I'm very pleased to note that you have an indubitable purpose in your life: to look after your parents in their hour of need. In our country, no such thing exists; when you're old and if you have money in your pocket, you could stay in a luxurious Assisted Living Facilities with all the amenities that one could think of, or otherwise, you could go to a place run by an NGO. We don't expect our children to be there for us when we need them most, nor were we there for our parents, so it pairs off. Having said that, you can bring your parents to this country, buy a decent place with an attached Multigenerational Home for your parents' stay, and hire the necessary help. Dany will help you organize everything. Let me tell you a few things about Dany. He's a kind-hearted and sensitive boy, and I'm proud that I gave birth to a wonderful human being. He's deeply in love with you and has informed me that besides looks, you're intelligent and disciplined, and you speak in low decibels, which he liked the most. It seems that the moment his eyes fell upon you, a spark ignited within him. He was immediately captivated, his heart affirming, 'She's the one.' He then inquired about you and learned of your brilliance and academic prowess. Fascinated, he resolved to delve deeper, investing ample time in observing your daily routines. These observations confirmed your discipline, evident even on weekends when you didn't stray from your path. This reinforcement only deepened his belief that you were his soulmate. He's my son, but allow me to tell you that missing a gem of a person like him is the most silly thing you could do. He has gone to the extent that if religion is a barrier, he will follow your faith. My husband didn't propose to me; instead, I proposed to him, as I thought such gems are hard to come by, and I should grab the opportunity. It's been over 25 years since we got married, and I'm very happy that I did the right thing; he's intelligent, hardworking, has no vices to talk about, and is a family man. My Dany is like his father, and I could bet my life that he will keep you happy and satisfied," Martha commented in her soft and melodious voice.

"Auntie, I believe every word you have said. First, religion is not an issue for me, or even it would be an issue for my folks.

My brother married a Japanese girl who practices both Shinto and Buddhism, yet both live happily and never complain.

"Based on my observations, I strongly believe that being a decent human being is not determined by the faith one follows. Instead, it is shaped by one's innate nature, upbringing, and the values instilled within, ultimately defining whether a person is good or bad. From my perspective, religion functions as a framework for engaging in good deeds. Still, it lacks the ability to embed itself in your system and bring about a fundamental transformation in your character.

"I have not interacted much with Dany, except spending ten or fifteen minutes while having our evening coffee, and still, I could tell that he has qualities that make him an ideal person to marry. Unfortunately, I cannot ask him to relocate to my place, as the research that he wants to do could be facilitated here only, and I cannot stay in this country for my own compulsions. Nonetheless, I have close to a year to spend here, and as you know, situations change, circumstances change, preferences change, and something unthinkable today could become very much conceivable. I'm not indicating anything or promising anything but signifying possibilities that could come up to make the improbable a reality," I expressed in my usual low-decibel soft voice.

"Fine, yet allow me to tell you not to miss an opportunity to marry a person who's dying to marry you and who could keep you happy and content as long as he's alive," Martha Auntie stated in her soft voice.

"It will be in my mind, Auntie, and as I said, you never know when, why, and how things could take a turn for better or worse. I hope we all will be at peace in the future," I stated earnestly.

Then we talked about her passion for scuba diving, and she informed me that she inherited it from her father, a schoolteacher who worked as a scuba diving coach on the weekends. Her mother was a personal trainer who taught aerobics and also taught scuba diving on the weekends. She met my dad through the scuba diving school that booked the students for the weekend practical sessions. After dating for a few months, they decided to settle down.

As for her own marriage, she explained that she and her husband knew each other from university but never interacted much. They reconnected at a deep-sea scuba diving session that he was attending as a participant, and she was there assisting her father because her mother was busy with her own students. They were both surprised to discover their shared passion for scuba diving; over time, she developed feelings for him and eventually proposed. He was thrilled by her proposal, and they married before finishing their doctorates.

The father-son duo returned from their stroll while our conversation moved from one topic to another.

The next three weeks passed without feedback about what I had discussed with his mother, and I did not inquire about his parents comments about me. Just before the third weekend, Dany inquired sheepishly, "Would you be available tomorrow night for dinner at the Maharaja? I really miss the butter chicken and the Nan."

Idiot, I was waiting for him to take me to dinner. Why Maharaja, and why not an expensive seafood restaurant where we could enjoy tiger prawns, lobster tail, and Norwegian

Saloman fillets? So, I said, "Let's go for a fine dining seafood eatery like Legal Sea Foods, which has 4.2 stars on Google or any other place of your choice, and this will be my treat."

"Thank you, Rukhs. Take me anywhere. I want to enjoy your company, look at your face, watch you laughing, smiling, or just talking. And mind you, I invited you, so it's on me. You pay the next bill when you invite. Since it's a weekend, you better book a table, or else we may have to stand in a queue," Dany said laughingly.

I was looking at him; his smiling eyes and relaxed facial muscles were heartwarming. My heart ached when I thought if I missed this boy to hold my hands and take me to my eternal peace, then life would be nothing but regret. He'll always remain in my dreams and will not let me leave a content life. I must find a way to marry him, and if I have to get my parents here, then I should do that.

"Your praising words of my looks are not appreciated. I have clarified that our friendship is strictly platonic, and I would prefer that we keep our interactions focused on our shared interests and activities. Even if we have decided to have a bite together as and when we want to, that doesn't mean you're free to express the romantic or intimate views you're harboring. Calm down, my friend, or you might miss the opportunity to interact with this Babe forever," I had to say this, or else he may become more aggressive and become a pain to handle. I'm equally or more in love with him, but a lot of things had to be ironed out before we decided to be together forever.

"Sorry, Rukhs. I got carried away and expressed my feelings for you. I'll be more careful in the future, but allow me to say that if you desert me for another man, you will see my dead body, period," Dany said in his usual low voice but with a hint of hurt.

"Save me from your emotional manipulation; I haven't made any commitments to you and don't welcome your sentiments, likely stemming from mere physical charm or a passing fancy. I'd prefer it if you avoided making comments that aren't within the scope of our friendship," I felt indescribable happiness with his comments. Still, I needed to maintain control until I was ready to commit.

"I've laid bare my genuine feelings, and it's entirely up to you how you interpret them," Dany expressed, keeping his composure.

It was almost over five months since we first met. Still, except for eating out on weekends, we were not putting any effort into paving the way for entering a relationship that could hold onto us forever. One day, while talking to Bro, I blurted out that a senior student is keenly interested in me and the whole lot that has happened since the day we first met.

"Not to worry, next week, I'm on the European tour with my wife, and I'll send her back at the end of our tour as our boy gives hard time to his grandparents. I'll come just for a day, so check with Dany whether he will be available to meet with me. Tell him to keep himself free from Saturday evening till I leave, most likely on Sunday noon," Bro made my day. The way he handled my hysteria was amazing; he was cool and never asked any questions, just said he'd come to meet Dany.

I informed Dany that my Bro is coming for a day and asked if he would be interested in meeting him on the coming weekend. Dany showed keen interest and confirmed that he's very much available and would love to meet him. I didn't tell him why my brother was coming and why he wanted to meet with him.

Bro came Saturday late at night and called me from the Hotel, informing me that I should come to his hotel tomorrow with Dany between 11 and 12 in the morning. He was staying at the Four Seasons Hotel, which was just a walking distance from the campus.

We were at Bro's hotel around 11:15 am the following day. A girl at the reception organized an escort to take us to Bro's room. As we walked to his room, the escort mentioned that he was staying in the hotel's most luxurious Royal Suite. This magnificent suite boasts three lavishly furnished bedrooms, a distinct living space, a formal dining room, a media room, and a fully equipped service kitchen.

My brother looked more dashing than I last saw. Marriage and money suit him well. He was wearing jeans and a round-neck light blue T-shirt. We spent the next 25-30 minutes talking about our education, future, families, and shared interests. He also briefed us about his company's activities and what they offer to their clients worldwide.

Bro suddenly changed the topic, addressed Dany, and said, "Dany, I don't want to beat around the bush, and will come straight to the topic of concern that drove me here. I was informed that you wanted to marry my sister. Since you belong to an educated family, raised in the shadow of loving parents, you must have been to an excellent educational institution that money can afford. Your brilliance is evident, as you are now pursuing postgraduate studies at the esteemed MIT. Considering your upbringing, education, and your plans for the future, I think you're suitable to marry my sister. However, my sister had a major concern: she did not want to settle in this country and wanted to be with her parents when they became frail and infirm.

"As a liberal, I'm skeptical about the idea that marrying someone from your faith automatically ensures happiness. However, navigating relationships that bridge different faiths, nationalities, and cultures has its own complexities. Both partners often need to make significant compromises to foster a harmonious and satisfying partnership.

"I suggest both of you open your hearts and discuss in depth whether you want to spend the rest of your life together or whether it's just a passing fling rooted in physical attraction. Either of you are highly intelligent and capable of making a well-thought-out decision. Talk about every minute issue that could surface and make you rethink your choice.

"I'll give my example of how silly things become challenging to overcome. After my marriage, we were very happy; however, my wife noticed I had lost a few kilos of weight in the first few months of our marriage. She wasn't a cook, but before our marriage, she learned how to cook delicious Japanese dishes from acclaimed cooks since I told her I loved Japanese food, particularly the Tempura prawns, Yakitori, Sukiyaki, Udon, and the world-famous Sushi.

"Eating different types of food can be a pleasure, as it allows us to explore new flavors and cultures. However, eating food that our taste buds are not used to all the time can be challenging. This is because our taste buds are accustomed to the foods that we have grown up eating, and they may not be able to accept the flavors of new foods on a regular basis, and that's what was happening to me. I wasn't eating a full meal, skipping the meals under flimsy excuses, which resulted in weight loss. My wife's exceptional intelligence and foresight enabled her to sense trouble brewing. She took proactive steps by engaging a recruiting company specialized in providing Indian cooks proficient in the Japanese language, a prerequisite for obtaining the Designated Activities Visa. Ever since the cook arrived, my weight loss journey came to a halt. My wife took it upon herself to teach her Japanese cooking while she learned the art of preparing Indian curries from her. Now, our dining table showcases a fusion of Indian curries and Japanese delicacies.

"This wasn't a minor concern, as it could have escalated into a significant problem that might have seriously jeopardized our marriage. So, discuss every significant or insignificant issue and determine whether it could be resolved and who would be willing to sacrifice to overcome it. Please finalize your decision when convenient and let me know whether you wish to proceed with marriage or choose to go your separate ways."

While we were talking, waiters came pushing several trolleys loaded with a variety of food and sweet dishes. We continued our discussion at the dining table and identified several issues that could surface only after marriage and become challenging to resolve. Dany asked multiple questions, and Bro answered them smiling; he even asked his wife's name, Emi Ito, which is easy to pronounce. After lunch, Dany called me to a corner and asked, "Can I leave now so you can spend some family time together?" I nodded.

Dany left after profusely thanking Bro for the lovely lunch and appreciating his approval for marrying me.

Bro's name was Jawad Jahangir, but I used to call him Jadoo. When Dany left, I excitedly asked Bro, "Jadoo, how did you find Dany? Did he meet your expectations?"

"Difficult to find any flaws in him, Rukhs. Having said that, I would like to remind you of a couple of Hindi sayings, 'First - Gold purity can only be established by rubbing it on the touchstone, and the next, 'To know a person, you must live with him.' A similar English saying is, 'You can't know a man until you've walked a mile in his shoes.'

"Marriage, whether arranged or after an elaborate courtship, is still a toss, and if you ask me, life itself is a toss; you never know when things could change for the worse or better. In such a scenario, you make a well-thought-out, meticulously measured pros and cons and decide whether to take the plunge or not, and once you decide to go ahead, have faith that things will work out as you expected, not exactly the way you wanted to be but close enough to be happy with your decision.

"I suggest ironing out every possible scenario and judging him by his approach to dealing with all your concerns; read between the lines to whatever he's saying. Try to understand how he wants to resolve all your concerns; is he trying to take a firm stand or wants to play it by ear? If he says we'll deal with it when we have to cross over that bridge, it means you could be in for a possibly disappointing stand.

"Allow me to share my own experience with you. Emi was dying to marry me during the courtship, and I was reluctant to settle with her. Emi was truly remarkable: educated, beautiful, intelligent, sharp- witted, had an excellent upbringing, held a prestigious position, and was probably making a fortune. Her love and constant reiteration to keep me happy made me take the bait; however, just after a few weeks of marriage, I realized it was a massive blunder. The cultural differences, language barrier, food preferences, and adjusting to various issues that wouldn't have existed if I had married a person of my origin. However, in a few months, both of us adjusted to our new way of life, and the love quotient that had disappeared immediately after the marriage slowly resurfaced when we noticed how much we cared for each other; she brought an Indian cook for me and installed a satellite dish that could allow me to watch Indian news and movie channels. We enrolled in language institutes to familiarize ourselves with each other's native languages, allowing us to appreciate Hindi or Japanese movies, reality shows, news, and more. Now, we have become more compatible and loving, and after the birth of our son, life has given us another reason to remain in love," Bro was always to the point and concise, and this sermon was also no exception.

We spent another hour talking about various things going on in our lives, and on his way to the airport, Bro dropped me at the hostel and left, leaving behind a vacuum in me.

The next day, Dany and I agreed to meet for dinner at the weekend and discuss what Bro had advised. Over this period, I drafted a list detailing what I desired from him if the prospect of marriage were to be entertained. To begin with, after the completion of his doctorate, he should relocate to my place so long as my parents are alive. Next, he'll not bring alcohol in the house or bring home any non-veg food that's not halal. Occasional drinks and any non-veg food of his choice outside the house are okay, but a big no inside the house. We will stick to our beliefs without any pressure to adopt the other's faith. I want at least two children; the first name will be a Muslim, selected by me, and the last name will be Daniel. Marriage is to be performed in a Mosque and Church.

During the weekend dinner, I opened the topic and asked him, "Dany, if you're really serious about marrying me, then you must agree to my marriage terms." I then informed him of what I wanted.

Dany waited for a few moments and, in his usual low decibel voice, said, "As I said earlier, I want to marry you at any cost, so I'll accept all the terms that you've put forth, and from my side, I've only one condition that you do a doctorate in this country, and then it will be your decision whether we work here or go to your country. If you want, I will sign a prenuptial agreement to confirm our understanding."

My heart warmed with his amorous words; however, I said, "Listen, it's not entirely up to me; I need to discuss it with my brother. If he can arrange for me to stay here for another four or five years, I'd be keen to pursue my doctorate. I'll talk to him in the next few days and let you know his response. Even if I must have to leave immediately after finishing my degree, you could join me once you secure your doctorate. I'll wait for you, but if you find a better chick, don't hesitate to stay and enjoy life here. I know the saying 'Out of sight, out of mind,' so I won't hold it against you if you find someone better than me. And please don't talk about the nonsense of any agreement; I don't believe in tying up my man with an agreement; if he finds love somewhere else, I'll let him go," I retorted crisply.

"Rukhs, with my prenuptial agreement, I wanted to give you the assurance that I want to grow old with you and die in your arms. My decision is not impulsive or love at first sight; I've watched you for weeks and observed your disciplined way of life, which made me decide that you're the person I want to marry. And, yes, your beauty is a bonus I would be proud of. Still, your inner beauty is worth weighing in gold, and I wanted to marry that beautiful person," Dany conveyed his feelings toward me passionately, and I ballooned with pleasure.

"Dany, don't spoil me with your flattery that could go to my head and inflate my devilish ego. No more discussion on this topic, and it's time to return to the hostel and study," I said with a grin.

I called Bro at the weekend and informed him about my discussion with Dany, and he said, "He looks genuine to me, as I thought about him for long and hard and couldn't find any motive to come after you. He belongs to an educated family and is the only child of his wealthy parents. Instead of squandering himself, he remained focused on his studies, and soon, he would earn a postgraduate degree from the prestigious MIT. I completely understand his aspiration to attain a doctorate; someone with his skills is naturally driven to aim for excellence. His desire for you to pursue a doctoral degree may be a strategic move to accomplish two objectives simultaneously. He genuinely wishes to see you achieve a level of qualification similar to that of his parents, and he might be hopeful that circumstances in the next five years could unfold in a way that eliminates the need to relocate to India. Wanting to be certain about his parents, I decided to do a little digging. I'm glad to say that my findings aligned perfectly with what he had told us about them."

"But I don't want to do the doctorate; I cannot be away for the next five years with my loving, aging, and ailing parents," I said, expressing my real concern.

"Honey, being the only male child in the house, taking care of our parents is my responsibility. For your peace of mind, I'm constantly in touch with our family doctor, who's getting a monthly retainer from me, and according to him, both are doing very well; they are regularly exercising and keeping them moving, doing lots of house chores, in addition going out to buy grocery, to watch a movie or meet with the friends. Every Sunday morning, the doctor visits them to check Auscultation, BP, and Glucose levels, and every month, he does a Comprehensive Metabolic Panel and sends the report to me with his comments. When you were in Hyderabad, I hardly called Mom and Dad, even once a week, but after you left, I talked to them almost once or twice daily. Being a Japanese citizen and part owner of a highly profitable company, with my contacts in government, I'm exploring the possibility of getting a resident visa for them. So, relax and go after all your aspirations and make sure to materialize them. If you want to marry Dany, my consent and blessings are with you. You could go ahead anytime you want to marry; inform me at least four weeks in advance, and I'll come and organize everything. And, at this stage, there is no need to inform Mom and Dad anything about whatever is going on in your personal life," Bro always treated me like his own child, which was the reason for his detailed input on how I should deal with the situation at hand.

"So, you think I should do the doctorate, and there's absolutely nothing to be concerned about, Mom and Dad?" I once again asked to ensure I heard him correctly.

"A big yes, honey. Go ahead, sit with Dany, chart out your road map, and inform me," Bro said solemnly.

Days passed by, but I failed to raise the topic with Dany. I was in a dilemma and failed to decide whether to do the doctorate or go back, minus Dany, in my life. I never envisioned staying here and doing a doctorate, but if I pursued it, I was sure that, give or take a few months more or less, I would secure the prestigious degree in a five-year timeframe. However, the million-dollar question was whether I really wanted to marry Dany. I didn't have a clear-cut answer, but yes, I may not be able to find a better person to spend a peaceful and happy life, and it would provide immense pleasure to raise his children. Today, he will give in to all my demands, but as the passage of time ensues, he may not feel the same way about me, and our once-solid foundation of emotional closeness and a vow to be together until death will erode.

During my teenage years, I spent all my holidays reading primarily romantic novels, and I still remember Nora Roberts's romance novels, which often feature strong-willed heroines and alpha heroes. Dany Boy is a typical example of an alpha hero, and if not now but in the future, I would be in danger of losing him, as any aggressive, alluring girl could chase him till he surrenders. However, my assessment of his characteristics tells me he's a strong-willed and hard-to-crack person; otherwise, he wouldn't have stopped dating at age fourteen when the teenage hormones were at their peak. Still, it is important to remember that love is a choice, and maintaining a relationship means a lot of care and respect for each other, communicating openly and honestly, and doing things that you enjoy together. It's a lot, and it's not easy, particularly when one becomes insensitive or gets addicted to annoying habits. If I heed my brother's counsel that life is a gamble, then seizing this opportunity and facing the outcomes seems logical. Enduring life with a compromised soul is far tougher than taking a leap of faith towards potential success. Here, it's not blind chance but a brightly lit, tempting environment with minimal risk of failure at present. I decided not to open anything to Dany; instead, I should spend more intimate time with him, like going for long drives, watching movies, dining, and doing anything he likes to do in his leisure time.

We began socializing on weekends, Saturdays reserved for dinners, and Sundays for the ocean in Winthrop, Massachusetts, close to our campus. There, he would rent a boat from the Boston Charter Boat Company, and we would venture two to three hundred meters into the deep waters to catch fish, eat snacks, drink coffee, and laugh at each other's silly jokes. He used to swim alone, even though I carried my swimsuit in my shoulder bag, a half-sleeved top, and knee-length plaid pajamas. He never invited me to swim with him. Perhaps he assumed I couldn't swim, but I've been an accomplished swimmer since I was twelve years old. I even competed in inter-school competitions and won several trophies. On the third week, when we were in the ocean, Dany was swimming close to the boat and asked me, "If you want to swim, I could teach you."

I asked him to turn and not look at the boat. I quickly changed into my swimsuit and dived, surfaced near Dany, who grinned and looked happy to see me swim close to him. We circled the boat for twenty minutes, and I came out of the water; it wasn't that cold, but now it made my body uncomfortable to swim further. Typically, our timings when we were in the waters were good as it was the time for spring tides, posing no difficulty for experienced swimmers like Dany and myself.

Another month passed, and neither of us raised the topic of a doctorate or how we would proceed. I noticed that he was afraid of even rubbing shoulders while we watched a movie or holding my hand while walking on the streets. One weekend, after our swim, we were having lunch at a beachside restaurant; Dany asked, "Have you talked to your brother about the doctorate?"

I replied, "Yes, and he asked me to decide what I wanted to do and not to worry about the parents, as he would take care of them."

"That's wonderful news. We should get married immediately or will not meet until you're ready to marry. Suppressing my urges to hold your hand, hug you, kiss you, and show my affection in various ways is becoming challenging with every passing day. If you want me to propose to you, I'm willing to do that right now, provided you happily agree and accept my proposal," Dany stated with pain and genuineness in his voice. I was over the moon, and I've no idea how and why, but I just blurted out, "Why not, Dany? Go ahead on your knee and propose."

Dany jumped from his seat and said, "Let me get a rose from the flower shop, which is just a few steps from here."

I saw him from the window. He went to his car, picked something, and then went toward the flower shop. He returned with a long-stem rose and a photographer in the toe, with a big camera hanging by his neck.

He shouted at the diners and said, "Ladies, gentlemen, could you please witness my proposal to this lovely lady." Everyone rose from their chair and surrounded our table. Dany went on one knee, holding in his left hand the flower and in his right hand a small box of Tiffany, in it a rose gold ring with a glittering large rock, must be at least three carats, and said, "Rukhs, you are the most amazing girl I have ever met. You are my love of life, my soulmate. I can't imagine my life without you. Will you marry me?"

Words couldn't come out of my mouth; I just extended my hand, and he pushed the ring onto my finger, kissed my hand, and rose. Everyone clapped and congratulated; the photographer was constantly clicking the photos. As he rose, he extended his arms, and I fulfilled his desire and wrapped myself in his warm body; first, he kissed me on my head, and when I looked at him, he gave me a peck to show gratitude, and everyone whistled, clapped, and laughed.

While returning, I complained, "Dany, why did you buy such an expensive solitaire ring, and how come you decided to buy it in gold? Another amazing thing I must appreciate is your keen eye, which perfectly measured my finger size."

Dany smiled and reverted, "Nothing is expensive when it comes to the love of my life. Next, I've seen most Indian girls wear gold jewelry, including rings, so I ordered the diamond set in rose gold. Regarding your last question, it was easy; I took a photo of your fingers, converted it to 3D, and measured the finger circumference."

"Very smart, and when did you purchase it?" I inquired.

"Upon conversing with your brother, I felt confident that he would endorse our alliance. Therefore, I made sure to be ready to solidify our bond with a few minutes' notice. Please speak with your brother and seek the earliest date when we could marry; I want to spend every spare moment with you," Dany cheerfully informed.

"You'll know in a few days. Please drop me off at the hostel, as all my energies have drained out from the unexpected bombshell that exploded into my body," I said equally cheerfully.

Upon reaching the hostel, I left a voice message for Bro to call me ASAP and lay on the not-so-comfortable hostel bed I had become used to. Within a few minutes, my intercom chimed; Bro was on the line. I briefed him on what had transpired while we were having our lunch.

Bro inquired, "When does he want to marry you?" "I believe yesterday," I said, and we laughed aloud.

Bro then seriously questioned me, "What about you?"

"It's better to go by his request and proceed with the marriage as soon as possible. However, I urge you to make your decision considering your engagements," I said seriously.

"Within the next two months, I'll come for a week and organize everything. Please inform him that it's critical that we adhere to both Muslim and Christian wedding rituals. Don't tell Mom or Dad; I'll break the news at a suitable time and make them come to the wedding," Bro's words were soothing and delightful, and I profoundly thanked him, even though he asked me to shut up and focus on my studies.

The next day, I informed Dany about my conversation with Bro. He was over the moon and asked me to give a tentative date of his arrival as soon as possible, as his parents, along with a few relatives and friends, would want to join. They need advance notice to be away from work.

Bro, along with his wife, child, our parents, and his wife's parents, arrived and checked into the same suite in Four Seasons. Prior to his arrival, he meticulously organized every event, from the Nikah ceremony in a mosque to the wedding in the church and the grand reception in his hotel. I suspect he collaborated on all the arrangements with Dany. Dany's parents and a dozen families of close relatives and friends stayed in a different hotel. Initially, my parents were nervous, but upon meeting Dany and his parents, they became relaxed and enthusiastically participated in every event.

I became a married woman and celebrated our three-day honeymoon in a hotel suite arranged by Bro. Everyone left within a week, and I felt it was difficult to overcome the vacuum when my folks left.

Every morning, I thanked Allah for giving me such a gem. Before tying the knot, my primary concern revolved around his masculinity, but it turned out to be far more exciting than I had ever imagined, almost overwhelming in its intensity. There were nights when exhaustion took its toll, and I wasn't particularly in the mood, yet my attempts to create space between us were consistently unsuccessful.

Only on the weekends do we go out for lunch; otherwise, in the morning, we have breakfast at the flat and lunch at the canteen and dinner I was preparing, and while I was in front of the stove, he was filling the dishwasher, vacuuming the house, throwing the garbage, and doing anything that I asked. Luckily, while coming to the USA, I learned cooking, Intercontinental, Chinese, and Indian cuisines from Mom as well as from a professional cook. My cooking skills made Dany delighted with everything I prepared, but he had a penchant for Chicken Tikka and Butter Chicken, requesting them every other day. Despite the effort and time it took to make these dishes, I enjoyed cooking for him and found joy in fulfilling his cravings.

He always stopped me from engaging in household chores, apart from preparing dinner, emphasizing the importance of staying focused on my studies. Preparing tea, coffee, and snacks fell under his purview. He disallowed me from shouldering any bills and provided me with a credit card to cover all my expenses, be it groceries or personal needs.

Every week after lunch in a decent restaurant, he used to forcibly take me to a shopping mall and pressure me to buy clothes, bags, or any items of my choice. Once, he told me, he had in his bank account over a million dollars, and the money had piled up since school days, as Mom was putting in a handsome amount every week, and he was spending hardly ten percent out of that. He bought a Mercedes-Benz C-Class sedan for me as my marriage gift. He never went anywhere alone unless I had to push him to go to a convenience store to fetch something. He respected the terms of our marriage, refraining from bringing any alcohol or non-vegetarian items into our home. He didn't even drink during our weekend lunches, even though several times I asked him to enjoy a drink of his choice, but he refused, saying he only occasionally had a glass of wine or beer.

I was taking pills to avoid pregnancy, and everything was moving smoothly on all fronts. Bro's company was doing extremely well, Mom and Dad were keeping well, and Dany and I were enjoying every moment. He offered to take me on a honeymoon for a week or ten days, but I refused as the pressure of studying increased with every passing day.

We were in our fourth month of marriage; as per our ritual of Saturday, we had lunch in an Indian restaurant; post lunch, he took me to a shopping mall catering to the upper-middle-class segment. It was a huge circular five-story building; its ground floor boasted a spacious open hall adorned with popup shops. Enveloping this central area were approximately twenty or more stores showcasing a diverse array of high-end branded merchandise. Dany insisted that I buy anything I needed, and I was checking at the shops when the sound of firing rattled. Dany pushed me to the floor and leaped on me to provide cover. While he was diving on me, a bullet penetrated his skull, and he died on the spot. I went with his dead body to the hospital and first called my parents and then Dany's parents, and then I collapsed. When I got conscious, I could see from the window that it was daytime, and next, I saw Bro, my parents, and Dany's parents sitting on a sofa staring at me, and I was on the hospital bed with several machines attached to my body. Again, I passed out; my eyes opened for a fraction and closed. In the evening, I opened my eyes, and this time, I recalled what had befallen, and my dear Dany is no more. Silently, tears streamed down my cheeks without restraint.

The next day, I was discharged from the hospital, and Bro took me to his hotel. Bro informed me that seventeen people were killed, and more than fifty got injured before the security staff killed the culprit.

On the fourth day, we laid Dany to rest, and with tearful eyes, his parents departed without uttering a single word of solace to me or my family.

Upon return from the graveyard, Bro asked me what plans I had for the future. I said, "Please take me home; I don't think I could ever go to a college or study any further. I want to be with Mom and Dad and nothing more."

Over the next three days, I remained in the suite while my brother handled the logistics. He engaged a movers and packers company to handle the shipment of both Danny's and my belongings; mine was bound for Hyderabad, and Danny's and his vehicles were sent to his parents' address. Additionally, he oversaw the closure of my bank account, transferring all funds to Dad's account in Hyderabad. Moreover, he directed Danny's bank to close his account due to his passing, arranging for the available funds to be transferred to his parents account.

I was in a state of shock and failing to come out of the grief and pain inflicted by the passing of my Dany. We buried him, and I'll never be able to see him again. Why did God do this to my Dany, and how am I going to live without him? I should commit suicide, as that's the only way to come out of angst; I must do that, meet my Dany, and live with him for eternity.

Bro stayed for three days with us in Hyderabad and left but was calling me every day. Reminding me that we're helpless against God's will and couldn't do anything but pray for his soul to land in heaven. Our faith says, 'INNA LILLAHI WA INNA ILAYHI RAJI'UN,' which means 'To Allah, we belong, and to HIM, we shall return.' Your Dany has gone back to Allah, and why HE called him, HE knows better. It was Dany's destiny; he came into the world briefly but has left you with his sweet memories. Please cherish them and move on with your life. Don't mourn, and don't cry, as he's not going to come back, and no force on earth could turn the table for you.

My life seemed worthless, and I thought of ending it, but I held on for the sake of my parents, whom I wanted to care for in their old age. However, living without Dany seemed unbearable; he showered me with his affection, support, generosity, and, most importantly, his love. He made me lose my strength and independence, which I valued, but I felt like a child in his presence. He always agreed to whatever I wanted and never let me do any chores in the house except for cooking since he loved my preparations.

Once, I told Mom, "Though Dany could have possibly saved himself, he selflessly pushed me to the ground and shielded me by leaping on top of me. This split-second act of protection resulted in a momentary delay that led to the unfortunate impact. He was cruel; he left me in this world to mourn for him. No, Mom, I'll go to him and stay with him forever," I said and wailed.

The next day, at noon, I felt nauseated; within a span of half an hour, I vomited twice. Everyone panicked, thinking I may have taken some form of poison, and rushed me to a hospital. They conducted all the needed tests to ensure my body was free from any toxic elements, and when they couldn't find anything, they conducted a few more tests, including pregnancy. While all the test results were within the normal range, the pregnancy test indicated a positive result for a six-week-old embryo. Everyone was silent in the room, and the only sound I could hear was the beating of my heart, with ecstasy. Dany has given me the privilege of raising his child, and I will dedicate my life to doing that. The same evening, Bro phoned me and asked whether I wanted to keep the baby or get rid of it, and he believed there was no point hanging on memories that would cause constant pain. I said not to utter such hurtful comments again; I wanted to dedicate my life to raising Dany's baby. No one said a single word after that about my baby, my Dany's baby.

To ensure I deliver a healthy baby, I initiated a regimen of consuming nutritious meals meticulously prepared by myself, harboring reservations about relying on household help to uphold cleanliness standards and hygiene. Embracing a wholesome lifestyle, I established a pattern of early bedtime and morning awakenings for refreshing walks, aiming to provide the baby with a dose of invigorating outdoor air. Meanwhile, I noticed my parents were often engrossed in discussions beyond my understanding or engaged in phone conversations with their son.

When I was in the fifth month, with a slight belly bulge, one day, Mom informed me that we were all moving to our farmhouse, where I could deliver a healthy baby. She had engaged the services of a well-known gynecologist who would make weekly visits; a 'Labor and Delivery Nurse' was hired to be in the farmhouse 24/7 to look after me. Our eight-acre farmhouse was situated at Gandipet Lake, which is famous for its scenic beauty. I noticed that all our old workers were replaced with new faces from UP and Bihar. Upon inquiry, Mom informed us that they were fired as they were collectively stealing the farm produce.

Days converted into months, and a few days after the scheduled date, I got into labor pains and rushed to a newly built hospital on the outskirts of the city. Before taking me to a labor room, a female gynecologist conducted a fetal position ultrasound and informed me that they would give me a mild sedative through an IV and inject an Epidural because the baby was too big. If the pain proves overwhelming, a C-section could become necessary. Furthermore, the expertise of a plastic surgeon would be sought to minimize the visibility of any resulting scar. While listening to them, I dozed off, and when I woke up, I saw Mom, Dad, and Bro sitting silently with concerned faces. They rushed to my bed as they heard the creaking sound of the bed when I tried to turn towards them. "Where's the baby?" I had to question them since I didn't see a baby cot in the room.

Bro left the room and returned with a doctor, who broke the bad news that they had reached a critical situation in which they could only save the mother or the child, and a collective decision was made to save the mother. The powerful sedatives administered during the delivery pains have caused me to sleep for the past two days. During that time, it was decided that the infant must be buried. She also stated that, as a young woman, I had ample time to have additional children.

Anger, frustration, and overwhelming emotions of hurt overpowered my senses, and in a pitched voice, I yelled at the doctor, my mother, father, and brother, accusing them of being insensitive. I felt they should have let me go so I could have been with my Dany or, at the very least, allowed me to see the baby's face. It was the epitome of insensitivity, never expected from my parents or brother. Tears flowed down my cheeks like a relentless river, and I found myself repeating that they should have allowed me to go to be with my Dany.

It's been almost six months since I returned home without my baby, a blonde girl with blue eyes like my Dany, informed me by Mom. My brother called me every day, offering his consolation and reminding me that I needed to move on and be on the path I had set for myself: being there for my ailing parents. He implored me to let them relish the last phase of their lives and provide them with the peace that comes from witnessing me overcome my sorrow.

Two years passed, and I almost returned to a routine. Dad transferred all the real estate in my name, including the part ownership of his construction company. I strongly protested that Bro must be given his share, but Bro refused and gave a legal undertaking that he has no claim on Dad's mobile/immobile assets and that everything should be given to me. While I almost overcame the grief, the pain turned into sweet memories of my time spent with my Dany.

I noticed that Mom was losing weight and complaining about fatigue and loss of appetite. I took her to our family physician, who conducted several tests and informed us to come the next day for results. Instead of giving the reports the following day, he conducted a few more tests, did a CT scan and MRI, and asked us to come the following day for the reports. On the third day, he informed me that he had to conduct a pancreas biopsy to complete the diagnosis. I suspected something bad he must have found or suspected, and to check it out, I went to his cabin, telling Mom that I was going to the comfort room. When he was free from the patient he was attending, I barged in and asked him why he had done so many tests and what he was suspecting.

"I'm afraid there's a likelihood your mother has pancreatic cancer. I'll share more information once I receive the biopsy report. I expect to have it within the next two days," the doctor conveyed without much emotion.

Leaving the doctor's office, I was left speechless by the alarming news. Once home, I reached out to my brother, who promised to arrive in two days. I was aware of the gravity of organ cancer, knowing that the survival rate is incredibly low, if not non-existent. If metastasis had already occurred, the prognosis became apparent and often swift.

Within two hours, Bro called and confirmed that he was arriving the next day evening, and I called the doctor to say I would come the following day with my brother, who was coming from Japan.

My educated and strong-willed Mom was informed about cancer that was in an advanced stage and the harsh reality that she had only six to twelve months to live. She decided to decline any treatment that could inflict more pain without altering the inevitable outcome. Instead, she requested potent analgesics and sleeping pills to alleviate her pain and provide some respite.

As expected, Mom passed away in just four months, leaving us to mourn forever. Bro and Dad were exerting pressure on me to marry, something I vehemently opposed. While I wished to join my Dany as soon as possible, I couldn't bear the thought of leaving Dad to the mercy of servants. Even after hundreds of moons had passed, life remained unbearable without Dany by my side.

Chapter Five

Samuel Thomas

Love's Melody

My Hindu grandmother, Rukmani Devi, was born in the second decade of the twentieth century, or you could say around 1920, in a village near Secunderabad, about five miles northeast of Hyderabad. The two cities are often referred to as the 'Twin Cities' Hyderabad-Secunderabad. Secunderabad was founded in 1806 as a British cantonment and named after Sikandar Jah, the third Nizam of Hyderabad. The encampment quickly grew to become one of the largest British cantonments in India.

My mom informed me about her Grandma's journey. Her mother passed away when she was ten. Her father owned a small agricultural piece of land and a few buffalos and hens.

Grandma's mom gave birth to three still babies; the fourth was Grandma and no more, and she was lucky to survive; she was underweight and came out in the seventh month. Since there was no boy in the house, her dad made her son of the house. Taking into account her frail physique, starting at the age of seven, he ensured she exercised with him every morning, helped milk the buffalos, and took them to the forest to graze and bathe in a small pond just half a mile from their home. Her daily regimen of push-ups, sit-ups, skipping, and tending to the buffaloes had become an inevitable routine, transforming her body into a powerhouse. Another advantage emerged from her rigorous workout and protein-rich dairy diet: she sculpted a remarkable physique. Her graceful figure highlighted finely honed muscles, complemented by sharp features and a complexion glowing with the warm hues of a summer sunset. All the young boys of the village were after her; however, they refrained from making any advances because they were well aware of her formidable physical strength and being the daughter of a wrestler.

Her household expenses were covered by the meager money her father was receiving from the sales/barter of milk, agri produce, and other dairy items, though that wasn't enough. It was still better than a lot of other villagers. After the death of her mother, her father failed to find a girl to remarry because he was picky and was waiting for a fairy to come from the sky; unfortunately, in his wait, he lost his right leg in an attempt to remove a large boulder that was hindering the buffalos' path fell on his leg and crushed the bones to the extent that it had to be imputed. Forget the chance of getting a fairy, having an elderly decrepit disappeared: who would marry a penniless handicapped?

When she turned thirteen, her life changed dramatically with her father's tragedy. From sunrise to sunset, she was tirelessly active. She began her day by milking the buffalos, fixing breakfast, and ensuring her dad and herself were fed. After that, she led the buffalos to the pond for a rejuvenating bath, guided them to verdant pastures for grazing, and scoured the forest for dry wood, tubers, and fruits to nourish them. Occasionally, she'd swap these hard-earned goods with fellow villagers.

One day, when she just crossed over the age of sixteen and was returning from the woods, she came across a horse-riding British squad of soldiers. One of the British soldiers, struggling with Telugu, asked where they could hunt deer and other animals. She directed them to a large pond about three to four miles away, where they might find what they sought, as animals often came there to quench their thirst. Curious, he inquired about her activities in the woods and her residence. She explained that she grazed her buffaloes, gathered dry wood, and resided in a village just half a mile away.

The following day, upon her return from the woods, she saw her dad sitting on the porch with two British soldiers. One of them was the same man who had spoken to her in inarticulate Telugu the previous day. The other was a tall and brutally handsome young man with many insignias on his chest, whom she remembered because of his unwavering gaze fixed on her throughout their encounter. Even as they moved on, he consistently turned to watch her.

With her slender frame and sharp features, she was a vision of grace and elegance. Her face glowed with the sun's kiss on her light, dusky skin, and her eyes sparkled with intelligence and curiosity. She was at the cusp of womanhood; her body changed its curves, which reflected beautifully but still retained a youthful innocence. It must have besotted the soldier.

They left, telling her dad they would return the next day. Dad informed her that the young officer wanted to hire her as domestic help and pay her a monthly salary of ten rupees, plus accommodation and food. He's willing to pay her father 100 rupees for relocation costs, which he must refund if she fails to work for him for at least five years.

Grandma was very intelligent; it seemed she thought that with 100 rupees, her father could buy a large piece of agricultural land and have a wife who could look after him, and her chances of getting a husband of her choice in the city would be enhanced. What was available in the village was a few urchins, good for nothing and more of a liability than an asset that could assist in sailing through life's ups and downs.

Grandma and her dad discussed the offer till late at night, and she successfully convinced him to let her go so both could enjoy life. Her dad agreed but showed his concern about how she could leave alone, and if something happened to her, he wouldn't be able to fight with these White people. She assured her that she would continue to do her morning one to two-hour exercise and keep her body strong to fend off any aggression. She will also make a monthly visit to him. By the time they slept, Dad was convinced that it would be sheer stupidity to pass up this golden opportunity.

Grandma sure wanted to escape from the village, which was nothing short of a hellhole where life was pathetically boring; you cannot differentiate from one day to the next. Each day, she had to venture into the jungle, armed with a long iron hook stick, hoe, trowel, and a concealed knife, for her work and to protect herself from deadly snakes, aggressive animals, and the potential sexual assault from boys who eyed her with a lascivious gaze.

The following day, as Grandma readied herself to lead the buffalos to the pond, the same two British soldiers arrived with her father and settled comfortably on the cots arranged on the verandah.

After the initial pleasantries, her father informed the Brits, "She's my only child, and it pains to think of sending her to the city and letting her live alone. But for a greater good, that's the money she would earn in the next five years; she could buy some agricultural land here and marry a decent boy. Considering this aspect, I'm willing to allow her to go with you for the domestic work only. If she's harmed in any way, she's not only fully capable of defending herself, but she could even become very dangerous and break a few bones of the aggressor. Moreover, I don't want you people to forget that the boys of my village could kill anyone if I tell them the village daughter was harmed or disrespected.

"I would visit her every week, and you must give her one day off every month so she can visit me. She needs two hours in the morning and one hour in the evening for exercises, which are essential for her to maintain her body strength. Her food must include dairy products and eggs."

They agreed to all her father's terms and gave him ten notes of ten rupees. They left, saying that tomorrow, they would send a horse carriage to pick her up and that her dad could accompany her to ensure that she was in good hands.

Her employer's name was Robert Samuel, a Second Lieutenant who graduated from Royal Military Academy Sandhurst (RMAS), and his first posting was in Secunderabad Military Cantonment. With the constant encouragement of Robert, within a year, she became fluent in spoken English.

In two years, she learned to read and write, and her skin color changed from light dusky to pale with the help of the sandalwood and turmeric powder mixture she was rubbing every day before her bath. She married Robert in a church before the end of her second year of employment, adopted a new name, Mary Samuel, and gave birth to an Anglo-Indian baby girl: my mom.

In the fourth year of their marriage, Robert was posted to one of the European war fronts and never returned. Fortunately, immediately after marriage, Robert had added her as a co-holder of his bank account, which had a sizable amount. Thanks to that money, she managed to buy a decent-sized house in Secunderabad. It was a place she could finally call her own, a sanctuary of stability in a world full of uncertainties. With careful planning, she ensured she had enough money to get by for the next few years, giving her a sense of security she had never felt. With the help of Robert's Indian officer friends, she managed to secure a job in the military's procurement department. After the war ended and India gained its independence, her attempts to learn of Robert's fate were met with silence from the British Military Administration Department, suggesting he might have lost his life. When she gave up the idea of Robert's return, she married one of her Indian colleagues when she was thirty-two years old; the groom was thirty-six and an issueless widower; his wife died from Malaria.

My Mom took a commerce degree and worked for a bank. She couldn't marry for long because she wanted a knight to come on a white horse to marry her. She got married when she was nearing thirty and managed to find a tall, good-looking hunk, but an absurd man working as a regional manager for a Bombay-based pharma manufacturer. He was already married and had a wife and son in Bombay; mom learned this after six years of marriage, and when I was hardly five years old, their fights escalated so much that he left for an unknown destination, leaving a note that he was going for good. She could use the attached signed blank papers to secure a divorce and marry a better person.

Mom's desire for a knight was not without merit. She was tall and slender, with piercing blue eyes set in a chiseled face and sharp features. Her pale skin was so flawless and radiant that it could take anyone's breath away.

I was a male version of my mom, except for my jet-black eyes. At the age of fourteen, I became passionate about jogging and building a muscular body; I believe my grandma filtered her passion down to me. Because of my tall, muscular body and sharp features, I stood out and noticed young girls looking at me in awe. At the age of seventeen, my world crumbled when my mother succumbed to a terminal illness. She displayed immense bravery throughout the two-year struggle, depleting almost all her savings in the process. Despite her valiant fight, she eventually lost the battle. She was more than just a mother to me; she was my universe: a friend, teacher, mentor, philosopher, and, above all, a source of inspiration and strength. Her sacrifices in raising me were immeasurable, as she chose the path of single parenthood after the cowardly and irresponsible person responsible for my birth abandoned her.

After her death, I received a small gratuity from Mom's employer that couldn't have lasted for a few years. With no source of income, I made the tough decision to sell my house along with all its furniture and fixtures. With the proceeds, I purchased a studio apartment on the third floor of a newly constructed building.

Mom wanted me to become an engineer, and there was no way I could have disrespected her. I completed my schooling with excellent grades and secured a seat in Mechanical Engineering at the city's prestigious government institution, where only top graders were admitted.

At the beginning of the final year of my master's degree in aerospace engineering, along with aircraft structures as a primary subject, I met with Aarti. It was my routine to spend 2-3 hours in the library after classes, and on that day, as usual, I left the library at my usual time of six in the evening, and I was about to kick my two-wheeler Jawa bike to start when a girl approached me. She was breathtakingly beautiful: slim, pale glowing skin, sharp features, around five feet six inches tall, wearing a blue kurta, a white salwar, and black rubber shoes.

"Excuse me. Can you please drop me off at the same place where you live?" she politely asked. It was impolite to drop a young girl late in the evening to a strange place, so I asked her, "Please tell me where you live, and I'll drop you there, and it won't be inconvenient."

"Thank you so much, but I'm certain you live in our colony," she whispered softly.

I gave my colony name and asked her whether she stayed in that colony, and she said, "Yes, that's where I live."

While we were on our way, she informed me that her car had gone for repairs, and the driver was supposed to bring Dad's car. He did not show up for reasons not known to her, so instead of looking for an autorickshaw, she asked me for a ride.

Aarti's house was six houses before my house. I stopped in front of a massive diecast iron gate and saw a beautiful two-story building, probably constructed on a thousand-square-yard area.

She thanked me and extended her hand, saying she was Aarti; we shook hands, and I gave her my name and left with a see you around.

On my way to college the next morning, I noticed Aarti standing in front of her house from a distance. As I approached, she waved me down. I steered my bike towards her and came to a halt right beside her, curious about what she wanted to say.

"Sam, I need your help for the next 2-3 days, as my car needs some spare parts that they don't have here and ordered from Bombay, which could take a few days to come. Is that okay with you?" she inquired.

"It's my pleasure, Ma'am, but after the classes, I spend 2-3 hours in the library. Is that okay with you?" I asked her.

"It's a pleasure to spend time in the library, and I've already informed Mom that I'll be late," Aarti said smilingly.

We strolled towards the lecture halls once I parked the bike in the parking area. Just before parting ways, she suggested, "Would you mind meeting me at the canteen before heading to the library? We could enjoy a cup of tea together."

I agreed, and we moved in the direction of our lecture halls.

After finishing my classes, I headed to the canteen as usual. I scanned the room, looking for Aarti, knowing she wanted to have a cup of tea with me. Eventually, I spotted her sitting at a corner table, completely absorbed in a book. I was positive that she must have turned down numerous advances, considering she belonged to the category of drop-dead beauty. I approached her, greeted her with a warm "Good Afternoon," and inquired if she'd care for a vegetable sandwich and how much milk and sugar she takes in her tea.

She wanted to come with me to pay for the purchase, but I asked her to sit and allow me the pleasure of paying the insignificant amount.

During our bite, she asked me what degree I was pursuing, and she was pleased with my answer. She then informed me that she's also in her final year of a master's in nuclear physics and plans to do a doctorate in the USA.

About her family, she mentioned she has an elder brother who went to do a masters in the USA, but it looks like he will never return. After his MS, he got a decent job at a multinational company and found his love in the same company. Mom is a homemaker, and Dad is a chartered accountant with his own company. She was shell-shocked when she learned about me all alone in this world. We didn't talk much after that, probably because she must have failed to digest me as a loner fighting it out to make something out of my miserable circumstances.

The following day, again, we met at the canteen, and this time, she insisted that she would pay for the drink and snack. While sipping the tea, she slowly asked me, "Do you eat in a restaurant or cook?"

"I cook, and I'm good at that. During my mom's illness, I had to learn how to cook. She used to instruct me step by step, and I used to follow her instructions. According to my mom, I became an excellent cook within six months. Today, I could prepare anything you want, from soups, curries, biryani, pulao, chapati, etc. Every day in the evening, I prepare curry and rice, enough for my dinner and breakfast. For lunch, I eat a veg sandwich with a cup of tea," I tried to make it as if I enjoyed cooking because I didn't want her to sympathize with me. Many people worldwide are suffering much more than I am, so neither should I feel unhappy with my situation nor allow her to sympathize with me.

"Me dumb, I know nothing about cooking, but I do have one talent in the kitchen: making the best tea in the world, according to my dad. He claims that a cup of my tea can melt away all the day's stress and relax his body, and I knew he was a liar. Besides that, I'm pretty useless in there," she chuckled, and I couldn't help but grin.

As the weekend came to a close, Aarti playfully asked, "So, are you planning to invite me over for lunch this Sunday?"

"It would be my pleasure but note that I live alone in my one-bedroom apartment, and I'm not sure you would feel comfortable sitting in my bedroom cum dining hall cum Kitchen. Compared to your palatial villa, it's a hole in the wall, with no comfortable sitting, and you need to climb close to 50 stairs," I said with a grin.

"Are you attempting to escape from offering a meal," she said smilingly.

"I love to cook for you, but I thought better to forewarn you of the perils. Tell me, are you a veg or non-veg?" I asked.

"We strictly adhere to a vegetarian diet at home, but Dad and I enjoy chicken when dining out or on Saturday nights when Dad sneaks in a few beer cans along with some chicken tandoori or chicken kababs. Mum is adamant about not allowing any trace of slaughtered birds or animals to enter the house, so the only permissible place for enjoying our chicken delicacies is at the terrace room, which Dad had furnished well with a music system and concealed lights so that he could hear his evergreen oldie songs while enjoying the cold beer," she shared with a chuckle.

"Wonderful! I'll prepare Chicken 65 and Kadai Chicken, along with Dhaba-style lentil dal, chapati, and Jeera (Cumin seeds) rice. If you need to eat anything else, tell me. Cooking is my passion, and preparing a couple more dishes is no bother," I said earnestly. I was thrilled that she had taken the initiative to come to my place; I wouldn't have mustered the courage to invite her, at least not in this lifetime.

"What you want to prepare is more than enough; there is no need to prepare anything else. Do you want me to bring something like a wine bottle, a few assorted juice bottles, cakes, puddings, or anything else you want?"

"Please don't bring anything; your presence will elevate my room's ambiance to new heights and transform my modest pad into a haven of warmth and joy. Just so you know, I don't drink. When my mom was alive, we had this tradition of cracking open a bottle of wine for Christmas, sipping half, and saving the rest for New Year. Apart from those special occasions, alcohol never found its way into our home," I said with a chuckle.

"Good to know that you don't consume alcohol, but why this flattery, Sam? "Aarti inquired with a smile.

"It's not mere flattery; rather, it's a genuine expression of my delight that someone of your stature will grace my humble abode," I conveyed earnestly.

"Please refrain from showering me with unmerited praise since it might go to my head and make me conceited and narcissistic. At what time do you want me to be at your pad?" Aarti inquired.

"You're welcome to come any time after one, and if the enticing aroma of spices and the rhythmic clatter of utensils don't bother you, feel free to come early," I expressed with a smile.

"Okay, I'll see you around one, and don't take too much stress; even if you cook, only Dal Fry and plain rice would be fine for me," Aarti said and left with a goodbye.

In the evening, I first went to the market and bought all the groceries, chicken, and fruit. After returning from the shopping, I took a little rest and went for a deep cleaning, which was a weekly ritual, but I used to do it on Sunday morning. Daily cleaning included making my bed, a little dusting, and cleaning the kitchen; no toilet, floor cleaning, or changing the bed sheet.

I methodically prepared each dish, aiming to enhance its flavors to the fullest by precisely selecting and adding all the necessary ingredients. I carefully balanced the level of spiciness, ensuring it was just right, and paid attention to every minute detail to make certain they were prepared to perfection. By twelve-thirty, all my preparations were ready, and I went for a quick shower, changed into my night suit, a light blue checkered pajama, and matching T-shirt, and sprayed my body with my favorite musk deodorant.

At one o'clock, I heard a soft knock, and an enchanting scent wafted in upon opening the door. She looked stunningly beautiful in her light blue cotton top paired with dark blue cotton trousers. She was holding a mixed flower bouquet in one hand and a small box of cake from a famous bakery in the other.

I guided her to sit on the three-seater sofa facing the TV. She looked curiously at my modest furniture and fixtures: a queen-sized bed, a small dining table with four chairs, a study desk with piles of books and notebooks, and two steel cabinets.

I sold my house with furniture and fixtures, except I carried some costly crockery and cutlery from my grandma's collection. She instructed Mom to look after the tableware and her jewelry and pass them on to her daughter-in-law.

A decorative wood wall partitioned the kitchen, and I excused myself, saying the food was warm and better to eat now. She followed me, telling me to allow her to help me.

Despite the undeniable deliciousness of the food, I began to feel uneasy at her overly effusive praise of my cooking abilities. With each bite, she commented that she never had more delicious non-vegetarian food in any of the city's restaurants. My mother received praise for her exceptional culinary skills and deserves much of the credit for raising me to be an excellent cook.

As I started clearing the dining table with the plates and dishes, she joined me and insisted on taking the plates to wash. With an exclamation, she said, "Damn it, you have some expensive taste. The Wedgwood crockery is crafted in the UK, and the sterling silver cutlery is made by Wallace Silversmiths in the USA. Nowadays, both of them are manufacturing most of their wares in China, but these are manufactured in the country of origin."

"This collection of tableware belonged to my grandmother and is possibly six or seven decades old. It is a family heirloom, and my grandmother instructed my mother to give it to her daughter-in-law. This is the first time I've used them in Her Highness Honor, who graced my humble residence," I informed her with a wide grin.

"Thank you. I really felt honored, and I'm not Her Highness, but an ordinary run-of-the-mill girlfriend. The next time I come, don't use this expensive tableware, and keep it safe for your Mom's daughter-in-law," she said with a laugh.

Every Sunday, she barged in without notice; twice, she took me out for lunch and didn't allow me to foot the bill. However, after those two outings, I started preparing meals substantial enough for the two, including dinner and breakfast. After lunch, she would linger for nearly two hours, helping with the dishes, making tea, and talking about her studies, family, etc. Up to this point, I hadn't mustered the courage to express my feelings for her, which was growing as the days passed, and she hadn't broached or hinted that we were more than friends. Our interactions were limited to a formal handshake and hug upon arrival and departure. Many times, I entertained the thought of giving her a warm hug and kissing her rosy lips adorned with subtle daytime pink lipstick. Yet, the fear of jeopardizing our companionship held me back, forcing me to suppress my desires with unwavering restraint.

Her weekly visits were becoming more and more unsettling. Every Sunday, she would show up dressed in her best, exuding the scent of mood-altering perfume and adorned with blush, mascara, and glossy lips. Picture a twenty-two-year-old, muscular hunk grappling with unruly hormones; reining them in was a considerable challenge. With an alluring Babe's presence in seclusion, even saints might lose their composure, and here I'm being tortured on a weekly basis. Was she subtly signaling, 'You fool, make a move, declare your deep love for me, embrace me, and promise a lifetime of happiness as we walk together, hand in hand, until our last breath?'

On the following Sunday, after we had devoured our lunch of egg-fried rice, Chicken-Manchurian, and pan-fried vegetables, I decided it was time to take the plunge. Even if she chose to end our friendship, I believed it would be preferable to this weekly torment.

In a composed, matter-of-fact tone, I began, "Artikins" (she asked me to use this affectionate nickname, as 'Aarti' felt too formal, and 'Dolly,' her childhood pet name, wasn't appealing to me), "Please allow me to open my heart. I understand it's a significant risk, and I might lose you, which is something I never wanted. I've always cherished our friendship despite our differing social standing and beliefs. But lately, it's becoming increasingly difficult to carry on as friends. My studies are suffering, as day by day, the fear of losing you is on the rise, taking my focus away from my studies. While I find great comfort in your weekly visits and eagerly look forward to them, the nagging thought of why I should get involved in a losing battle is damaging my brain cells.

"I think I'm experiencing profound love for you, Artikins, but you're free to interpret my feelings as mere physical attraction or infatuation. This affection drives me to do things I'd rather avoid, as I hold a deep respect for all women in general and, especially, for you, someone who has become the love of my life. I wish I could hold you close, embrace you, and gaze at you forever. However, my desires exceed my standing, so I must implore you to spare me from this torment and never cross paths with me again. Life has already dealt me a harsh hand, so adding one more blow would be an unbearable burden. Artikins, you will remain engraved in my mind until my dying day, like a transient moonbeam that graced my life and left behind the loveliest memories to sustain me for the remainder of my days. Please forgive me if I have ever offended you."

"Sam, you idiot, you think I come here all dolled up to show my looks to the four walls. I was doing everything for you, dumbo, and instead of holding my hands and committing to love, respect, and care till the last breath, you were talking about our different beliefs, social standing, losing focus on studies, and whatnot. I'm taking you with me to the US, and together, we'll do doctorates in our fields and earn enough money so we can enjoy our lives as we want. My brother has already applied for my parents' and my residence visas, and hopefully, we will get them soon; you could come on a student visa, but you leave that to me. What do you have to say now?" As Artikins spoke, her words felt like sipping on sweet nectar, filling me with warmth and joy. It was as if my brain was flooded with happiness, and my heart raced with excitement, overwhelmed by this unexpected stroke of good fortune. I don't know how and why a couple of tears dropped from my eyes, and she saw them come, jumped to her feet, took a paper napkin, and cleaned my face. "So, you're a crybaby? Grow up, boy, and face the ups and downs of life like a brave man. I don't like crying men; it's the forte of women," she admonished.

"I remember the last time tears fell when my mom passed, tears of devastation and profound pain. Now, these tears cascade from the sheer pleasure and gratitude for the divine mercy that has bestowed upon me, something I feel undeserving of. Artikins, my tears mirrored the overflow of happiness, and I thank you; I never anticipated you accepting me as your life partner," I shared with a smile.

"Get up and give me a bear hug; I want to feel your happiness," she exclaimed with a grin. Taking my hand, she drew me close, enveloping me in a tight embrace that revealed her excited heartbeat. I gently rubbed her back and whispered, "Thank you, Artikins; I've longed for this moment. I'm overjoyed, floating on cloud nine, and so grateful for my incredible luck that words fail to capture," I confessed earnestly. She lifted her head, gazing into my eyes, and then pulled my head down for a warm, lingering kiss that sent indescribable delight coursing through my body.

The following week, I organized a lavish lunch of her favorite dishes and bought a small cake. I wanted to propose to her and give her a diamond ring that mom had asked me to give her daughter-in-law.

After lunch and our tea, I knelt before her and said, "Today, as I kneel before you, my heart is brimming with affection and anticipation. You have brought me happiness, hilarity, and unending affection from the instant we met. I cannot fathom spending the rest of my life with anyone other than you. Will you accept this ring as a symbol of our love and commitment?"

She looked at me for a couple of minutes and slowly extended her hand. I gently pushed my grandma's large diamond ring onto her finger. Then she rose from the sofa and said, "Yes, Sam, I'll marry you and stay with you till my last breath."

I whispered thank you, took her in my arms, and planted a passionate kiss on her warm lips.

She returned the ring, telling me it was safe in my possession, as she wouldn't be wearing it, and keeping it in a safe place in the house was impossible.

Days passed by, and our final exams were hardly a few months away when she informed me, "Sam, my mother is mad at me because I'm not bringing my boyfriend or his family home, and I should tell her what exactly is going on or no Sunday outings, and I'll be only allowed to go to college, and rest of the places she'll accompany me. Sam, my parents are religious people, especially my mom, and for her religious family lineage, the Gotra, or purity of blood is of prime importance. She permitted Bro to marry when she learned that the girl belonged to our Gotra; to prove it, Bro sent a passport copy of the girl he intended to marry. Between you and me, the girl was Punjabi, and Bro forged the name on her passport that my dad and I noticed but didn't inform Mom about it. Mom's a tigress in the house; no one could dare to go against her, not even Dad, even though she's not very literate, couldn't complete her upper school, but more worldly wise than any of us. She forced Dad to sell his business, which he had recently done because the company was making more than reasonable profits and could fetch an excellent amount if sold now, and that's exactly what had happened. She has recently put our home up for sale as she and Dad wish to spend their remaining days under their son's roof in the USA.

"If I shared with my parents my plan to marry a Christian boy, I'm certain it would cause them anguish, even though you also have Hindu heritage. Introducing you to them seems impossible, and discontinuing my visits here is not an option. Don't worry, I'll handle this. Just give me a couple of weeks to figure things out and devise a solid plan for moving forward."

I didn't comment as there was nothing positive I could have contributed except by wishing her good luck.

I recall a conversation with Artikins when she mentioned she belonged to an upper-caste Hindu community and held a prestigious position in the social hierarchy. If her mother insists on having a son-in-law who is well-educated from a respectable family and shares their ancestry, then she is right in her asking. It was only fair if she turned me down; she had no reason to take in a penniless Christian boy with no living family members.

My mistake was encouraging Artikins to spend time with me; in that process, I got hooked on her intelligence, beauty, and organizational skills. If she leaves my life, I don't think I would ever be happy with any girl or marry anyone to fulfill my manly desires.

After two weeks, on a Sunday, when she came for lunch, she told me, "I found the solution to overcome the hurdle that mom would create for our marriage. And don't you say no to it!"

"Why would I say no to any sensible solution that could allow us to spend our lives together?" I responded impassively.

"Sensible or not, this is the only solution that should prove effective. I want you to make me pregnant; then my mom will have no choice but to accept you," Artikins exclaimed.

"Artikins, your suggestion is irrational, and I won't accept it. Have you thought about the repercussions of your suggestion? Your parents will be devastated, and possibly your dad or mom may have a heart attack or a stroke. If you love them, don't do this to them, and I refuse to be a part of your brilliant idea. Besides, there's no need to hurry into marriage. We can resolve everything once we're in the US, and I'm sure that with patience, we can convince your parents of our commitment," I expressed decisively.

"I anticipated your opposition, but it's a carefully considered plan. Our immigration visas to the USA will arrive in the next few weeks. The application has been approved and is in the issuance process. Final exams are in two months, and let's hope you work hard and plant the seed successfully; within the next three months, nothing will be visible. I'll explain what occurred when we were in the USA and when the belly bulge became visible. In the USA, my parents won't have a choice but to accept you as their son-in-law and happily marry me; otherwise, we could pursue a civil marriage. Following my suggestion will protect both of us from any unforeseen events that might tear us apart forever," Artikins expressed firmly and in an even tone.

"Please spare me from this crazy suggestion of yours. I don't want to hurt your parents under any circumstances. It's better if you kill me so you can live a peaceful and happy life with a suitable person of your parent's choice," my statement was firm and uncompromising.

"Shall I assume with your statement that you have no interest in marrying me?" hurt reflected in her voice.

"Your comment is baseless. I'm merely pointing out that your plan would inflict significant pain on your parents, and I'm unwilling to be the cause of their suffering, even if it means foregoing your presence in my life. I refuse to build my happiness upon the anguish of others," I stated firmly, maintaining my resolve.

"I implore you not to put me through this; I feel incomplete without you. It's impossible to express the depth of my affection for you. From the first day I laid eyes on you on the campus, my heart and mind whispered, this is the person I must spend my life with, and believe me, it wasn't that I got hooked on your looks, but something that I couldn't exactly comprehend. I inquired about you with one of your fellow classmates, and she described you as a reserved and disciplined person, seldom interacting with others. Both male and female peers attempted to be friends with you, but your responses consistently dissuaded them. You had informed them that your studies and family commitments spare no time to socialize. Your living circumstances and family background remain a mystery to all. You arrive early at college and depart late, maintaining silence when questioned about your personal life. However, you were exceptional in academics, consistently ranking at the top of the class.

"After hearing these comments, I became more attracted to you. I wanted a person of integrity who subscribed to a disciplined life, apart from being intelligent, and I could foresee those qualities in you. I struggled for weeks to establish contact with you, and luckily, when I saw you in our locality,

I succeeded in finding a way to connect with you. The narrative about my car repair was a product of my creative mind, which was to achieve the intended results, and it worked perfectly fine.

"If you think I can live without you, then you're wrong. I'd rather die than give up on marrying you. You have become an integral part of me, and if that goes away, I won't survive," she stated with tears rolling down her cheeks.

I gently wiped her cheeks with a paper napkin and whispered, "Artikins, I want to express my deep gratitude for sharing your love for me. I want you to know that my love for you is not equal but far more profound. It would undoubtedly amaze you if I could reveal the depths of my love for you by baring my heart. Believe me, I express this with sincerity: I am committed to either marrying you or embracing a single life for the remainder of my existence. These words are not mere utterances but rather a heartfelt pledge that echoes the passionate truth of my feelings. However, we must both acknowledge that we shouldn't take any steps that might hurt your parents. Let's explore alternative paths that are appropriate and respectful from every perspective."

"Alright, let's strike a deal. Give me one week to ponder over this, and if I decide to go ahead with my current proposal or come up with an alternative, you must agree without any fuss. I contemplated a court marriage, but that's also unfeasible due to the extensive documentation requirement, including proof of residence, not to mention the mandatory 30-day waiting period. There's a potential for being exposed before marriage. My solution is practical; parents can handle their children's choices without suffering a lethal shock. Children aren't bound to always adhere to their parents' wishes; they possess their own lives, thoughts, and preferences. In our situation, we've moved past adolescence and beyond mere childish infatuations. We're adults on the verge of earning master's degrees in our respective professional fields; if anyone asserts that we lack the capacity to make informed decisions about our lives is mistaken. I have thoroughly envisioned this situation and assure you that I will arrive at a conclusive way to move forward," Artikins conveyed her thoughts with remarkable brevity and confidence.

"Okay, my love, I sincerely hope and pray that you discover a path that allows us to navigate easily and brings joy to others when they see us as a respected couple. I plead with you to take your time, ponder thoroughly, and avoid the temptation to choose a fast and easy way out," I conveyed earnestly.

On the following Sunday, Artikins arrived wearing a rather cheerful expression. I sensed that she must have found a positive solution, but I kept quiet and let her tell me.

We had a quiet lunch, briefly discussing exams and studies. In the midst of our tea, she brought up the subject, "Sam, a couple of days ago, I casually asked Mom and Dad what they would think if I found a decent boy from a different faith to marry. Mom got upset, exclaiming she'd either kill herself or the bastard wanting to marry me, refusing to compromise the purity of our lineage. Dad echoed her sentiments, suggesting either they find a suitable match or I choose, as long as he belongs to our ancestry.

"Upon receiving a resolute refusal from my parents, I pondered deeply and crafted a solution. Don't you dare reject it or be prepared to be killed," Artikins added with a playful frown.

"Firstly, I have no desire to meet my end at your hands, as it would imply; I've somehow provoked your ire, a scenario I aim to avoid throughout my existence. Additionally, I aspire to cherish several years alongside the love of my life before bidding farewell to this fleeting existence. Jokes aside, tell me what you're proposing, and I'm keeping my fingers crossed in the hope that your suggestion will be prudent," I expressed earnestly.

"Tomorrow, we are getting married in an Arya Samaj temple. If you're unfamiliar with Arya Samaj, let me give you a brief overview. Founded by Swami Dayanand Saraswati in 1875 in Bombay, Arya Samaj is a Hindu reform movement. The movement's primary objective was to reform Hinduism and restore its original Vedic teachings. Dayanand Saraswati asserted that the Vedas were the only infallible source of religious truth, and any later additions were corrupt and degenerate. The movement also advocated for social reform, including women's education and widow remarriage.

"They simplified marriages, making them unrestricted, devoid of elaborate rituals or ceremonies. The process includes the couple exchanging vows in the presence of a priest and two witnesses. The priest recites Vedic hymns, and the couple takes seven rounds (pheras) around the sacred fire. A distinctive aspect of Arya Samaj marriages lies in their inclusivity, permitting the union of inter-cast, interfaith couples; the marriage between a Hindu upper-caste girl and a Christian boy is though discouraged but not considered a forbidden fruit. "After the marriage ceremony, the couple will be presented with a marriage certificate. This certificate is legally valid, and all courts of law recognize it.

"This morning, I visited an Arya Samaj Temple and briefed the priests on the whole situation, emphasizing your Hindu heritage. They agreed to conduct the marriage ceremony and asked me to come tomorrow with the groom. They have offered to provide us with two witnesses in case we cannot arrange them. The priest mentioned that he maintains a list of willing witnesses who dedicate their time to assisting those in need. They need proof of identity and age and to fill out a marriage registration form, so come laced with their requirement.

"I'll pick you up sharp at nine tomorrow at your building gate. Do you have any questions?" Artikins conveyed a sense of determination and firmness.

"Artikins, I don't know what to say. This solution is not the best, and I'm unwilling to proceed. However, I won't say no if you insist since we're legally getting married. If upset people kill me for this irresponsible action of mine, I won't blame them. Now you decide, and I'll accept whatever you say," I poured my thoughts in a muted voice.

"Take heart, my love; tomorrow, you'll be marrying a girl who is making significant sacrifices to spend her life with you. Take pride in yourself and make me a promise to bring happiness and contentment into my life. Let us also beseech the Supreme Force to bless us with beautiful children, just like you," I sensed her joy in the way she spoke.

I approached her, took a seat beside her, gently held her hands, kissed them, and with teary eyes, in a soft tone, expressed, "I am filled with joy, yet the fears loom just as large.

I am committed to not causing harm or disrespect to anyone, values instilled by my mother that I fervently adhere to. My primary worry revolves around not having your parents' approval of your marriage. Despite this, I will heed your request to marry you tomorrow and assure you that I'll invest all the money that I earn and time to keep you happy."

Artikins took my face in the palm of her hands and said, "Boy, don't be a crybaby. I want my man to be a very strong person, not only physically but mentally."

After delivering this sentiment, she rose from the sofa, pulled me into a bear hug, pecked my lips, and announced, "I must leave now, as I have quite a few errands to run before the end of the day. Please don't fail to bring a small wedding gift for me." With that, she left.

The next day, Artikins picked me up and brought me to an Arya Samaj temple. There, we were directed to a designated area for the wedding ceremonies. In the center of the area, the sacred fire burned brightly within the mandap. A photographer stood ready with a large camera hanging from his neck while another person held a pair of garlands. Two witnesses, an elderly man and a woman who appeared to be retirees, patiently awaited the commencement of the ceremony.

Artikins excused herself for a few minutes, carrying her sizable bag with her. Within a few minutes, both the priest and Artikins appeared. Artikins was wearing a red pure silk saree and covered her head and upper body with a large red dupatta decorated with golden embroidery. She appeared stunningly beautiful in the saree, an ensemble I had never seen her wear before. The vibrant crimson lipstick and coordinating bindi elevated her beauty to breathtaking levels.

In under an hour, we were out with a certificate confirming we were married. While coming out of the temple, Artikins replaced the dupatta with a wool shawl, and once on the road, I asked her to stop by the bank for a few minutes (I wanted to take my Grandma's diamond bangles to give Artikins as my wedding gift). From the bank, she drove the car to a famous hotel and gave the car key to the attendant for parking. At the reception, she informed the receptionist that a suite had been booked for Mrs. Aarti Thomas. With the key in hand, we rode the elevator up to the fourth floor, reaching our suite. It was a spacious place with a TV lounge and a bedroom. The bedroom was decorated with various flowers. The bed had a large heart made of red rose petals. "Honey, please wait in the living room and come when I call you," Artikins instructed me.

I sat in the TV lounge for about fifteen minutes when she asked me to come to the bedroom.

Artikins sat squatting on the bed in the exact center of the rose petal heart, her head and face veiled by the blood-red dupatta she donned for the nuptials. Seated beside her, I whispered gently, "Artikins, I simply yearn to embrace you. You looked incredibly captivating in that saree, and my breathing became irregular, and my heart almost stopped beating. And I feared I could not withstand your beauty for long, so I averted my gaze. But now, I crave to see you, to hold you close, and to take pride in being the husband of the most beautiful woman in the world."

"Liar, you could see, hold, and be naughty only after giving my wedding gift," Artikins expressed in a happy tone.

I took out the two diamond bangles made by Garrard, the famous Jeweler of the UK who was the crown jeweler for the British Royal Family. It seems one of the King's daughters presented them to Grandma's husband when she was camping with her husband for hunting, and he saved her from a python's attack. My mom asked me to give them to my wife on the wedding night.

As I placed the bangles in Artikins's hands, she exclaimed delightedly, "Oh my goodness, these bangles are absolutely stunning! They must be from your mom's collection, as they are made from large solitaire rocks. Thank you so much, my love. Now you have my permission to unveil the dupatta, gaze upon me, and embrace me as much as your heart desires."

Our results were out two months post-exams, and both of us achieved our master's degrees with outstanding marks. Simultaneously, Artikins shared the joyous news that she was expecting, with an estimated delivery date of less than eight months from then. According to her gynecologist, if she needed to make her pregnancy invisible until the beginning of the third trimester, which starts at the 28th week, she should keep herself highly active. Basically, she should be on foot all the time, walk, do house chores, or do anything that could keep her moving. But it's only a chance with no guarantee of the outcome.

Every day in the evening, we met at a garden for a brisk walk of ninety minutes. Another way she found herself to be on her feet was to learn how to cook and spend at least two hours in the kitchen.

Artikins US visa hasn't come yet, and according to her bro, it's in the pipeline for issuance, but when it is issued, no one can tell.

The primary subject of my master's degree was Aerospace Engineering, and a few related subjects are secondary.

Artikins pressed me to apply to several universities. Still, she preferred that I do it at the California Institute of Technology (Caltech), which is among the best universities in aerospace technology. Because of the baby, she may have to delay her admission for at least a year or more, so I should proceed.

I secured a priority phone connection in just a few days. I was aware that the process involved an initial interview before they made their decision. I applied to several Universities, and luckily, the first call came from Caltech. A girl called me and asked me whether I would be free the following day, late at night, for an interview with the teachers who would decide on my application.

The next day, at 2:30 am, I found myself engaged in a stimulating two hour intense questioning session with four Caltech faculty professors. Their questions were tough, probing my knowledge, dedication, and vision. Thankfully, luck favored me as I answered accurate and satisfactory responses to all their queries. Their emphasis extended beyond evaluating my proficiency in the subjects; they were intent on confirming not just my diligence but also my lack of personal ambition, highlighting a wholehearted dedication to serving humanity through the creation of innovative and safe products for the world.

In ten days, I got a letter confirming my admission. In eight weeks, I flew to Los Angeles, and during this time, I made Artikins a joint account holder with access to my locker that had the mom's pricey jewelry. I transferred all the money to a US bank, which I could collect by showing my passport. I gave the key to my flat to Artikins and introduced her to the owner of our building from whom I had bought the apartment, informing him that she was my wife and that when needed, she would come to stay or for whatever purpose she would want to use the place. Artikins gave me the original marriage certificate, telling me it would be safe in my custody. With tears, we bid goodbye.

Chapter Six

Aarti Anya

Betrayal & Loss

I opened my eyes within the confines of an affluent Hindu household belonging to the upper caste. Everyone called me Dolly since my folks believed I looked like a doll. How true it was, a question that only my family could answer in affirmation; whether others agreed or not was not my family's concern.

I had a brother who was six years older than me. He was my mom's favorite, while I was Dad's darling. My brother and I attended the city's most prestigious and highly sought-after convent school, owned and operated by a Church. This resulted in us learning more about Christianity than our own faith, as most of the teachers and headmistress were Nuns.

My brother was the opposite of me; I was very organized, studious, and no-nonsense like my mother, whereas my brother was only good in his studies but was all over the house. You could never find his shoes, socks, clothes, books, or even toys in one place. Mom always used to hunt him for beating but never touched him, whereas she never thought for a moment to slap my back over a minor slight.

My bro left for the US for his PG immediately after securing his Electrical Engineering degree. A brilliant student, he earned an excellent GPA in his master's, secured a job in a prestigious MNC, and decided to settle in the USA, even though all of us opposed his crazy idea.

In my master's final year, I saw Sam and became enamored with him. He had a striking appearance: a handsome figure with a muscular V-shaped body, distinct features, ethereal eyes, and a fair complexion, standing around six feet tall. However, my interest in him went much beyond his physical attractiveness. Something about him distinguished him from every other boy I had ever met.

He had a habit of walking with his gaze lowered, always by himself and always alone, whether in the canteen, library or elsewhere. It struck me as peculiar; how did none of his female classmates, or boys, find him appealing enough even for friendship? And how he survived without any friends. I'm also not fond of having many friends, but I have a few friends in college and a few close friends from school. He's either a lunatic or wants to hide something from everyone. After the classes, he goes to the canteen, has a bite and a cup of tea, spends the rest of the evening in the library till closing time, and leaves on his motorbike to his unknown destination.

One day, I decided to find out more about him from a girl in his class. She informed me he's a very reserved person; even if you go to him and introduce yourself to make friends, he won't encourage you. Answer every question politely, and that's it; never bother to ask anything about you. No boy has dared to pull a prank on him or just pass any nasty comments. His weird attitude and muscular body have instilled fear in everyone, which is very plausible because he looks so strong that he could beat up three or four boys at once. He's the only boy in the class who asks highly complicated questions from the lecturers, and a few times, they told him that they would answer his query in the next class, which means they didn't know the answer. The entire class is aware of his exceptional intelligence and acknowledges that he outshines everyone else. It's clear that he's destined for great things.

This heightened my curiosity, prompting me to explore more deeply to unravel everything there was to know about him. I contemplated tirelessly, seeking an unconventional approach to connect with him, steering clear of the usual methods that I believed would inevitably lead to failure like others. One evening, as I stood on my house's balcony, relishing the fresh air while sipping my evening tea, staring at the sparsely traversed road below. Only the occasional car, motorcycle, and pedestrian were in the traffic, with or without their dogs. To my amazement, I spotted Sam passing by our house on his motorbike, focused on the road. I wondered whether he was visiting someone or if this was the route to his residence. Over the next several days, it became a ritual for me to stand on my balcony at the same time, and without fail, Sam passed by at almost around the same time each day. This solidified my hunch that he either lived in our neighborhood or worked for one of our colony residents.

During my usual routine of observing him pass by our house, a sudden idea struck me on how to initiate a conversation with him. The next morning, I told my driver not to pick me up, explaining that I'd be staying late at the library.

The next day, I waited close to his bike, and when he came and sat on it, I approached him for a ride to my house, which worked and marked the initiation of our friendship. The first thing I found out about him is that he's all alone in this wide world, without any immediate family members or other relatives, which could be why he shies away from making friends. The next, I noticed that he was a person of remarkable discipline and organization; he strictly adhered to a routine of early sleep and rising, allocating ninety minutes of his mornings to bodybuilding exercises. Under the expansive canopy of his room, he had his gym, complete with a treadmill, a set of dumbbells of various weights, and a sturdy bench press with a barbell and multiple weight plates. He confided in me that he had sold his substantial house after his mother's passing, as their entire savings were spent on her medical expenses. From the sale of his house, he purchased his studio apartment and still had ample funds to sustain his studies and live comfortably. He desired to secure employment after completing his postgraduate studies or immigrate to a foreign land.

Grounded in her spirituality, my mother fervently upheld the principles of a vegetarian diet and was deeply committed to preserving the purity of our family lineage. She belongs to the school of thought that believes in reincarnation and achieving Moksha, liberation that takes seven births to achieve. She also believes that the soul is eternal and transmigrates from one body to another after death. To continue being born into the 'Swarn Zat,' a term referring to the Noble Caste, it is essential to uphold the purity of lineage through adherence to traditional practices and preserving ancestral heritage.

Being a certified idiot, I forgot all the valuable teachings my mom imparted and ended up head over heels in love with Sam, who had Hindu blood, as her grandma converted from Hinduism to Christianity. Once my mom catches wind of my irresponsible behavior, I'm certain she'll be enraged and leave me out to dry. However, no one should blame me for being drawn to a boy who was an absolute gem, a solid 24-carat pure bar of gold. After thoroughly evaluating him from every possible angle, I concluded that I couldn't find a better companion to spend my life with, so I encouraged him to commit to me.

Today, he left for the USA to pursue his doctorate, a decision I strongly encouraged. We got married just before our final exams, and now I'm three months pregnant with our child. To quell my fears of losing him, I insisted on our marriage. Given that we will be studying in different states, I worry about the possibility of him being enticed by assertive girls who might try to lure him away from me.

Still, our US visa didn't come, and there was no way to expedite it. We sold our house and moved to our farmhouse. It was spread on a 60-acre piece of land and, in the center, a lovely four-bedroom, fully furnished house. The farmhouse was also up for sale, but we had yet to find a reasonable offer since it was far from the city.

Before Sam's departure, I gave him the address of my close friend from school days. I received one letter from him, informing me that he had reached safely and opted for a shared room in the hostel with another boy who had come from Singapore for his doctorate in his subject only. He closed the letter asking me to take good care of myself and waiting to hear the good news of my arrival in the USA. I responded to him, asking him not to write until he heard from me because his letter ended up in the hands of my friend's father, who didn't like her to be a messenger.

My morning sickness, which is nausea and vomiting, didn't stop even at the end of the third month; in fact, it increased. My gynecologist informed me there was nothing to worry about and that I should keep myself hydrated and stop eating spicy food. I was at the end of my fifth month when one day, Mom came to me and said, get ready; I'm taking you to meet someone. She brought me to a female gynecologist, where she voiced her concern about my diminishing appetite, tired appearance, and lack of energy.

The gynecologist asked me to lie on the examination table as she needed to perform an ultrasound. After finishing the procedure, she asked me to wait outside. Mom came out within a few minutes but didn't utter a word until we returned. When I was sitting in the TV lounge, surfing the channels, Mom came with Dad, sat on the sofa on my left, and asked me to switch off the TV.

Mom cleared her throat and said, "I'm sure you're aware of your pregnancy, which is in an advanced stage and cannot be terminated, legally or otherwise. Tell me why this happened and who's responsible for your pregnancy," Mom was holding herself from bursting, and Dad looked in pain.

"Mom, I got married seven months ago, and I know I've just entered my six-month pregnancy. You wouldn't have agreed to our marriage, so I decided to marry the love of my life in an Arya Samaj temple. My husband's grandma was a Hindu and converted to Christianity to marry a British soldier stationed at the Secunderabad cantonment. He's pursuing his doctorate in the USA now. Mom, he's truly amazing, and I couldn't have asked for a better partner to share my life with," I expressed in a muted voice.

"Why did you assume we wouldn't have approved of your choice of a life partner?" Dad scowled, his voice sharp and stern.

"Dad, a few weeks before my marriage, I asked both of you whether you would accept if I wanted to marry a person of different faith, and Mom said she'd kill herself or the person who wanted to marry me, and you also agreed with her. This was the reason I didn't seek your permission. Look, there is no need to blow the issue out of proportion.

If you believe I've brought shame upon you, or if you don't want me in the house, I'll leave right away. I'm qualified; I could find a decent job and earn enough to live an independent life. However, I'm your baby and will always be available if I can be of any service," I expressed earnestly.

"Can I see evidence of your marriage," Dad asked.

"Sure, give me a couple of minutes to fetch the marriage certificate copy and photos," I said and went to my room.

Both saw the photos with keen eyes and carefully read the marriage certificate.

After a while, Mom said, "You haven't brought shame on us but buried us alive. I don't know how I could live with this taboo and what would happen to us when we faced our Lord. If I get permission from your father, I'll wring your neck with my hands. You have destroyed us and our future generations, and your cardinal sin is unpardonable here or in the next world. I pray to my Lord to meet out a miserable death here and eternally punish you in the next world."

"Mom, feel free to express your frustration or curse me as much as you want, but bear in mind that everyone is responsible for their actions. Children's or parent's' choices are their own, and they will face the consequences alone. Instead of concerning yourself with me, focus on your deeds to help you achieve the outcome you seek. If killing me is what you believe will benefit you or Dad, go ahead.

"But before you eliminate me, think of the possible aftermath if my death isn't kept under wraps, which seems quite plausible. If you don't know the consequences, allow me to brief you: you could be locked away in prison during your final days, far from the comfort of your son's roof, surrounded by hardcore criminals, and forced into hard labor."

Tears filled my eyes, revealing my genuine concern, my voice trembling with emotion.

Mom and Dad didn't react to my statement or the tears; they must have been badly hurt because they couldn't have imagined that I would do something like this.

After a long pause, Mom said, "You're our daughter, and this is your house; you have hurt us deeply, and this wound will go with me to the other world. For me, my faith is everything. However, I never said believers of other faiths are evil, but they have their own God to answer, and I've my own Lord to answer. My faith doesn't permit me to accept a person of another faith as my son-in-law, but as you said, I wouldn't be held accountable for your actions, and you would pay alone for your deeds. However, allow us a few days to tell you how we intend to move forward."

Dad didn't say anything, but both quietly walked out of the living room.

Time was moving at its usual fast pace, and I entered my ninth month now; it's a matter of weeks for delivery. During these last three months, I was feeling lethargic and excessively sleeping; I asked Mom to take me to the gynecologist, but she said it was normal and everyone felt like this. I wrote several letters to Sam, informing him that the cat was out of the bag and there was nothing to worry about, and asked him to mail directly to my new address, but I received no response, which was strange.

Mom took me to a newly built small hospital for the delivery; the same gynecologist who attended to me before but in a different hospital was there to handle my delivery. She asked me to relax, and the delivery should be within a few hours. When I was crying with the pain waves coming in droves, she came to check the baby's position, did an ultrasound, and informed me that she must go for a C-section because the baby was in distress, not getting enough oxygen, resulting in abnormal heart rate, which is called fetal distress. They rushed me to the operating theater and gave me anesthesia, and when I woke up in the morning, I was informed that they couldn't save the baby, a male child. I asked the Doctor to show me the dead baby, but she said my mom and dad took the baby early in the morning and performed electric cremation. I cried incessantly; Mom and Dad also cried with me and consoled me with the Lord's will.

Just eight days after returning home, Mom broke the news that our US visas had arrived. The very next day, she gave me a sizable envelope couriered from LA by Sam, explaining it had been in her possession for over a month, with Dad having already opened it. Upon reviewing its contents, he instructed me to hand it over to you after your delivery. I've no clue why he made this request and what was in it.

The envelope held a stack of papers, the first of which was addressed to me. I began to read it slowly.

Dear Artikins,

I trust this message reaches you in good health. With profound sorrow and overwhelming remorse, I convey the most agonizing declaration, tearing my heart and rending my very being.

I envisioned a lifetime spent in your company, and the prospect of leaving this world in your arms was a beautiful dream I held dear. Alas, life has unfolded in a way that has led me down, forcing me to take steps I never thought I would. Please know that the love I have for you has not diminished; it remains an unwavering presence in my heart.

I understand the gravity of the situation and the pain my decision could cause, and I am truly sorry for that. I assure you that this decision was not made lightly, and it pains me to see the distress it would bring upon you. In the face of an indescribable situation, I found myself at a crossroads, and regrettably, the path I had to take diverged from the dreams we once shared.

I implore you to forgive me, not as a plea for exoneration but as an earnest request from someone who still cares deeply for you. If it were within my power to rewrite our story, I would, in a heartbeat. Life is often unpredictable, and we find ourselves grappling with circumstances beyond our control.

Enclosed is the formal divorce letter prepared by my attorney and authenticated by The Indian Consulate General in San Francisco. In the divorce document, I have legally bestowed upon you all my worldly possessions, including the ownership of my studio apartment and my mom's jewelry kept in the bank's locker.

I am quite aware that this gesture may not alleviate the burden of our parting. However, it stands as my final tribute to you, a symbol of my profound gratitude for your overwhelming impact on my life. The moments we shared are etched in my heart, and I will forever hold them dear, treasuring them as some of life's most beautiful memories.

It tears me apart to think of how much anguish my action would cause you, and I want to emphasize that you are not alone in bearing this torment. I, too, am involved in a deep battle in which I am attempting to come to terms with the weight of the act I was driven to make and the far-reaching ramifications. I beseech you not to keep my picture as a malevolent person in your heart but rather that of a fallible human who stumbled amidst the intricate tapestry of life's difficult complexities.

My envisioned future has taken a different course from my hopes and dreams. Instead, I now foresee my days concluding in a starkly different manner, far from the aspirations I had held dear. I foresee a solitary path that may end in a care center or in a hospital bed. My fervent prayers and hopes are now directed toward this conclusion arriving sooner, as I believe it may offer some measure of respite from the anguish that is tearing me apart.

I wish you nothing but peace and happiness in the days ahead. May you find the strength to move forward, and may life grant you the joys and serenity that you deserve.

With deepest regrets,
Samuel Thomas

As I completed reading the letter, cold sweat began to bead upon my entire body, and I felt a numbing shock envelop me. My beloved Sam had divorced me and left me for what? What had I done to warrant such a decision? We had shared a profound love that had compelled us to unite in matrimony. Confusion and pain gripped my heart, and I yearned for answers to the unfathomable void that had emerged between us.

For the next ten days, I confined myself to my room, finding solace in the comforting presence of Mom and Dad. Dad devoted a substantial amount of time to cheering me up by luring me into the television lounge that I flatly rejected. He told me silly quips and brief stories to root me up. There were poignant instances when he, overcome with sorrow, let out heartfelt wails, took me in his arms, tenderly kissed my forehead, and held me close, mourning the unrelenting cruelty of destiny that had cast its shadow upon me.

With care, Mom ensured I consumed dry fruit and fenugreek seed ladoos (sweet balls), though they weren't easy to swallow. She insisted they would aid in my quick recovery from the strains of childbirth. She took it upon herself to prepare all my favorite dishes and even arranged for a twenty-four-hour nurse to be with me in the room all the time. Through it all, not once did she shed a tear. Instead, she consistently reminded me that we couldn't challenge the will of the Lord. With unwavering strength, she encouraged me to gather the remnants and forge ahead, constructing a new and grander castle. Her words resonated with the wisdom that life persists even when someone exits our narrative, and so the journey continues, ever unfolding.

After two months of my delivery, we left for the USA, where Bro arranged for a rented four-bedroom house, which was hardly a few hundred steps from his house. All of us were hugely disappointed that he didn't even ask us to stay with him for a few days. Dad and Mom didn't say a word, but it wasn't difficult to figure out that they were angry and disappointed.

Dad bought a luxurious house beside a large park within a few weeks. Bro wanted to pay for the mortgage, but Dad said there was no need; he'd pay the whole amount, and he has enough to live a comfortable life as long as he's alive.

A few days after purchasing the house, Dad informed me that he had invested most of his company's annual profits in purchasing shares of Blue-Chip American companies through an American share trading house that one of his clients recommended. His investment had multiplied beyond his expectations, and I am the sole beneficiary of all his investments.

I became a silent spectator; words were refusing to come out of my mouth. I was eating and drinking when someone was reminding me of it. Dad was forcing me to sit with him and watch TV, which I was doing but watching with no focus on what was happening on the screen. Dad took me to the park every evening for a walk and some fresh air. Somehow, Dad looked very worried about my health, and I felt he wanted to tell me something, but holding himself since it was only a hunch, I never inquired. One night, Mom came to my room and said, Dad is complaining about an acute pain in his chest. I asked Mom to stay with Dad, and I'll call for an ambulance and Bro. Within a few minutes, an ambulance arrived, and the paramedics rushed him to a hospital near our house. I went with the ambulance and asked Mom to come with Bro. Paramedics didn't do much except console me that he'd be fine, and they had already requested a cardiologist to be available as we were bringing an unconscious patient who complained of acute chest pain.

In a matter of minutes, my brother arrived with Mom, and we gathered across from the emergency room. After a while, a physician emerged from the emergency room and told us that they were diligently working to stabilize the patient despite the severe damage to his heart muscles. Over the course of two long hours, a team of four doctors tirelessly tried to stabilize Dad's condition, but sadly, despite their efforts, Dad died, leaving us to grieve his loss.

The day Dad passed, it felt like the ground beneath my feet had vanished. I was lost, adrift in a sea of grief. But then, something strange happened. It was as if his passing, as painful as it was, became a spark. It woke me from my numbness and ignited a new fire. A determination filled my body to face life's challenges head-on and be the person I was, full of energy and zest. It was a bittersweet strength, born out of loss and laced with the memory of his love. And I don't have to feel sorry for myself just because someone has ditched me.

First and foremost, I decided to find a decent job, as working would help me understand that life is much more than weeping or feeling dejected. Mom wasn't happy with my decision to work. She kept reminding me about a lot of money Dad had left behind that would bring all the material pleasure I was seeking. I loved how she was looking out for me, but honestly, the thought of staying home all day felt suffocating. I craved some normalcy, a routine that would get me out of bed and face the day. Work wouldn't erase the pain of losing Dad, but maybe it would give me a sense of purpose. I convinced Mom that earning money was not the aim, but keeping engaged was the objective.

In a matter of weeks, I secured a decent position as a research assistant in a massive organization dedicated to exploring diverse fields, including nuclear physics and engineering. The salary was good, and the commute to the lab, a mere 40-minute train ride, wasn't inconvenient.

The job made me embark on a journey of self-care. I invested in quality business attire, cosmetics, and various accessories to present myself sharp and polished. I also committed to a rigorous exercise routine to shed the extra pounds I had gained during pregnancy and the subsequent sedentary months.

Every day, Mom was pressing me to find a person and settle down, but I refused, saying I got married once and that was enough. Days were converting into weeks, and weeks were turning into months, and it was almost five years since we landed in the land of opportunity.

One day, while I was busy in the office with my routines, my boss came along with a brown guy. Since he had moved to another department, I was introduced to him as my new supervisor. The brown guy introduced himself as Kabir

Sharma, who has been working for the company for the past 12 years.

Initially, Kabir exhibited a certain degree of presumption, possibly expecting me to grovel to secure his favor. Frankly, I had no intention of ingratiating myself with him, nor did I see any reason to do so. In fact, I'm already in line for a promotion to the very position he occupies, and I anticipate achieving it within the next year. My job performance reviews for the last four years have regularly made me the top performer in every category. My ability to meticulously record my work, provide exhaustive presentations, and defend my study with solid evidence earned me a lot of praise. These successes put me ahead of many more seasoned coworkers in the competition for promotion.

Realizing that I cared little for his expectations, he adopted a more amiable demeanor. He began lauding my work and frequently invited me to his meetings to seek my feedback on various research projects my colleagues and I were working on. One day, when I was in his chamber discussing some of the issues I was facing in delivering an assignment, he extended an invitation for a weekend dinner. Instead of immediately refusing, I informed him that I would get back to him the day before Saturday.

I mentioned the dinner invitation from my Indian boss to Mom for the upcoming weekend. Intrigued, she inquired about my boss and, upon learning, encouraged me to accept the invitation. Her rationale was that he was a widower and I should check him out. She emphasized that the age gap wasn't substantial, and he was well-educated, had a stable job, and must be making good money. I protested that I was not interested in marriage and wanted to die as a loner.

Mom calmly stated, "Dolly, I'd like to share the story of my journey with you. Your father and I were never a good match. He was educated, while I barely completed school. Our marriage was arranged; your dad was striving to establish his own business, and my father, being a rich landlord, offered financial support as my dowry, even though I was still a schoolgirl. Back then, parents were eager to rid themselves of the responsibility of a pubescent daughter.

"Post our marriage, I witnessed his unwavering dedication to work and accumulating wealth, often leaving me feeling neglected. Yet, he never uttered a word of criticism about my cooking or my occasional mishaps. His remarkable kindness and affection were evident in his willingness to fulfill my every request. In gratitude, I made sure to serve his favorite meals and relaxed in his preferred manner.

"Since I was a misfit at a party of educated people where they spoke in English and drank wine, he never attended any of his client's parties. I was grateful for the respect he gave me in the house and in the family. When he noticed that I was an efficient and organized person, he left everything to me except for earning and investing money. When he became financially sound, he spoiled me and never refused anything that I asked for, clothes, jewelry, a new car, or whatever, but we hardly spoke. He came home late, tired, and exhausted; after dinner, he watched TV for an hour or two, mostly the news or financial channels, and slept like a log. We seldom had a meaningful conversation; if I decided on anything, he never challenged me, and when he decided to do anything, I never questioned him. We never had a bond of any kind, yet today, I feel so lonely that I'm praying to the Lord to call me so I can be with him; he was the purpose of my life, my strength, and seeing him was enough for me to rejuvenate my energies and spend my days with zeal and vigor. You know, we decided to relocate to this country only to live under the roof of our son. We had too much money and didn't come here to be a parasite, but when our beloved son put us into a separate house, we were hugely disappointed and even thought of going back. Your father reacted with deep anguish and designated you as the sole recipient of his entire wealth. He made you the sole beneficiary of his investment in the US stock market, which he claims is worth millions of dollars. Additionally, he instructed me to appoint you as the beneficiary of all the funds held in both US and Indian bank accounts and the substantial jewelry that I have kept in Indian bank lockers. He wanted you not to give a penny to your brother, and if he hasn't told you, then you promise me that you don't disobey your father's will.

"I appreciated my son's effort to check in every other evening, even if the visits were brief. It meant a lot. However, I can't find happiness in this, as I firmly believe my beloved husband died due to his mistreatment. I'm simply biding my time until you marry so I can peacefully depart from this world for good." She stopped the sermon and started wailing loudly, and I joined her, remembering Dad, who was holding back from telling me his disappointment and maybe more. The pain inflicted by his son may have killed him; otherwise, he didn't have any unhealthy habits or health issues, except for BP and diabetes, which he got when he was in his mid-forties.

Anyhow, now Dad has gone, and Mom is unhappy, and to make her happy, I mustn't disrespect her desires. So, I decided to accept Kabir's invitation to the dinner.

Kabir took me to an Indian restaurant; it was not fancy, but okay. He ordered several dishes, more than enough for two people. During the bite, he informed me that he had done his PG in this country and had joined this company. He is the only son of his parents; his father died, and his mother has a few poor relatives who look after her. He wedded an ambitious American-born and bred woman of Indian origin who was employed at an investment firm, and the initial years of their marriage flowed smoothly. However, after her promotion, her job demanded frequent travel to Europe and the Middle East to woo potential investors. Spending almost half of the month away from home, I eventually voiced my discontent, being a young man with physical needs. She said she has no issues if we open our marriage; in any case, her job is such that certain super-rich clients are only willing to give business if I keep them happy, which I do all the time. Feel free to bring girls of your choice and have fun or have a study girlfriend to serve you in my absence. It wasn't acceptable to me, and we agreed to an uncontested divorce. The conversation turned to my past marriage. I answered his questions honestly and openly. He then expressed his interest in dating to see if we were a good fit. He even offered to move in with me, but I politely requested some time to consider everything.

There was an inexplicable aspect about him that I couldn't quite pinpoint. By all standards, he was attractive, well-educated, had a substantial income, and drove a Honda Accord, even though he could easily afford a BMW or a Mercedes. He displayed his wealth in a restrained manner, which is good. Yet, despite these qualities, I found myself lacking a genuine attraction or a desire to engage in meaningful conversations with him.

After two weeks, again, he took me for dinner to another Indian restaurant frequented by middle-class folks, whereas he could have taken me to a classy fine dining restaurant. I just listened to him without getting into a conversation and spoke when he asked for my comments. Why was I not getting attracted to him, or was I waiting for a better man? What other option could be available for a working-class widower of over thirty years? I'm not a celebrity model to get lucky in fishing for a wealthy businessman or a top-notch executive. I was so confused that I decided to invite him for dinner at our house so Mom could meet, interact, and give her feedback on how she found him.

Mom commented that he's an excellent man and that I'm lucky that such a decent person is desirous of marrying me.

We started going out for dinner almost every Saturday, and on our fifth or sixth dinner in a similar restaurant, I offered to pay the bill, and he didn't object.

I mentioned this to Mom, and she said, "Remember, you're a rich girl. To learn about your wealth, tomorrow you speak with the investment company; your dad has given me a file in which you'll find the company name and the contact person's phone number, various documents pertaining to the invested amount, and so on. So, even if he's a little tight, let him be; you don't need his money."

"Mom, I don't need his or anyone's money. I've got my savings, plus what Dad has left in his US account is more than enough to enjoy a comfortable life. I haven't felt the spark that would push me towards marriage," I confessed, wanting to be completely transparent.

Upon Mom's pressure, I spoke with Dad's investment company, based in New York, the next day. The person handling Dad's account informed me that he'd mail me all the details in the next few hours. Before I left the office, I received an email with an attachment containing the requested information.

In the evening, while having dinner, I informed Mom that the shares were worth more than fifty-five million US dollars, which is a massive amount, and it would be unfair if I didn't split it equally with my brother.

"No, you won't be giving a single penny to your brother and causing pain to your dad and me. Your brother's actions led to my husband's demise; he felt so humiliated that it resulted in his death. He could have asked us if he wanted a bigger house; instead, he callously left us in a dismal situation, neglecting any responsibility. He treated us horribly, displaying a level of cruelty that I can never forgive; you know your dad believed he abandoned us in a metaphorical dungeon. This is why, within weeks, he bought a new house of his liking. Consider yourself disowned if you even think about splitting the money with your brother," Mom's voice resonated with frustration and indignation.

"Okay, Mom, whatever you say, but I suggest you think about it when your anger settles down. You don't know why he behaved this way," I calmly said.

One evening, I opened up to Mom and said that Kabir was pressuring her to marry, but I couldn't shake the feeling that he wasn't the right fit for me. While Kabir is a decent person, there's just something missing, some spark of attraction that I can't seem to find. Mom laughed and said, "It's because of your Sam. I assure you it would be impossible for anyone to come to your expectations because of him. So, settle with someone keen on marrying you, and mind you, he's educated, good-looking, and earning in five figures."

Almost every week, Kabir reminded me that we should settle down. In the third month, when Mom started spitting fire, I had to agree to his proposal to get married, but I put two conditions: one, he would move with us, and two, no children unless I decide to have. He gladly agreed to both conditions.

After three months of marriage, Mom and I agreed that this bloody idiot was a pest and a freeloader. Since he started living with us, he hasn't contributed a penny towards house expenses, and he has never asked us to go out to dinner or go shopping. In the house, he reads magazines that he brought from the office or watches TV. He never asked Mom or me to help with the house chores. One day, I decided to have a showdown.

I asked him to follow me to the living room, explicitly instructing Mom to refrain from entering. With a stern tone, I addressed him, "Kabir, I'm sure you're aware that this isn't a philanthropic dwelling where one can reside without compensating for the sustenance, lodging, and utilities. Kindly issue a check for $12,000 covering the living expenses of the past three months. Beginning next month, ensure a monthly transfer of $4,000 to Mom's account on the first. In addition, you will be responsible for vacuuming, dishwashing, and throwing garbage. On Saturdays and Sundays, your duties extend to tending to the garden, mowing the lawn, cleaning the backyard, pruning the plants, and maintaining the backyard in impeccable condition."

"Don't you think four thousand is stiff? Settle for 2500, and the rest is fine," Kabir stated in a muted voice.

"No, Kabir, it's not possible to accommodate your request. You're getting 1500 dollars toward the rent of your house, and what you're paying is just 2500 dollars, which is nothing compared to what you earn monthly. Additionally, you must take us to a fine dining restaurant every week, not to the subpar places you previously took me. You must also buy me at least ten thousand dollars worth of jewelry, clothes, or accessories every three months. If these terms are acceptable to you, you're welcome to stay and enjoy the benefits you're getting," I was firm in my expression.

"I believe you're unfair to me. Be reasonable so I can feel happy to contribute and comply with your other terms," Kabir expressed in the same muted voice.

"Please, don't bargain. This is not a flea market to seek discounts, and you're not a poor person to haggle," I knew I was harsh, but he pushed me to become one.

"Okay, Aarti, I don't have a choice but to agree with whatever you're asking," he said depressingly.

"Great, go and write the check and give it to Mom," I didn't want to give an inch to the idiot for his insensitive attitude.

Somehow, I developed an aversion to Kabir. He seemed disinterested in everything, never suggesting activities like going to the movies, embarking on a long drive, hosting a backyard BBQ, or enjoying a day by the lake. His sex drive was also limited to once a week, and most of the weeks, I excused under some pretext. Never asked me once to have at least a child, though I wouldn't have agreed to it. He had no friends and no relatives in the USA, or maybe he was hiding from them for reasons best known to him. No vices: liquor, cigars, cigarettes, gambling, or at least watching movies. He never complimented me once, not while we were dating and not after marriage; he was a pathetic soul! I failed to understand the purpose of his living and why he married me.

The yearning for Sam persisted within me, unabated. I wanted to meet him at least once but was unwilling to initiate the steps to do so. I could let him come to me or hope we meet through a serendipitous crossing of paths, perhaps on a flight or elsewhere. I had a nagging suspicion that some compelling factors had influenced Sam's action, as the Sam I knew couldn't be the one who could bring me so much grief and torment and abandon me to face misery eternally.

After spending almost twenty years in the USA, my mother peacefully passed away as her health had been deteriorating for the past several years. Just eight days before her passing, she asked me to sit by her side and spoke in a faint voice, saying, "Dolly, I'm nearing the end, and any day, any minute, I'll come face to face with my Lord. I wish to meet HIM without the weight of guilt. If you can, please find it in your heart to forgive me for the choices I made, thinking they were for your salvation, to shield you from divine retribution. As I lie on my deathbed, I've come to understand that HE won't judge me for the actions of my husband, children, or anyone else but solely for my deeds. Now, in this final moment, when it's evident to me that everyone will be answerable for their own actions, I deeply regret my decisions and believe I should have accepted your husband and the pregnancy and allowed you to live your life on your terms.

"You were sedated during the birth so that you couldn't see the baby's face. Regrettably, I decided to place your baby boy in an orphanage in Shankarpally village and to give him his father's Christian identity; I adorned him with a gold chain featuring a pendant of Jesus. I must also bear the responsibility for your divorce. It was easy for our lawyer to track your hubby with the name that I retained from the marriage certificate you had shown us and the name of the University you mentioned where he was pursuing his doctorate.

"With the help of our lawyer, I spoke to him and asked him to divorce you. He begged me not to force him to divorce because it would inflict too much pain on you, and he didn't want to hurt you emotionally or otherwise. Your husband was a wonderful person, and he only agreed to the divorce after I threatened to execute you. He pleaded and wept like a child, begging me not to cause you any harm. He agreed to divorce you, provided I promise not to inflict any harm on you. Your father opposed my decision, but I remained steadfast in my resolve, and everything unfolded as I had planned.

"The cruelty of my actions torments me, and I doubt I will ever find redemption. Even if you forgive me, your father will not, for since we arrived here, he has held me responsible for the destruction of his baby's life. I am certain that due to my brutal actions and his son's mistreatment, he suffered silently and ultimately passed away.

"I've prepared my will with your brother's assistance, who arranged for a lawyer to visit and record my instructions for the will. In the will, I've bequeathed the farmhouse, all the money, and jewelry in my bank account and locker in India to you. Your brother and I signed the will, and the lawyer witnessed it. Your brother's signature confirms his voluntary agreement to the terms, with no coercion involved, and he has undertaken not to contest it or allow any member of his family to contest the will in any court of law. The lawyer has taken the document for authentication from local authorities and the Indian Embassy. He will deliver it to you in a few days.

"I am deeply aware of the wrongs I have committed, and I hold genuine remorse in my heart. I fully understand the immense pain I have caused you, and my regret surpasses what words can convey. Needless to say, I am departing from this world with a heavy heart, leaving my child unhappy, and that is the most profound regret I carry with me." Both of us started shedding tears; my tears were a product of anger and frustration while she wept in deep remorse for the unjust treatment she had inflicted on her own child. I silently cried without commenting; she was my mother, and even beyond that, the values I've been raised with and the principles I adhere to forbid me from showing disrespect to someone on the edge of life.

Mom became almost unconscious till she died, and during this period, whenever she opened her eyes and saw me, instead of saying something, she dropped tears.

I was right; my Sam could never hurt me, and it wasn't him, but the gun that was kept on his head made him act callously. For the next six months, I debated how to move forward; I became fairly rich because of my own savings and the share value that had increased significantly, and there was no need for me to work. I was now a middle-aged woman, and it was better to hang my boots and do something to my liking. While debating what I should do to keep me engaged and happy, it dawned on me to go back to my roots and do something for my people. The thought came as a bolt of lightning struck me, and I decided to act without any further contemplation.

I resigned from my job, ended my marriage with my idiot husband, sold my house, liquidated the shares that had brought me unimaginable wealth, established an account with an American bank having a branch in Hyderabad, transferred my entire fortune to this new USD account, air-freighted all my possessions to Hyderabad, and finally returned to my beloved city.

Upon reaching Hyderabad, I headed directly to the Farmhouse, which was now surrounded by towering buildings. I learned from our farmhouse staff that the vicinity was transformed into an upscale neighborhood. Our longtime farmhouse caretaker, Vijay Uncle, had passed away, but now his two sons and three other families were maintaining the farmhouse. The next day, the sons of Vijay's uncle informed me that they faced increasing challenges in protecting the premises from the land-grabbing mafia and developers that relentlessly pressured them to sell the property.

Armed with my bank account details the following day, I went to the Chief Minister's residence. I informed the staff that I was an Indian American interested in investing in some social causes and would like to meet the CM for a few minutes to discuss my project. I was there at five in the evening and patiently waited there until ten, when he finally got free from his engagements and agreed to grant me a brief audience. I introduced myself, presented my bank statement, and sought his assistance in establishing on the farmhouse land an ultra-modern Higher Secondary School for the super-rich kids, a medical college, an engineering college, a nursing college, hospital with 200 suits for the elite, an Orphanage to accommodate at least 200 newborn abandoned babies, a Senior Citizen Luxury home, a Vocational Institute for the woman, and at least 100 two-bedroom apartments for support staff, and fifty or more apartments for senior staff. In concluding my address, I pleaded for his aid in securing the necessary permissions and sparing me from the harassment inflicted by land grabbers and developers.

He was very pleased with the idea and asked me to prepare the drawings and meet with his chief secretary, who would assist in getting the needed approvals from various government departments. Regarding the harassment, he said I need not worry about it, as he'll instruct the Director General of Police (DGP) to make sure that no one can get close to the premises. As per CM's instructions, I wrote the complete address of the property, my name, and my contact number and gave it to him. The next day at noon, I got a call from the DGP himself, who assured me that no one would come close to the property and that he was sending the area Circle Inspector to meet with me. Within half an hour, the CI came with a couple of junior officers and several constables. He gave me his and other officers' direct contact numbers and said all of them were available to take my call around the clock whenever I needed help sorting out any issues. He also assured me that they would instruct all the property developers and land mafia to stay away from this land.

The following day, I went to Shankarpally village and found the only orphanage located a little away from the village. I met with a senior caretaker of the institution. She informed me that the couple who established the orphanage had passed away, and she was appointed by an NGO based in Hyderabad, which now owns this facility. She has been working here for the past few years. I asked her whether they had a record of babies in and out with dates. She informed me prior to her joining, the owners didn't maintain a proper record, but since she joined and as per the guidelines of the NGO, a record is maintained of all children's admissions date and the date they left the facility, which is generally when they're sixteen years old. I thanked her and left. My visit's outcome was on the expected lines; to believe more than twenty-five years of record from a village establishment was too much to ask.

I initiated my search for a well-regarded builder and consulted with four top builders recommended by Google who work throughout India. They all told me they were too occupied to accept new projects that required strict timelines for completion. One executive of a builder asked me to meet with a builder who is growing very fast and has a reputation for excellent workmanship and on-time delivery. I took the address and went to their office, and after a wait of approximately forty minutes, a woman came and took me to a meeting room.

In a few minutes, a young, breathtakingly beautiful blonde girl entered the room, sat opposite me, and gave me her business card, which read Angelina Daniel, President, Rajesh Builders, and her contact details.

In a low ear-pleasing voice, she asked how she could help. I explained the purpose of the visit.

She was surprised and, to reassure herself, asked, "You have more than a 60-acre farmhouse in that prime locality, which has become affordable to only super rich?"

"Yes, that's what I said, and I want you to take up the project and finish it in an agreed time frame. Can you do that?" I stated.

"We are working more than our capacity, but I'll take up your project to support you in doing admirable philanthropic work. On my way to the office, I want to visit the site tomorrow between 9 and 9.30 am. Will anyone be there to show me the whole premises?" Angie's response was heartwarming.

I said, smiling, "I stay at the farmhouse, so please come whenever it's convenient and give me the pleasure of hosting you for breakfast."

"Thank you for the breakfast offer, but don't bother, as I don't eat much early in the morning," Angie remarked.

"Okay, then I'll leave now, and thank you for seeing me without an appointment," I expressed with a grin, shook hands, and left.

The following day, Angie was at the farmhouse gate at sharp nine in the morning, and I welcomed her at my door and asked her to have at least a cup of milk tea before we could walk around the premises. She agreed with a smile.

"Can I call you Auntie?" Angie asked me with a smile.

"Please, it would be not only ear-pleasing but uplifting to have a talented girl like you as my niece," I said cheerfully.

"Auntie, how long have you been living here," Angie inquired.

"Upon my recent return from the USA, I didn't have a place to stay, so I temporarily chose to reside in the farmhouse. This land was gifted to my mother by my maternal grandfather as part of her dowry, and it wasn't a farmhouse but a barren land unsuitable for agriculture. The terrain was rough and unfit for living or cultivation, with only a single track, poorly constructed road heading toward the city directly in front of the farmhouse's main gate. Grandpa likely acquired it for a bargain and passed it on to his daughter. Nonetheless, my father decided to transform it into a farmhouse, investing heavily in the process. He fenced the property, drilled two borewells very deep to get the water, converted some of the land for farming, and constructed this four-bedroom house and staff accommodation. Employed several families to reside here, oversee the estate, and cultivate rice and pulses.

"Before leaving for the USA, we used to come once or twice a month, but since we were gone, no family member has stepped in as the entire family was in the US. While we were leaving for the USA, Dad retained the services of only four families who were hardworking and loyal. They took care of the premises and reside here. Dad paid them well, looked after their children's education and medical, and allowed them to sell the agricultural produce and divide the earnings equally. After coming, I promised them that I'd take care of them and their children as long as I'm alive," I stated solemnly.

"What about your immediate family? Are they going to stay in the US or join you soon?" Angie inquired. Before taking up the project, she wanted to make sure that no one could bring a stay order on the construction. Otherwise, she would lose money because she would mobilize lots of resources, and the progressive payment wouldn't suffice the losses she would incur.

"I have only one brother, but Mom gave this land to me through her WILL attested by a US court and the Indian Embassy. I will give you a copy of it for your records. I was married while I was in the USA but never had any children, and six months back, I legally separated from my husband. To give you comfort, you're not getting into murky waters; I'll pay you not only the needed advance payment but, in addition to that, will provide you with a bank guarantee confirming that in case of delay in receiving due payments for forty-five days, the bank would pay you. Honey, I'm financially very sound, and I've shown my bank statement to the Chief Minister; because of that, he gave me the go-ahead with my project and not only provided police protection against land grabbers and aggressive builders but asked me to visit his principal secretary with the engineering drawings, who would facilitate all the needed permits, licenses or whatever I need to execute the project. Please treat it as one of your star projects and allocate maximum resources, as I want the facility to be up and running as soon as possible," I expressed.

"Okay, Auntie, I'll start my work immediately. Tomorrow, I'll come with my team of experienced engineers to conduct a comprehensive site assessment. The assessment will commence with precise land measurements and a thorough soil survey. This survey will meticulously evaluate crucial soil characteristics, including soil-bearing capacity, soil stability, potential for liquefaction, groundwater levels, and other essential factors. The gathered data will determine the soil's suitability for development in accordance with your specific requirements.

"Once it is established that we can go ahead with the construction, our architects and I will sit with you to effectively grasp your vision for this project and ensure we're aligned throughout the design process. We will spend at least two hours asking questions and gathering your feedback. This initial consultation will help us develop a basic 3D preview, allowing you to identify any necessary additions, deletions, or refinements. We'll make as many revisions as needed until you're fully satisfied with the design.

"Next, we'll craft a comprehensive offer for the construction and landscaping. Once you give the green light to proceed, we'll move forward by sculpting a clay model for your additional scrutiny and approval. After the project kicks off, we prefer to stick to the plan without significant alterations; however, we're open to minor adjustments. Since it's a massive project, I strongly suggest you engage a Construction Management Company to oversee the project, ensuring that the buildings are erected according to plan and the materials used align with the specifications outlined in the proposal.

"We charge for the initial work, and considering the work involved, we would bill you for twenty lakhs, which you must pay tomorrow when I come with the engineers and architects," Angie expressed calmly.

"Please give me your bank account details, and I'll transfer the amount before the end of the day," I remarked.

Angie gave me the account number, bank name, and address and left with a 'See you tomorrow.' The following day, she arrived with a team of eight, armed with various tools and equipment. They toiled for nearly six hours, measuring the land, digging deep into various places, taking samples, and a lot I didn't know as I decided not to spend my time looking at their work. Ten days later, Angie rang me up with the good news that the land was good to go ahead with construction. The next task was to create a 3D video clip according to my requirements. She scheduled a meeting at her office for the next day at ten and asked me to be prepared to spend at least two hours detailing my vision for the project.

Four weeks later, I again met Angie at her office to review the 3D file. Before the review, I asked Angie, "Can you ask the person who has prepared the file to join us so I can seek clarification on anything that I could fail to understand."

"Auntie, the file was prepared under my supervision. I want you to know that I hold a master's degree in construction engineering and management from IIT Delhi. So, please don't hesitate to ask questions or suggest modifications."

I was absolutely stunned by the meticulously thought-out work in which I couldn't find a single flaw. Given the school's elite nature, she managed to create an impressive indoor environment with a swimming pool and games arena for indoor sports like badminton, shuttle, table tennis, and volleyball. She also designated ample space for outdoor activities with cricket and football fields. The building itself, a fully air- conditioned five-story structure, was designed to accommodate two thousand students and featured three separate entrances for Kindergarten, Primary, and Secondary classes. The total school was sprawled across 18 acres. She allocated five acres each for Medical, Engineering, and Nursing colleges. For the Senior Citizens, Orphanage and Vocational Institute, 3 acres each. For the central kitchen, she allocated one acre. For junior and senior staff apartments, 2 acres each were allocated, and she designated one acre each for two dormitories, one for unmarried male staff and the other for unmarried female staff, each capable of accommodating 200 or more workers. Separate entrances and dedicated parking spaces for two and four-wheel vehicles were part of the plan, and she ensured ample open space for children's playgrounds at the orphanage and staff quarters. She kept the remaining space of 12 acres for the hospital.

My only suggestion was that she allocate a plot of one acre for me to build a two-story luxury Bungalow.

"Sure, Auntie, I'll attend to it. Please allow me to give you a rough estimate for construction alone. If you opt for the best material to be used, it could easily cross one thousand crores. Are you prepared to spend this much?" Angie inquired.

Nearly 19 years ago, Dad's share value stood at $55 million. Having attended a thought-provoking talk show where experts elucidated the far-reaching impacts of advancements such as smartphones, high-speed internet, cloud computing, and artificial intelligence, I became convinced of the immense potential for growth in the digital sector. In light of this, I strategically decided to redirect my investments away from traditional Blue-Chip companies toward the upcoming giants like Apple, Microsoft, and Google. My decision turned out to be a tremendous success, significantly boosting earnings from the previous five percent to above fifteen percent yearly. When I finally sold all the shares, the total amount far surpassed my expectations, reaching above four hundred million dollars. Combined with my savings and the funds I received from Mom, my bank account had little over three thousand five hundred crores.

"My love, please don't worry about the finances. I require the final 3D file prepared for my review and approval as soon as possible," I expressed with a smile.

While returning to the farmhouse, I stopped at Sam's house. The moment I entered the gate, a young man approached me and asked what I wanted.

"I'm going to Sam's room on the third floor, which he had given to me, being his wife," I stated.

"Papa once told me that uncle got married before leaving for the USA and introduced his wife to him. Are you the same?" He inquired.

"Yes, can I meet with your Papa, as he knows me," I commented.

"Papa passed away five years ago, and I'm his only son, and I believe you if you provide some authentic documentation to prove your claim. Please understand; you would do the same if you were in my position," he earnestly stated.

"No issues. Give me until tomorrow so I can show you our marriage photos. What work do you do, sir?" I stated.

"I have a factory to manufacture auto rubber washers, and I mostly work from home as I must look after my ailing mom. My wife is a business executive in a private company, and I have two school-going children. If you need any help, please inform me," he said.

"Sam came twice to Hyderabad for work but never stayed here because he found the room full of dust. I wanted to get it cleaned, and I may stay here for a few weeks or more since I've got to deal with a few issues that could take time," I said. I wanted to know whether Sam had ever come to Hyderabad and stayed here.

"I or anyone in the family never saw him coming. Maybe he just assumed that the room must be full of dust and stayed at a hotel to attend to his work," he said.

"I believe you're right. My name is Aarti. What's your name?" I asked inquisitively.

"I'm Prashant. Please note down my phone number and feel free to call me for any assistance," Prashant said.

I recorded his contact number and left him with a thanks.

As expected, the room was nothing but a dust pool, and I couldn't spend a single minute fearing my lungs would collapse.

The following day, I got in touch with Angie, seeking her support in cleaning and renovating my studio apartment. The only valuable item left was Sam's family heirloom, the tableware; I instructed Angie to have it packed under the watchful eye of a reliable person and delivered to me. I granted her the flexibility to allocate funds as necessary, emphasizing the importance of the final result reflecting a job well done. For the buildings and landscaping, Angie quoted a price of 1340 crores since she would use only the best material available in the market, which I accepted without asking for a lower offer. The construction would be completed within three years, allowing an additional six-month buffer supported by a performance bond.

Angie gave me the complete layout plan, detailed drawings, and the clay model. I went to the CM's Principal Secretary and showed him everything. He asked me to come in two days to collect letters addressed to the concerned departments to issue you the permission and licenses needed to proceed with the construction. In addition, he said he'll personally call the concerned people to facilitate the process as a priority.

Construction started in three months, and I moved to Sam's apartment, which Angie turned into a palace. I bought the entire building from Prashant at a price that he quoted far above what it could fetch him and moved with the farmhouse workers into the building.

Living in Sam's apartment became an absolute pleasure; the best part was that I could smell and feel him. I've often thought about trying to track down him, but then I've imagined he's probably married with grown-up kids. Even if I found him, it would be like intruding on his world, disrupting the peace he's built. Let him enjoy his life wherever he may be, but I'm happy he didn't just disappear on me.

Since I had no activity to spend my time on, I worked on outsourcing all the institutions except the orphanage and senior citizen home that I wanted to keep under my charge. Fortunately, I came across esteemed institutions known for their stellar track record in managing similar enterprises. All of them demonstrated significant interest in taking charge of my prestigious hospital, school, and colleges. Their senior representatives conducted a site visit and examined the clay model and copies of the construction drawings. For every institution, I drafted a scope of work document with the aid of a lawyer exclusively hired for this task. I entered extensive negotiations with the selected companies on profit sharing and, upon agreement, signed a legally binding contract for them to run the institutions for an initial ten-year period, with the option of extending it for an additional five years and in confirmation of their commitment they submitted the required performance bonds. I assigned the selected companies to recommend the necessary equipment and furniture, underscoring the importance of suggesting only the finest options available.

My project represented a prestigious endeavor for both Angie's office and the Construction Management Company, as their relentless efforts drove the project to near completion of all the buildings' structures within the agreed completion period.

I was left with one major task: finding a reliable source to run the institutions' canteens and supplying food to Hospital, Orphanage and Senior Citizen Home. I didn't want a high-end but a mid-range reputed institution to run so that they could cater quality food at a price that no one could find as stiff. I spoke with Angie, and she said she knows someone who's very good and fully capable of meeting all my conditions, but whether he has the time to take up the massive assignment or not is the question she needs to ask and get back to me.

Three days later, she reached out to me, inquiring if I'd be available to join her for lunch the upcoming Sunday at an upscale restaurant. The purpose was to meet with the owner and explore the possibility of him taking on the project. I agreed and asked her to send me the restaurant's name and location and mention what time I had to be there.

I purchased a high-end automobile and hired a chauffeur due to the inconvenience of navigating through heavy traffic and searching for parking spaces. It was three days until Sunday, and in my spare moment, I searched the restaurant and noticed that it had several outlets present in numerous high-end shopping malls and upscale areas. Okay, so I would be meeting with an experienced person, and even if he couldn't take up the job, at least he could guide me to some other reliable institutions that could be of help.

I reached the restaurant on time, informed the attendant that I'd come to meet Mahendra Reddy, and was guided to a cozy room where Angie was sitting. I gave her a warm hug and conveyed my blessings. I don't know why, but every time I met her, I developed an increased affection for her and wished I had a daughter like her. Suddenly, thoughts of my son flooded my mind, bringing tears to my eyes, which Angie noticed. She tenderly grasped my hands and asked about the source of my emotions. With a fragile smile, I softly said, "I remembered my lost son and the unfulfilled desire of having a daughter akin to you."

"Auntie, please consider me as your daughter. I've never experienced what a mother is like since I never had one, but when I met you, I couldn't help but imagine how wonderful life would have been with a mother like you. I didn't express my feelings, fearing it might upset you. But from this point forward, I want you to treat me like your baby. I may not be your biological child but don't think any less of me. While I may not possess the same wealth as you, I still fall under the super-rich category, so the bond is devoid of any material motives," Angie candidly shared her heartfelt emotions.

Please allow me to add, "Taking on your venture was not my initial intention, as I was tightly engaged in executing more than our capacity, but the instant you spoke to me, I felt an immediate connection that led me to take up the project."

"My love, I want to express my deepest gratitude. I was feeling incredibly lonely, with no friends or family to turn to for companionship. You've become like my own child, not just figuratively but in the truest sense. And please never discuss money between us; I'm aware that you're incredibly wealthy, and I have much more than my needs. Please find some time to spend with me on a weekend or whenever it's convenient for you to have me around," I confessed, my emotions running high. I may have been carried away by overwhelming feelings and possibly saying things that aren't entirely relevant, but in my eyes, I've found a daughter.

"You don't have to say anything; just allow me to be with you when I can and take you for an outing, a movie, or just binge and talk about our frustrations or uplifting moments." Angie was an upright person, and hearing her such comments was heartwarming.

Before I could respond to her, a young man entered the room, and the moment I set my eyes on him, I fainted, just slumped on the adjacent chairs.

I heard Angie say, "Maddy, please get some water and check if there's a doctor dining here. If not, we might need to take her to the nearest hospital."

Maddy returned with a middle-aged man who checked Auntie's pulse and eyes. He then took a little water in his hand and sprinkled it on her face. She slowly opened her eyes. The doctor left saying she was fine; maybe she had become weak because of excessive dieting and exercise.

Angie asked me what had happened to me and why I fainted, and I expressed my ignorance. How could I tell her that I saw a young Sam, identical to my ex-husband, same height, same features, same skin color, and same exercised V-shaped body?

The young man sat beside Angie, and she introduced him as Mahendra Reddy, owner of several upscale restaurants and another chain of eateries for the lower segment.

I murmured, "It's Good to meet you, Mahendra. I believe I don't have to introduce myself, as Angie must have told you about me. You have an excellent place, and I hope the food will be more praiseworthy. Could you tell me about your business in detail, and are you open to taking up my project?"

"Sure, but first, tell me how you're feeling now. You have scared us. I'll be more than happy to take you to a hospital for a thorough checkup," Mahendra stated with serious concern, reflecting his tone.

"I'm perfectly fine, and don't you worry a bit; it's probably just a fatigue attack. Still, tomorrow, I'll visit a hospital for a checkup," I stated smilingly.

"That's Good to know; however, if you need any help, just let us know. Regarding your needs, let's plan a meeting in the next few days to discuss the project details at your place, here, or wherever suits you best. But for now, please enjoy the meal and share your comments on the presentation, taste, portions, and service. Your feedback matters," Mahendra added with a chuckle.

Chapter Seven

Mahendra Reddy

Unrequited Love

While searching for an apartment to purchase, I came across an advertisement for an ultra-luxurious residential building to be ready in less than 16 months for occupation. A nine-floor building in an upscale colony, one apartment of eight thousand square feet on each floor with all the amenities one could think of. On the ninth floor is a twelve thousand square feet penthouse with open space for hosting a party of 100 people and a dedicated elevator. The ad was from a reputed builder, so I decided to visit them immediately, as generally, the high-end villas and apartments vanish within hours.

I informed the receptionist of the purpose of my visit, and she asked me to take a seat. A young girl approached me within a few minutes and requested that I follow her. The girl took me to the top floor, which was the third floor. I was guided to a twelve-person meeting room, a teakwood gleaming table surrounded by twelve luxurious leather chairs. The room was well equipped with the latest AV presentations and conferencing. While I was checking the gadgets and wall hangings, a server came in a crisp white dress and asked for my preference for a drink. I ordered a glass of water at room temperature.

In a few minutes, a remarkable young girl who possessed striking beauty, slim and around five feet and five inches or a little more, blonde with milky glowing skin, golden hair, and blue eyes, entered the room. She sat opposite me and gave me two cards; one read Rajesh Gupta, President, and the other had the name of Angelina Daniel, Vice President. She politely asked me, "How could I be of any help?"

I said, "I've come to find out about the possibility of buying the penthouse in your venture for which you have placed an advertisement in today's newspaper."

"Sure, but unfortunately, I look after a different department. Papa is the only one who handles the residential buildings, but unfortunately, he didn't come today. I'll check with him whether the penthouse is available, as his old customers book the penthouses in advance. Please give me a few minutes to speak with him and get back to you," she politely expressed and walked out.

I was unsure of hearing her call Papa to Rajesh Gupta. If I heard her right, then it would be a mystery. I was scratching my head at the puzzling relationship when the fairy entered the room again.

"Sorry to keep you waiting. I spoke with my Papa, and the situation is that a couple of old customers have already booked the penthouse, and in a day or two, they would pay the 10% booking advance, as per the terms. However, he's willing to sell you provided you pay 50% advance now, 25% when the structure is ready, and the balance prior to registration of the property. All amounts are to be paid by check, and for paying

50% in advance, you could enjoy a discounted price, which would be on par with the lower-floor apartments. You need to make the decision now; otherwise, there's a good possibility that the property will not be available tomorrow." Then, the horse trading started, and she took her Papa on a conference call; after twenty minutes of haggling, we settled for 70% advance payable today and the balance 30% before registration. The price I negotiated was almost below 12% of what they quoted initially. I signed the sales deed and gave her the check, and she asked me to come tomorrow evening to collect the signed sales deed from Papa.

The next evening, I was with Rajesh Gupta to collect the duly signed sales deed. While sipping the coffee he insisted on, he asked me whether I was studying or working. I replied, "I own Dum Pukht Darbar, a fine-dining chain of restaurants, plus I also own Desi Dhaba restaurants that primarily cater to the lower segment of the market."

"Was it your parent's business that you're running now?" Rajesh Sir inquired.

"No, I developed the entire business myself, and it was because of my passion for cooking. First, I worked as a cook for a small restaurant in a lower-middle-class locality, and later, I took over it, renamed it Desi Dhaba, and expanded the business," I informed him.

Then, we discussed the various topics related to the construction and handover date for over fifteen minutes.

When I rose from the chair to leave, Rajesh Sri asked me, "Do you have any special requirements for the flat, or are you happy with the design given on the brochure?"

"Yes, I want many changes, and I would appreciate it if you recommended an architect who could design according to my requirements."

"I believe my daughter could help you, and there's no need to go to an architect. Angie has a master's in construction engineering and management from IIT, New Delhi; my baby's brilliant. She will give you a drawing for your approval within no time. If she's available, I'll ask her to come," Rajesh Sir proudly said, calling Angie from the intercom to join us if she's not engaged.

Angie joined us within a few minutes and noted my requirements of two large bedrooms with sizeable dressers and washrooms, a sports room cum gym to accommodate a snooker table, table tennis table, and gym equipment, a TV lounge, visitor room, an office-cum-meeting room with a separate entrance.

After noting my requirements, Angie asked me, "How many members do you have in the family?"

"I'm single, and my wife will stay with me when I marry. And after marriage, I intend to have only one child, so one more room is enough," I said with a smile.

"I suggest you have one more bedroom to host relatives and friends. A guest room would be of great help," Angie suggested, smiling.

"Thank you. I appreciate your input and go by your suggestion," I expressed earnestly.

"Fine. Call me after one week, and I'll show you the drawing so you can make any changes or accept and sign it. Once that's done, we'll calculate the cost of the changes compared to our budgeted cost. If it's more, you need to pay the difference; we will give you a credit if it's less.

"Additionally, if you want us to do the interiors, then inform us as soon as possible. We use the best quality materials and exceptional craftsmanship. There's no rush to inform us now, but the earlier, the better, as it helps particularly with the electric wiring and organizing the sockets and plugs according to the needs," Angie expressed with a grin.

"I accept your offer. Please prepare a quotation for the interiors and choose the best quality materials and accessories. I don't want to compromise on anything." It was a genuine expression.

I met Angie again after eight days and approved the drawings, as there was nothing to object to since she did a marvelous job. She said she'll provide a 3D video for the interior, which could take around six to eight weeks.

Every night, before I drifted off to sleep, I found solace in gazing at a photo of Angie that I had taken surreptitiously with my mobile phone. Her beauty was nothing short of mesmerizing, leaving me in awe: Her slender figure and resplendent golden blonde hair perfectly matched her captivating blue eyes and porcelain skin. Her delicate nose and a smile that could brighten the world adorned with impeccable, pearl- white teeth and inviting full lips. Until now, the thought of having a life partner had never crossed my mind, but now, it wasn't just a mere desire; I yearned for Angie to be that life partner.

I knew this desire might be a far-fetched dream, almost like reaching for the moon. To begin with, I was clueless about her relationship status, and even if she happened to be single, why would she consider me for marriage? With her vast riches, formidable intellect and education, and breathtaking beauty, she possessed qualities that could enchant even the most discerning admirers. What odds did a boy like me, raised in an orphanage without formal education, stand? None at all. It would be sheer folly to chase after such an unattainable goal, subjecting myself to the potentially unbearable pain of rejection. Instead, I must be content with the nightly routine of gazing at her photograph, seeking comfort in those moments that brought warmth to my heart and eased me into slumber while yearning to encounter her in my dreams.

After six weeks, Angie called me to check the interior drawings and a 3D video that would show every item from various angles. The next day at eleven, I was at her office. She took me to the meeting room and called her Papa to join.

First, she showed me the impressive colored drawings and then a four-minute 3D video, which showed the house as breathtakingly beautiful and, most likely, highly comfortable. In under an hour, I signed the drawings in approval of everything as presented, with no changes whatsoever. While leaving, I said to Rajesh Sir, "If you have time, can I take you and Angie Ma'am for lunch at one of my restaurants, which is hardly three kilometers away?"

"Thank you, Mahendra, but I eat only home-cooked food with minimal salt and oil. You could take Angie if she agrees to avail your offer," Rajesh Sir conveyed his unwillingness.

"You must excuse me; I've been swamped with pressing paperwork, but I assure you, some other time, I will take you up on your offer," Angie stated with a smile.

Rajesh Sir intervened, "Angie, take a break and get some fresh air; spending twelve hours in front of the desk daily is detrimental to your health."

"Papa, I need to prepare two bid documents that are due for submission early next week. Please excuse me, Mahendra Sir, for this time, but I promise to accept your offer when you visit us next," Angie conveyed her reluctance in her usual subdued tone.

"Angie, go outside and take a breather; there's no need to stress about the work," Rajesh Sir asserted firmly.

"Papa, you're too much. Don't blame me if I miss the bid submission dates." She then addressed me, "Mahendra, Sir, give me a few minutes, and I'll be right with you."

Rajesh, Sir, left the meeting room and asked me to wait for Angie. I called the manager of our recently opened star restaurant and asked him to keep the VIP room available and prepare a lavish lunch, as I was coming with a VVIP guest.

I asked Angie to come in my car, and while driving toward the restaurant, the scent of Angie's body and the delicate fragrance she wore filled my nostrils, bringing a sense of elation and overwhelming joy.

I was engrossed in my own thoughts when I heard Angie say, "Papa informed me you have a chain of restaurants, and you're a self-made person; how did you manage to accomplish so much at such a young age?"

I responded to her inquiry: "I was passionate about cooking from a young age, and to hone the skills I acquired at home, I worked as an assistant cook at a 'Greasy Spoon.' The restaurant owner suffered a Hemiplegia attack, which left the entire left side of his body paralyzed a couple of years after my joining. Unfortunately, he didn't have any immediate family members to take over, so they sold the business and the property to me at a bargain price. I built my modest empire through this little outlet, which I renamed 'Desi Dhaba."

I wanted to ask about the mystery of how Rajesh Gupta could be the Papa of Angelina Daniel, but I refrained.

"That was commendable. A few months back, one of my assistants told me she had dinner at one of your Dum Pukht Darbar restaurants. She said the food is amazing, but it's a pricy place, and one can only go occasionally," Angie commented smilingly.

"Our price goes up because of two factors: one, the high overheads, and next, we base our food pricing on a sixty percent table occupancy. Still, we don't make much money out of food; instead, our major chunk of profits comes from the sale of desserts and drinks. However, if we have a steady table occupancy of 80% throughout the weekdays, for lunch and dinner, we will make substantial profits," I informed her earnestly.

The restaurant's ambiance allured her, and she sought a tour of the whole place, including the kitchen. She was intrigued by the smart use of every available space, and she appreciated how lovely everything was, from the opulent seating and lighting to the drapes and wall hangings.

The VIP room had a large single table for twelve people, with a lovely red rose bouquet in the middle. The manager ensured he seated Angie and politely asked for the preferred drink, which was water for both.

"I hope that the food will be much more amazing than the impressive ambiance. I must commend you for crafting this remarkable place, skillfully optimizing the space to accommodate a maximum number of tables." Her praise, which carried additional weight because it came from an accomplished Construction Engineer, was truly uplifting.

"It's wonderful to hear you liked the place! I'm eagerly anticipating that the food will exceed your expectations and be mouthwateringly good," I said, grinning.

The meal commenced with a platter featuring a variety of grilled non-vegetarian items and baked exotic vegetables. Vegetarian and non-vegetarian curries, an assorted Indian breadbasket, and a lamb Biryani followed it. To conclude the lunch, three classic Hyderabadi desserts graced the table. To counter any post-feast drowsiness, a delightful tea infused with saffron, ginger, and cardamom, with a dash of honey but without the addition of milk, was served. She relished each course with the sharp palate of a true connoisseur, and her lavish admiration knew no limits. I dropped her off and only heard from her after thirteen months when she informed me that Dad had asked her to show you the flat, which was getting the final touches.

The following day, I picked her up to check the flat around eleven in the morning. While driving, I asked her, "How come the flat is ready before the committed time period?"

"All the flats were sold within three days with a 70% advance, which helped Papa assign the maximum number of contractors to accomplish the task in such a short period. We prioritized completing your flat's interior as too much work was involved, and then we had to do the furnishings and fixtures, which could also take time," Angie commented.

"Thank you. I appreciate your efforts in completing my flat as a priority," I expressed earnestly.

We drove silently for the rest of the passage. The building was almost ready from the outside, except for a little debris here and there. The dedicated elevator to my flat was at the extreme end, and adjacent to the elevator, it had four car parking spaces for the occupants of the penthouse: the flat needed painting, and the open area needed to be cleaned. She mentioned the installation of a spacious motorized canopy in the open terrace area, offering the opportunity to enjoy the outdoors and fresh air on cooler days. While returning, I invited her to have lunch with me, but she refused vehemently and said, "Maddy, your last lunch I couldn't forget; you fed me so much that I had to sleep for an hour before coming to my senses. Today, I cannot come because of the workload piled up on my desk, which must be cleared before the end of the day."

I chuckled and declared, "Today, I swear to let you choose and savor whatever you desire."

She laughed and said, "Thank you, but I'll stick to Papa's home-cooked food."

That night, on the bed as usual, I took out my mobile to watch Angie's photo, and while gazing at her beauty, it occurred to me that she said 'home-cooked food from Papa's house.' It means she's not living with her papa, and she must be from a second Caucasian Christian wife who lives in another house with Angie. Whatever, she's highly educated and rich, so she won't look at me even if I become very wealthy. If she had any interest in me, she would have called me at least once since we last met, which indicates she has different plans for her partner. Today's refusal of lunch is also a clear indication that she wants to maintain only a business relationship. I don't blame her since I would have done the same thing if I were in her shoes. So, dear Maddy, be happy and content with gazing at her photo, I said to myself, and a tear rolled down my cheeks.

Chapter Eight

Angelina Daniel

Heart of Cold Stone

I first met Maddy when he came to purchase the penthouse. He appeared to be in his mid-twenties, possessing a commanding stature, with fair and radiant skin that seemed to capture the warmth of the sunlight. His features were finely chiseled, akin to a work of art. His eyes resembled sapphire pools, exuding intelligence and charm, and his smile was a glowing beam of sunshine that could illuminate any space. His youthful, unbridled, and invigorating vitality held such allure that it captivated and brought my heart in hand.

I never had a desire to get married, but after meeting Maddy, I found it hard to imagine turning down a proposal from him. Setting aside his physical attributes, he is a highly successful businessperson, making him a prized catch; many girls must have chased him, and it would be a surprise if he had no girlfriend. Even if he were single, I questioned why he would make me his girlfriend. This orphaned girl was abandoned by her biological parents and left on the streets, only to be rescued by a compassionate soul who ensured I had a home in an orphanage, sparing me from death or a life on the streets.

He never called me after he took me for lunch, and his failure to initiate contact or inquire whether I would be interested in spending an evening with him was unequivocal confirmation that he was not interested in me.

For some reason, I found myself deeply invested in making sure that Maddy's flat had an interior décor worth cherishing. I procured fixtures and furniture from a nationally recognized vendor renowned for their superior craftsmanship. I assigned two of my most capable assistants to oversee the project and made frequent visits to the flat to ensure we delivered much more than what was committed. While we typically maintain a 40% profit margin; our profits dwindled to single digits in Maddy's case. I informed Papa that I intended to use the flat as a showcase for potential clients, and in order to achieve that, I wouldn't be able to maintain the margins calculated in the quotation. He gave me the go-ahead, and in fact, he was pleased with the idea. Once the project was completed, I hired a top-tier videographer to create a stunning five-minute video, and my father was thoroughly impressed with the exceptional results of my efforts.

Before the property registration and the official handover of the flat key, I forwarded Maddy the video clip for his review and comments. I also offered to arrange a physical tour if he preferred. In response, he messaged me expressing his interest in seeing the flat in person and asked if he could pick me up the next day at eleven in the morning, to which I agreed. The next day, he arrived precisely at eleven, his excitement bubbling over as he complimented everything he'd seen in the video. I kicked off our tour by guiding him down to the expansive second basement, a subterranean sanctuary boasting a temperature-controlled oasis. Here, a plush club room offered a haven for relaxation, a state-of-the-art gym, a professional-grade snooker table, high-bounce table tennis, and four poker tables with plush chairs. The open area offered a dedicated court for badminton and a sparkling heated swimming pool.

Next, I took him to inspect his flat. Maddy's eyes shone with gratitude as he said, "I want to extend my heartfelt thanks for all you've done to transform this place into a paradise for me. I couldn't have envisioned anything better, and I genuinely believe no one could have accomplished a better job than what you've done. Your efforts have earned you a special gift, which I'll present at my housewarming ceremony." His smile stretched from ear to ear.

"Your appreciation of my work is more than a pricy gift for me. Thank you for liking my work, and I wish you good luck in enjoying this prestigious place. However, I need a favor from you for your appreciation," I commented.

"I would be more than happy to extend any favor that you need, and even in the future, please never hesitate to reach out if I could be of any service to you," Maddy said with a smile.

"If some of our serious customers want to see the décor of your flat, will you allow me to show them?" I asked in a muted voice.

"I'll give you the password of the digital lock. Please feel free to show the flat to whichever customer you want to. There is no need to get permission from me," Maddy said with a big grin.

"Thank you, Maddy, but I don't want to take responsibility for knowing the password. I'll call you in advance to make an appointment to bring a customer who's not satisfied with the VC," I commented.

"I'm okay with whatever you say," He then abruptly changed the topic and expressed, "I realize you might say no, but I'd still like to extend an invitation to have lunch with me. We'll go to a different restaurant to dine among fellow patrons, and you're free to order any dish you desire. I'm in high spirits today, so I'd be delighted if you'd join me for a bite."

Apologizing to Maddy, I expressed, "I had to decline the offer. I've got a lot to catch up on. Since it's your special occasion, I believe it's best for you to celebrate with your girlfriend rather than with a business contact." I couldn't help but feel I was being a bit blunt in my attempt to find his status.

"You're right. Unfortunately, I don't have a girlfriend yet, and since I've no plans to marry, there's no chance of having one. But you never know when someone will force me to change my mind," Maddy said with a grin.

"How sad! You're a catch, dear, and how come no one attempted to hook you beats me to understand. Anyhow, let's go for lunch, that must be quick. If you could order a small platter of assorted grilled veg and a few bits of non-veg items with a mixed vegetable curry and a bowl of plain rice, I would be fine," I asserted.

Maddy expressed his happiness, called someone from his mobile, and instructed the person to keep a table vacant and prepare the dishes I mentioned.

While in the car, Maddy inquired, "Can I ask you a personal question? You don't have to answer if you find it offensive, but don't be mad at me."

"You could ask, and I promise not to get offended. However, it will be my prerogative to answer your question or to ignore it," I remarked dispassionately.

"Thank you. Are you married, or do you have a steady boyfriend?" Maddy inquired.

"I'm not married, never had a boyfriend, and have no intention of having one in the future. Like you, for some very personal reasons, I've decided to enjoy my life alone without anyone's interference or undesirable dictates," I proclaimed firmly.

"Instead of a boyfriend and girlfriend relationship, can we be just friends and share our lows and highs, or seek opinions on matters where you're hesitant to make decisions? You could use me as your punching bag and an errand runner besides being your friend," Maddy mentioned sheepishly. I believe he was very nervous while he was asking for me to be his friend; his voice was a little over a hiss, indicative of his nervousness.

"Maddy, your suggestion is good for a person who's not engaged heavily, like me, who works six days a week and gets exhausted when returned home in the evening. I don't find the energy to speak a single word; I have my evening meal, surf news channels for half an hour, and go to bed. I have quite a few people taking care of the house and kitchen, and occasionally, on a Sunday, I go to a shopping mall to pick up dresses or accessories; otherwise, I do most of my shopping through online portals. Being a successful young man, you would find plenty of girls who would be more than willing to be your friend or enter a relationship," I commented in my usual tone, which was a little above a whisper.

"I think as friends, we can be a source of strength for each other. Please don't feel pressured to make a quick decision; take all the time you need and reach out whenever you have a change of heart. I'll be at your disposal around the clock, ready to offer whatever means I possess. I realize that your wealth is considerable, making my modest assets appear insignificant by comparison. Nevertheless, having a friend like me can only enrich your life without causing any harm or regrets in knowing me," Maddy's voice reflected disappointment and hurt.

I didn't respond; there was nothing to comment on since my fears cautioned me that I would be better off without his friendship, which has a strong potential of growing into a relationship that could become a disaster. He's a Hindu, and his parents must be rich landlords in a village and could have the power to impose their will upon him. He may be good as gold, but very few have the courage to go against their families. Take the example of my Papa, who told me that he couldn't take me to his home because he didn't want me to be raised by a maid. What BS! He preferred to leave a child in the orphanage instead of raising her in the four walls of his home where she could have felt safe, secure, and loved. You don't have to be a genius to understand why he did that. His wife wouldn't have allowed him to bring home a girl found on the street, so he dumped her in an orphanage. I don't blame him; when it's clear that you'd be fighting a losing battle, it's better to 'let sleeping dogs lie' and go for the safe options at your disposal.

It was yet another exquisite fine-dining restaurant in Maddy's repertoire. At this place, you willingly embrace the higher costs for exceptional service, captivating ambiance, and the delight of indulging in visually stunning, calorie-laden, delectable cuisine.

We had the food, mostly talking about business, the city's breakneck expansion, and the cropping up of new malls and high-rise buildings. Also, I informed him that I take care of large projects, mostly in the Government and private sectors. Dad was taking care of high-end gated communities or luxurious apartment buildings, but for the past two years, he was doing only one or two projects at a time, as he had developed quite a few chronic diseases. The purpose of telling him about Dad's ill health was to know about his parents, but he didn't say a word about them, and I didn't poke further.

He dropped me off after lunch, and we hardly spoke during the ride. He must have been upset and hurt by my refusal to be friends.

After two weeks, Dad and I received an invitation from Maddy to attend the housewarming ceremony on the coming Saturday night. As expected, Dad asked me to attend, which I didn't want. Still, he forced me and asked me to take an expensive gift, stay for a few minutes, and come back.

By eight o'clock, I had arrived at Maddy's apartment, holding a bouquet of red roses and a silver idol of Lord Shiva encased in an acrylic box.

No one was in the apartment, so I surprisingly asked him, "Are I on time or too early, as I don't see any of your guests?"

"First, allow me to thank you for coming and for the lovely gift. Next, I invited you and your dad only, as I don't invite staff to my residence, and I don't have any friends or relatives to invite," Maddy commented with a chuckle.

"Alright, I'll leave, as I don't drink, and my dinner consists of only a bowl of salad with two boiled eggs. Best wishes for your new home. May it be a haven of comfort and tranquility for you and your family, and may you be blessed with good health, happiness, love, and prosperity," I expressed my best wishes in a single breath and made my way to the door. Maddy softly murmured his gratitude and asked me to wait for a moment. He went to his bedroom, came out holding a jewelry box, gave it to me, and stated, "Thank you for the lovely interior decor, which was way above my expectations and breathlessly beautiful. Please, I beg you not to say no to my humble way of thanking you for your exceptional work."

Upon opening it, I found a diamond necklace inside. Judging by the size of each diamond, roughly 0.5 or 0.6 carats, along with a sizable emerald pendant and earrings encircled by small diamonds, it must be pricy. By looking at the diamonds, I could say they were flawless with an E or F color. They were similar to the two E-color diamond necklaces Dad gave and educated me about the three C's of diamond - color, clarity, and cut. I returned the box to Maddy, telling him I didn't deserve such an expensive gift, as we did our job, and you paid us for it.

"You're making me unhappy," Maddy pleaded earnestly. "I bought this gift with genuine pleasure to express my gratitude, no ulterior motive whatsoever. Please reconsider your decision; rejecting it would truly break my heart." Despite Maddy's plea, I remained steadfast. Why should I accept such a pricy gift from a client to fulfill our side of the agreement?

"Maddy, I need to be upfront with you about my stance on accepting costly gifts, particularly from clients; it's something I simply cannot do. Please don't take it wrong; my refusal of your gift is solely based on my principles, and I hope you can appreciate my honesty." I said, maintaining a warm smile. With that, I made my way towards the door. Maddy didn't utter a word but quietly followed, making sure I was settled comfortably in the car.

For the next two months, I didn't hear from Maddy. On one Saturday evening, while I was relaxing in front of the TV watching a comedy show, my mobile buzzed, announcing that Maddy was calling. I answered the call, and he asked, "Is it a good time to speak with you for a few minutes?"

"Go ahead, I'm all ears," I stated, reflecting no emotions.

"I was waiting to hear from you regarding my request to be on your list of pals," Maddy expressed.

"Maddy, I don't have any friends, so the question of having a list doesn't exist. Anyhow, I gave thought to your request but failed to see the merits of having a male friend since I cannot discuss the trending fashions or the biological issues with you. To serve my needs, I have a platoon of workers, and some of them stay in my house to be available around the clock. Finally, I don't have time to socialize; I get only Sundays, which I spend mostly with servants to ensure the house is immaculately cleaned and prepare the list of groceries needed for the next week. Then, on some Sundays, I have to go to a mall to purchase what I need, and that's it. Now you tell me where the time to give to friends is," I stated crisply.

"Ma'am, you maintain a demanding six-day workweek while I, an unwavering toiler, dedicate 12 to 14 hours throughout the 365 days of the year. With our exhaustive work hours, it's evident that both of us require an avenue to address our daily challenges and triumphs. While our financial stability is assured, it prompts us to consider whether we are genuinely embracing a healthy, fulfilling existence. Unfortunately, it seems that we probably are not. If I keep going down this stressful career route, I'll be putting my own mental health at risk, and you may not be too far behind. I propose we become each other's pillars of support, sharing our dreams, plans, and achievements openly. We should provide feedback on difficult decisions and, most importantly, encourage one another to overcome the inevitable low points in life, especially those moments when loneliness strikes. I recommend giving me a three-month trial. Should you find that my companionship falls short of your expectations during this period, please feel free to part ways without the necessity for an explanation. I eagerly await your affirmative response, and if it doesn't materialize, I'll consider it as part of my destiny and move forward. I'll reach out to you in two weeks to take your feedback," Maddy confidently articulated.

"I don't know what to say to you. Anyhow, I've got two weeks to decide, and you keep your fingers crossed that I come up with something satisfying for either of us," I said, showing neither enthusiasm nor indifference.

"Wonderful, good night, and you take good care of yourself," Maddy remarked, disconnecting the line.

Ever since my college days are over, I've experienced a growing sense of loneliness as each night unfolds, evoking the poignant Chinese proverb, 'The King is alone at night.'

My day was filled with interactions with sellers, buyers, and some government officials. Then, I had to find time to spend with the team, crafting bids for new ventures, meeting with purchasing staff to ensure fulfillment of all site needs, scrutinizing drawings for upcoming sites, and, lastly, delving into the intricacies of accounts, various bank positions, and the unexpected issues that invariably cropped up.

Days passed in a whirlwind, but the nights felt interminable and dishearteningly dull; the weight of solitude was an insurmountable burden. This situation could remain a perpetual, agonizing void: a void that is destined to stretch till I say goodbye to this transient world. Regrettably, it's my decision to remain single and be in this situation. Even if I find a caring partner like Maddy, I don't think he would marry me after knowing I'm a love child who was thrown on the street and raised in an orphanage. There was not an iota of chance that I would find someone who would hold my hand, stand by me through all of life's challenges, let me relish the days and nights in his affectionate companionship, and raise his babies.

While on the bed, I thought Maddy seemed a good person, a man of character and discipline, earning excellent money. To top it off, his charismatic personality is the cherry on the cake. It's puzzling that a young and financially successful entrepreneur like him might lead a celibate life. I'm left wondering about his sexual orientation, whether he's heterosexual or if he identifies differently. Unfortunately, I would need to establish a closer connection with him to find answers to these questions. However, I must avoid getting too personally involved to protect myself from potential emotional harm. He's insisting, and I also need someone to talk to; all my orphanage friends have vanished, and I didn't make any friends at college to hide the past and stay dignified. I must find a way to have him as my friend without developing any form of intimacy; I continued my thinking and dozed off without establishing a firm path.

This went on for the next two weeks. While sleeping, I was thinking about how to be friends with Maddy without getting too close to him. Exactly two weeks later, on Saturday night, around nine, Maddy called and asked me for my input on his request.

Suddenly, something clicked, and I informed him, "Okay, Maddy, I'm willing to accommodate your request. To begin with, let's limit our friendship to two or three weekly phone conversations, each lasting no more than half an hour. When you'd like to talk, send me a message after 9 PM, asking if I'm available to speak, and I'll either call or reply with my unavailability. If things go well over time, we can also consider occasionally meeting up for a meal or a movie," I asserted.

"Thank you, Ma'am; I'm absolutely thrilled and can't wait to speak with you next week. I'm so excited right now that my heart is pounding like it might leap out of my chest. So, for now, goodbye," Maddy exclaimed before disconnecting.

His behavior, resembling that of an adolescent despite his success and maturity as an entrepreneur, hinted at the possibility that he had never been in a romantic relationship before. Typically, someone with more experience or a few past relationships under their belt wouldn't exhibit such excitement. To them, any new relationship is just another conquest, unlikely to evoke the intense emotions that make one's heart race. Even though it could be a speculative assumption on my part, I had a strong intuition that this was the case, and it inexplicably pleased me, bringing a smile to my face.

The following week, on Tuesday night at nine, I received Maddy's message about whether I was available to take his call. I called him, and on the second ring, he answered.

I opened the conversation and asked, "Hello, Maddy. How're you? How's everything?"

"I'm doing very well. Business is in full throttle, and health is as good as any other guy in his prime. And since you've made me too comfortable in the house, I'm having a ball. My typical workday unfolds within the confines of my home office, checking the stocks received, bank positions, and so on till late afternoon. Then, I go to the office, which is primarily an accounts and audit department, and spend at least an hour or more. Next, I take up the responsibilities of a quality control inspector. My first stop is at the warehouse, where I check hygiene and ensure that the work in progress is being done in accordance with our set standards. I then go to one of my fine dining restaurants as the evening approaches. Here, I meticulously assess kitchen cleanliness, stock levels, and timing of the chefs' order preparations and, at times, taste the dishes. Then I spend at least half an hour behind the bar counter, and before calling it a day, I take my usual dinner in the restaurant. You tell me how everything is at your end," Maddy proclaimed.

"Maddy, I don't have the luxury of working from home. Each day, I had to attend several meetings either with staff or clients, existing or potential. Occasionally, I needed to produce precise CAD drawings for important projects, but I reserved this effort exclusively for large clients. It's always a hectic day; I hardly get a chance to join Dad for lunch, who had to eat on time, being a diabetic patient. But I enjoy the work, which perfectly aligns with my education. You tell me, apart from making money, do you have any hobbies, what you eat daily, what you love the most to eat, and how you spend your spare time," I commented.

"Due to my busy schedule, I've had to give up my only hobby of reading. Since I started making money, my eating habits have significantly transformed. My day typically begins around six in the morning. After a glass of milk, I engage in a ninety-minute session of jogging and various exercises.

"Gone are the days of consuming greasy, unhealthy food. My breakfast and lunch are sourced from one of my restaurants. For breakfast, I eat a bowl of fresh fruits, followed by three soft-boiled eggs, two lightly buttered slices of whole-wheat bread, and a bowl of mixed avocado, cherry tomatoes, and iceberg lettuce leaves, all seasoned with a dash of lemon and salt. After the meal, I take a large mug of lightly roasted Ethiopian Yirgacheffe coffee with a dash of honey to cleanse my palate.

"Lunch usually consists of grilled chicken breast, fish fillet, or lamb steak once a week. I take these proteins with mashed potatoes, boiled carrots, beans, broccoli, and zucchini. To add some zest to the meal, I use a mustard sauce made from honey, Dijon mustard, and a touch of mayonnaise.

"My dinner, which I eat in one of my restaurants, usually consists of a bowl of salad blended with boiled vegetables, a single egg, and strands of chicken, fish, or prawns.

"I usually return home between nine and ten in the evening, where I spend an hour or so catching up on the latest news channels before retiring to bed. Occasionally, once or twice a week, I find myself obliged to partake in lunch with VIP suppliers, which is generally in one of my restaurants, and I indulge in the preferences of my guests. I don't drink anything other than water, milk, tea, or coffee, no fizzy drinks or spirits.

"What about your hobbies and food preferences," Maddy inquired.

"Oh, I eat whatever is prepared by my domestic help, but my dinner quantity is much less when compared to breakfast and lunch. I prefer to eat home-cooked food; occasionally, I binge when I've got to attend a business lunch or dinner. Like you, I've no time for hobbies, and when I get little time before I close my eyes for the night, I read a journal related to my industry," I affirmed.

Then we talked for a few minutes more about our routines, likes, and so on, and under the pretext of sleep time, I disconnected the line. As we had agreed, Maddy faithfully adhered to our three-day-a-week call schedule, but our conversations revolved around trivial and inconsequential subjects. He never shared anything about his parents or upbringing, never inquired about my childhood, and never sought clarification on why I had a Hindu father despite having a Christian name and why I didn't stay with my Papa. This routine continued smoothly, and soon, I became addicted to his calls, making sure to return home early, finish my dinner, and be available for our chat.

From our various conversations, I noticed that he possesses remarkable organizational skills and unwavering discipline, which was the reason he single-handedly established his empire. He sticks to his schedule religiously in his daily routines and carefully monitors the performance of each restaurant. The restaurant managers are on profit-sharing arrangements, thus motivated to keep expenses in check and put in a dedicated effort to ensure customer satisfaction with the food and services. He has an internal audit team consisting of two auditors and a manager, who make surprise checks of inventory versus consumption, particularly the alcohol bottles, which tend to disappear. He has no college education, but he has an amazing knowledge of computer hardware and software; all his restaurants are connected to a central server placed in his office with a backup server in his house, giving him minute-to-minute input on the cash register and table occupancy. He had CCTV cameras installed throughout, allowing him to monitor activities in the warehouse, central kitchen, restaurants, and other areas.

Dad was frequently absent from work and seemed to be losing weight. When I asked him about it, he mentioned that his blood sugar levels had risen significantly, and he feared he might need to quit coming to the office soon. I suspected he was hiding something but didn't ask anything further. He didn't come to the office for the next week but called every day to inquire about how I was doing. He never asked about my projects or his projects at all.

When he didn't come the first couple of days of the next week, I panicked and reached out to his family physician to check on his health. At first, the doctor was reluctant to share any information. Still, with some insistence, he finally revealed the truth, "Your father was diagnosed with Acute Myeloid Leukemia (AML) two months ago, and it was in its advanced stage, spread in the body. Unfortunately, AML is typically resistant to chemotherapy and radiation therapy, especially when it has reached an advanced stage. We consulted with renowned oncologists worldwide who specialize in treating AML patients. Their unanimous conclusion is that the prognosis is quite grim, and any treatment would likely cause more harm than good. They've recommended providing him with tranquilizers to keep him comfortable. He has approximately six months left, with a little less or more margin."

As I listened to the doctors, my eyes welled up, and tears streamed down my cheeks incessantly. After conveying my gratitude for providing updates on Papa's health, I hung up the phone. I wept until there were no more tears to shed, and in that moment, any grievances I held against Papa melted away. It was as if the safety of the roof over my head had vanished, exposing me to all potential harm sources. My body felt drained of strength, and I was overwhelmed by a sense of emptiness, making it seem impossible to even rise from my chair.

Papa was only sixty-one years old, and in this day and age, that's not an age at which anyone is expected to bid farewell to this world. I've always considered myself independent, but ever since joining the company, I've grown heavily reliant on Papa. His guidance, support, and encouragement have been the cornerstone of my success in all my ventures. Without him, I doubt I could continue to perform at the same level of success. Life will undoubtedly become incredibly challenging without him by my side, even though he's provided me with such wealth that several future generations will lead comfortable lives without earning a single penny.

The prospect of life without Papa and how I could manage the business felt daunting. However, for the past two years, I realized that nearly ninety percent of our business comes from my own efforts, and I have a competent team to assist me with project execution. Still, I couldn't escape the fact that Papa was the unwavering support that allowed me to take risks and confidently tackle demanding projects. Papa was my backbone in running the business, and I would find it incredibly demanding to continue to run it successfully.

I left the office early and went to Papa's house. He was sleeping in his bedroom, a nurse was sitting in his room reading a magazine, and no family members were around him. I asked the nurse for permission to wake him up, and she nodded in agreement. I took Papa's hand in my hand and gently rubbed it. In a few moments, he opened his eyes, looked at me, and smiled. Tears were rolling down my cheeks, my throat choked, and words failed to come out of my mouth. Instead of saying anything, I just buried my head in his chest. He rubbed my back with his fragile palm and, in a faint voice, expressed, "Don't cry, Honey; I know you have learned about my incurable ailment, and seeing me in this condition is undoubtedly painful. Please remember that life is a journey, and my destination is rapidly approaching. While the burden of leaving you to sail across this world alone weighs heavily on me, I am certain that my child's inner strength and resilience will enable her to confront and overcome any trials that may attempt to undermine her. I depart with a steadfast faith that my child will persist in achieving her goals with brilliance, courage, and innate talent. However, I carry one regret: I failed to persuade you to consider marriage despite my numerous attempts, as you chose to remain unmarried."

"Papa, I can't fathom a life without you. Your love and support have always been my rock, and the idea of tackling life's ordeals without you by my side is too much to bear. I've faced considerable challenges starting from my birth, and just when things seemed to be getting better, I'm now confronted with the prospect of unbearable pain and suffering. I believe I've come to the world with only one purpose: to suffer. I won't hold anyone accountable for my suffering; I see it as part of my journey. Papa, you may not know, but I'm a non-believer, so I won't pray to any God, as I don't believe there's a higher force orchestrating cruelties on my Papa and me. I strongly believe that diseases stem from our imperfect evolutionary process; otherwise, if a brilliant being created all living things in this world, he could have also created disease-free bodies. And my sufferings aren't the outcome of a cosmic plan; it's inflicted by humanoids that are imperfect and, at times, inhumane," I confessed, tears streaming down my face, overwhelmed by emotion.

Papa didn't comment; he held my hand in his hand, and I noticed his body had weakened substantially because of his poor grip and inability to respond to my comments.

While engulfed in my thoughts, I heard the sound of steps getting closer to the room. Ridhi Ma'am entered, and I, in a muted voice, wished her a good evening. She pulled a chair and sat beside the bed, formally announcing that she had come straight to the room from work.

In a somber tone, she conveyed, "Raj, tomorrow we have two specialized oncologists arriving, one from Paris and another from Atlanta. After an exhaustive examination of your medical records, they're optimistic about fostering a treatment strategy to make your body free from the disease. Please don't lose your fighting spirit and assure your beloved daughter that you'll be back on your feet and soon be with her in the office full of zest and energy."

With a grin, Papa softly said, "Don't waste your time and money, my dear. You're fighting an unwinnable battle, a reality that the best doctors globally confirmed. Still, you continue to bring in doctors from around the world who appear solely motivated to earn their hefty fees and enjoy an all-expenses-paid trip to our city."

"Giving up is not in my nature, and when it comes to my loving husband, I don't want any stone to remain unturned. You don't lose your fighting spirit, and don't discourage me from what I want to do. As for the money, it's not even peanuts for me to be concerned about," Ridhi Ma'am stated and dropped a few tears without a sound of wailing. She was famous for being made of steel nerves, but she still failed to control her emotions and cried for her beloved husband in front of me. Papa took Ma'am's hand in his and stated faintly, "Please don't cry. We all have to die one day, and if I'm going a little early, then it's okay. But you stay strong, as you have to marry our boys and ensure they are well settled in their lives."

"Don't worry about the boys," she assured him, her eyes filled with tenderness. "They're well settled and have even started dating. But, my love, how can I go on without you by my side? You've been my pillar of strength, the source of my pleasure, and the one who granted me the freedom and courage to become a resilient businessperson. You've held my hand through the toughest times, supporting and lifting me when I felt like falling apart. The heights my business has achieved today are a testament to your constant support and encouragement. You shaped me into an administrator, teaching me how to master every facet of business. Please, my love, don't leave me here or take me along with you, for I cannot imagine surviving without you by my side."

Ridhi Ma'am's wailing echoed her deep affection and reverence for her hubby. The room was filled with her agonized sobbing, moving evidence of the profound nature of their bond. With tears welling in my eyes, I stood up and gave her a few paper napkins, but she didn't clean her face and continued her wailing, and only stopped when the tears dried. I noticed Papa silently shedding tears instead of telling us to stop our wailing.

A heartbreaking silence engulfed the room after all of us stopped the water shedding. Papa was the first one to break the silence and addressed his wife, "Rids, I want you to promise me one thing. You'll look after my daughter as long as you're alive. You provide her with whatever she asks for and speak with her regularly so she won't feel that she's alone in this world. She has enough money but is bidding for large government and private sector projects, so when needed, please arrange loans and bank guarantees or provide any help she needs to execute her projects. Finally, treat her like your own biological daughter and convince her to marry."

"Raj, as long as I'm alive, I'll treat her like my own daughter, and she should feel free to ask me anything that she wants," Mom gloomily expressed.

Days passed by at their usual pace; I was handling both Papa's and my own workload, which was making me buried in the paperwork. Each passing day saw Dad's health deteriorating as he became increasingly frail, spending most of his time in slumber due to the potent painkillers and tranquilizers. Each evening after work, I visited Papa; Mom and I would sit in Papa's room for at least two hours, often engrossed in our mobile phones to avoid disturbing him.

Finally, the day we had dreaded arrived, not after six months, but just a little over three. In the early hours, Papa peacefully embraced eternal rest. He had been a devoted husband, a loving father, and a compassionate man who had done so much for an orphaned girl left to fend for herself on a desolate street. I will never be able to shake off the weight of his boundless empathy for me.

The cremation was set for the following noon, awaiting the arrival of the sons. Mom and I were overwhelmed with grief, offering each other solace. In the hall, the mortal remains were placed, and quickly, it got filled with throngs of VIPs, staff, relatives, and business associates, all there to bid their final farewell and pay their respects to the departed soul.

Initially, I was calling Ridhi Ma'am every day, but slowly, it tapered to once a week. She was always busy on the phone, even in the house. To alleviate the burden of Papa's work, I hired two well-experienced assistants, who relieved me from working a few extra hours daily.

I don't know why, but I was aggressively bidding for large projects. Because of our track records and my impeccable presentations, I was appreciated and awarded almost 70% of the projects I bid on. My first huge project request came from a corporate house that called for bids to construct a massive mall featuring five hundred shops, ten sit-down restaurants, an ice-skating arena, bowling alleys, a twelve-screen multiplex, a food court, adult and children's game areas, space for numerous pop-up shops, four parking basements. In addition, there was a five-star hotel with a connecting corridor to the mall featuring 200 rooms, 20 suites, and two Royal suites. The project was so big that my team and I had to spend at least a couple of hundred hours preparing the bid. My PowerPoint presentation was unmatched: I used all my skills to prepare detailed, error-free slides, making the attendees not pick any slights. I set a slim margin of just twenty percent, aware of the high risk it entailed, but I was eager to secure this prestigious project for our portfolio. On the day of the bid presentation, I discovered that a consortium of investors was backing the project. The audience included not only the investors but also representatives from the Architectural firm and the Construction Management firm. The presentation lasted over ten hours, and I faced intense questioning that nearly tested my nerves to the breaking point. Nonetheless, I felt content knowing that I had given my all. Whether I win or lose, the outcome doesn't weigh heavily on me.

After a fortnight, I received a call from a representative of the consortium, inviting me to meet them the next day. During our meeting, they provided me with the letter of intent and a preliminary draft of the contract. The issuance of the letter of intent confirmed their intention to award the contract, and prior to that, within two weeks, company should submit performance, liquidated damages, advance payment, and retention money guarantees; the amounts of each guarantee were mentioned in an annexure. Presentation of these guarantees was mandatory prior to signing the contract.

All our banks refused to give the required guarantees because we didn't have enough collateral. The only way left to get the guarantees was to pledge my shares in Ridhi Ma'am's company. I felt it was important to let her know my plans, so I called her to arrange a meeting. I asked her to suggest a convenient time for my visit. She invited me to join her for dinner that same evening.

Before I could utter a word at the dinner table, Ma'am enthusiastically said, "Congratulations on clinching the shopping mall contract! Your presentation was truly remarkable, leaving everyone in awe. Your meticulous attention to detail garnered widespread admiration. People also admired your composed responses to their queries, and the three-dimensional mall view, along with your impactful PowerPoint slides, made a lasting impression."

"Thank you, but how did you learn about it," I responded, taken aback by her insight.

"Honey, I own a 51% stake in the project and didn't attend your presentation as I wanted you to secure the contract on your own strength," Mom expressed with a chuckle.

"I'm glad to hear that, and I appreciate your absence from my presentation. Otherwise, seeing you would have made me nervous," I stated sincerely.

"I watched your presentation live and appreciate your impeccable work. Just a few days ago, a unanimous decision was made to award the contract to your company. Tell me, is there a hurdle you're facing in taking up the project?" Mom joyfully expressed.

"Mom, I need your permission to pledge my shares in your company to obtain the bank guarantees. The banks have refused to give them because we don't have enough collateral," I softly expressed.

Mom thought for a few minutes and then slowly said, "You can do that, but I have a better idea. I'll buy forty-nine percent of your company shares, and whatever you need, my company will provide, and you don't have to use the shares for any business needs. This will also help you with very large projects, as my company will be behind you. I'm extremely confident that you're fully capable of undertaking any large projects and comfortably executing them. Your confidence and clarity in understanding customer requirements are amazing, and I'm making this offer considering your abilities and not because you're my daughter. Don't feel any pressure to decide favorably; make a well-thought-out decision and inform me. Don't worry about the guarantees; I would arrange them even without you accepting my offer."

"Thank you, Mom; your appreciation of my abilities means the world to me, and it'll keep me under pressure not to let you down. Mom, you know very well that this is your husband's company, and I'm working on it because of Papa's instructions. Whatever you want to do with the company is your prerogative, and I'll sign on the dotted lines without raising any questions," I expressed humbly.

"Honey, it's your company, and my investment comes from a place of genuine belief. I truly think I'm backing a winning horse. I have complete confidence that you'll steer the company to great success and make everyone envious of your business acumen and accomplishments," Mom said with a warm smile.

"Mom, please call me when the documents are ready for signature," I expressed with deep gratification.

"Honey, my accountants will review all your financials tomorrow at noon. Based on their assessment, we will determine the net present value of your company, including the goodwill amount. Once you agree to this valuation, you'll receive my company shares, which would be equal to a 49% stake in your company. We will issue the shares at face value, which means you'll receive a significant bonus because the current market value of our shares far exceeds the face value. This process will take approximately one week, and I'll instruct the consortium to wait for two to three weeks to receive the necessary guarantees. We'll also need to obtain acquisition approval from various organizations, which may take some time. However, as this is a relatively minor transaction, I don't anticipate it will take more than a week to complete the entire process," Mom explained.

I thanked her with teary eyes, and she rose from the chair, hugged me, and said, "I'm doing this for my baby and to make your Papa happy, who would be watching how I treat his daughter."

Within three weeks, I submitted the guarantees that my bank issued based on the collateral provided by Mom's company. Ever since then, it's been a whirlwind of success. I've been landing one major project after another worth thousands of crores.

My addiction to Maddy's calls was increasing with every passing day, but still, we never moved beyond the formal discussion. However, one day, in a trembling voice, Maddy asked me whether I would care to have dinner with him. I had been contemplating this scenario for the past few weeks, and I had decided not to refuse the invitation, so I agreed. My routine life was so hectic and mundane that I was not getting a leisure moment to unwind or do something relaxing.

Dinner in a restaurant provided an opportunity to unwind and discuss other than business.

On Saturday night, Maddy picked me up from my place at eight o'clock. Maddy proposed we go to a renowned five-star hotel offering a selection of Indian, Japanese, and Chinese cuisine. However, I declined his offer and requested that we dine at one of his own eateries. We ended up at another of his upscale restaurants, featuring impressive furnishings, plush chairs, elegant tables, exquisite tapestries, magnificent padded carpets, and aesthetically designed lighting arrangements. The wall decorations were stunning. Like his other eateries, this one was bustling with diners. Even though it had a larger seating capacity than his other eateries, all the tables were occupied.

Maddy asked me my choice between sitting in the restaurant with a waiting time or in his office. The restaurant was noisy, so I opted for the compact office: a small desk and chair with a desktop computer, a four-drawer steel filing cabinet, and a comfortable three-seater sofa in front of his desk. A waiter promptly appeared to take our food order. I asked for crab soup and lobster risotto, and Maddy asked to have the same dishes. He then inquired if I would prefer a glass of wine or a refreshing mixed fruit punch with ginger ale, and I opted for the punch.

We sat there for more than an hour; our conversation revolved mostly around our businesses and briefly touched on current local and global happenings. Notably absent were any discussions about his family or inquiries into my own past, including the demise of my beloved Papa or anything related to family members. It struck me as odd, but perhaps he shared similar thoughts about me. Nevertheless, one thing was crystal clear: he had developed strong feelings for me. Otherwise, there'd be no explanation for his unwavering interest in our weekly three tele-conversations, his jubilant mood, and the constant grin on his face. It was as if he were a child who had just received his most coveted toy.

I developed a liking for him: he was an upright, diligent, and intelligent person. My emotions for him were complicated, and I wasn't sure whether they qualified as romantic love or mere veneration. Even as I explored the depths of my feelings for him, I encountered only emptiness; to me, he was merely a release valve for my bottled-up emotions. This inclination may stem from my instinct to shield myself, as I've always guarded my dreams from prying eyes. From a young age, while other girls indulged in discussions about romance, tender embraces, and the allure of love, I resolved to fortify my heart, rendering it impervious, a symbol of my stanch resilience.

An orphanage-raised girl's heart must be a cold stone.

Chapter Nine

Samuel Thomas

Love Across the Divide

With a heavy heart, I left for the USA to pursue my doctorate and to be with my Artikins as soon as possible and remain with her till I took my last breath.

The California Institute of Technology (Caltech) is a private research university in Pasadena, California. It was founded in 1891 as Throop Polytechnic Institute, a vocational school. In 1921, the school was renamed Caltech and began to focus on scientific research and engineering education. The school's faculty included some of the most renowned scientists of the time, such as Albert Einstein, Robert Oppenheimer, and Linus Pauling.

Caltech has played a major role in many important scientific and technological advancements. Caltech researchers developed the first jet-propelled aircraft and helped to develop the atomic bomb. Caltech is a highly selective university, with an acceptance rate of just 3.9%. The university's student body is small, with around 2,500, and the students are known for their intelligence and academic rigor.

I was very happy to be among the brightest students. I had to work hard and secure my doctorate in four to five years to prove that my selection was not an oversight.

Artikins wrote only one letter and asked me to stop writing until I heard from her, which never happened. It had been close to nine months since we were married, and I hadn't received a call or letter, which was depressing. However, I consoled myself that my Artikins is much smarter than me and must have compelling reasons for not communicating. One evening, when I was in my room, the intercom chime and I answered the call; a male voice announced that he was a lawyer representing Aarti's parents regarding my marriage with their daughter. He asked me to hold the line and speak with Aarti's mother.

A woman's voice boomed over the phone, saying angrily, "This is Aarti's mother speaking, and I'm extremely annoyed and unhappy. You have married my daughter without our consent, and it's not acceptable to us. Although you may be a wonderful person, we cannot accept this marriage since it goes against our religious beliefs. To uphold our honor, maintain our faith with integrity, preserve our dignity within our social sphere, and face ourselves proudly before our Lord as adherents to HIS teachings, we have decided to execute our daughter and drink poison to end our lives. The alternative to save her life is for you to divorce her. For your information, in her sixth month, she miscarried because of excessive hemorrhaging that had caused the loss of her child and allowed us to conceal her negligent behavior. The choice is yours, and I won't pressure you to accept my request. However, it's definite that we won't approve your marriage, and to save our faces, we'll end our lives."

I pleaded with her through impassioned cries and tears, imploring mercy. I urged her to send Aarti on a tourist visa so I could take her to a foreign land where our identities could remain concealed. I begged her to spare both her and them from the implications of this irrational decision. A divorce from me would inflict overwhelming pain upon Aarti, possibly leading to dire consequences such as self-harm or a perpetual inability to lead a happy life, given the trust she has placed in me. I earnestly intreated her to show compassion, as the aftermath of such a divorce would not only shatter the love of my life but could also bring about the ruin of my own life, and I fear I may not be able to endure such agony.

However, her heart seemed unyielding, impervious to reason, my pleas, the pain of her child, or the devastation that awaited in my life. She insisted that within a month, if the divorce papers were not received, news of their tragic death would reach me.

Immediately after sending the divorce papers, I thought of committing suicide. The anguish was so overwhelming that thoughts of ending life looked a better option, but I decided against it as I wanted to inform my Artikins what had happened and how I was strongarmed into divorcing her. I'll live a miserable life; she made me addicted to her intellect, beauty, and the magnetic aura she exuded. Her scent lingered in my nostrils, and her captivating smile haunted my thoughts incessantly. I had no idea whether I could focus on my studies with my aching heart and starved eyes to see her, which was too much of a pain to keep my focus on anything other than my beloved Artikins. Focusing on the intricacies of academia amidst the agony of inner turmoil felt like being crushed under a ton of bricks. However, she wanted to see me secure the doctorate, earn lots of money, pamper her with pricy gifts, and take her to exotic places across the globe. So, I must earn my doctorate and save lots of money to give her if I ever meet her.

My daily routine had evolved into spending 12 to 16 hours at the institution, returning home, and collapsing into bed, yearning for a few hours of sleep. However, true rest remained elusive, as each time I closed my eyes, Artikins appeared, tears streaming down her face. She questioned the reasons behind divorcing her, pledging to pursue me even beyond this world to unravel the truth. She was puzzled and failed to recall ever causing me distress with her words or actions.

I decided to complete my doctorate as soon as possible and leave this place where I had the chance to face my Artikins. My dedication and passion for securing the doctorate helped me to achieve my aim in four years and a few months. I got job offers from several reputable organizations but turned them down as the postings were only in the US. I achieved my objective when Airbus Societas Europaea, headquartered in the Netherlands, offered me attractive employment at their Airbus Corporate Research Center in Filton, UK, working on aerodynamics, propulsion, and systems integration research.

Close to 25 years ago, I joined as a Research Scientist in Aerodynamics, and now, I proudly hold the position of Vice President, leading a sizable team. Despite acquiring British nationality, I chose to remain single, turning down numerous expressions of interest from female coworkers and their friends. In the face of remarks like being labeled as queer, homophobic, or a part of the LGBT community, I opted not to defend myself. Instead, I maintained my dedication to my job, consistently put in more than 16 hours daily, and stayed in a rented studio apartment near the research center rather than purchasing a house. I diligently saved every penny, all with the hopeful anticipation of one day meeting Artikins and being able to give her all my savings.

For the past several weeks, my mom has been coming into my dreams and telling me why I haven't come to see her. I've remained dedicated to my responsibilities throughout my tenure without taking any extended leave. On only three occasions, I visited Paris, Switzerland, and Italy. These vacations were unplanned, prompted by the suggestion of close colleagues to unwind together during the Christmas and New Year holidays.

After a few days of deliberation, I took six weeks' leave to spend time with my mom. I reached Hyderabad around four in the morning and reached home at six. Luckily, the gate was opened; someone probably woke up to take the milk delivery and failed to close the gate. I climbed the stairs with my trolley and shoulder bag and took out the key to open the padlock, which was missing. In its place stood an unfamiliar door equipped with a digital lock. I was taken aback, wondering who could have replaced the door and the lock. With caution, I attempted to open the door, but it remained closed. As a last resort, I knocked, anticipating that someone might be inside. After a few knocks, a weak, sleepy woman's voice asked who's there? I said I'm Sam, owner of the apartment. A few moments later, the door was slowly opened by a woman in her nightdress; she looked at me and slumped on my body. She was my Artikins; I took her in my arms and gently laid her on the bed, took the glass of water from the side table, and sprinkled it on her face. With half-open eyes, she said, "Is this my Sam, or am I dreaming?"

"No, you're not dreaming, and I'm your Sam," I calmly stated.

"Lie down beside me and take me in your arms as I want this dream never to end," Artikins expressed in a sleepy voice with closed eyes.

I closed the door, removed my shoes, and lay down beside her, and she nestled, gripping my body. I took her in my left arm firmly; probably, I never wanted her to leave me again. Kissed her forehead several times, involuntarily, tears were rolling down my cheeks. Within a few minutes, I noticed she was in deep slumber, but her hold on me was firm. I couldn't bring myself to close my eyes; gazing at the love of my life was both heartwarming and visually delightful. Though she had gained a bit of weight and was not as slender as before, she maintained a well-toned body, with slightly puffy cheeks showing the subtle effects of time elapse. She remained as beautiful as the day we got married, and the reality of having her in my arms, breathing on my body, was almost too much to sink in. I found myself unable to look away from her, feeling deeply grateful to have her in my arms. Again and again, I pinched my arm and leg, confirming that my Artikins was indeed with me, not a figment of my imagination.

She slept for almost thirty minutes, then suddenly shivered, opened her eyes, touched my face and body, and said, "Sam, is it real that I'm in your arms, and I'm not dreaming? Don't wake me up if it's a dream."

"This is real; I'm actually embracing you. I arrived this morning, and you fainted when you opened the door and saw me. It's hard to describe my overwhelming joy. Even if this were my last moment alive, I would still be grateful to my creator for this opportunity to see you and hold you close," I expressed with heartfelt sincerity.

She came out of my hold and sat on the bed, took my face in her hand, rubbed my body, and then bent on me and kissed my forehead, cheeks, and lips and started wailing violently.

"Artikins, why you're crying? You should hate me, beat me up for dumping you, or at least complain to me for my sickeningly treacherous act," I stated, holding her hands.

"Sam, a few years ago, my mother passed away. On her deathbed, she revealed the reason behind our divorce. Papa passed away just a couple of years after we relocated to the US. Following Mom's demise, I moved here," she shared, standing up from the bed. "I'll prepare some tea; you can wash up. Afterward, we can update our respective journeys."

While sipping the tea with buttered toast, Artikins inquired about my family.

"Artikins, promises are to be kept for me, and I believe I stated many times that either you or no one. Therefore, I'm still a divorcee and single," I informed her.

"Sam, you idiot, you should have married and enjoyed your life instead of sulking for me. How did you overcome the loneliness of the weekends and holidays? You're insane, Sam darling!" Artikins expressed, and I noticed a hint of happiness in her voice.

"My research work was tedious and time-consuming, and sixteen-plus hours each day didn't allow me to think of what was missing from my life," I commented honestly.

After chatting for over three hours and enjoying several cups of tea, we caught up on our separate journeys. Artikins proposed heading out for lunch and giving me a tour of the ST Group Institutions she had established. Instead of a restaurant, the car took us to an upscale colony, and we entered through the imposing gate of a villa. Boldly engraved on white marble at the gatepost was the name 'ST. STONEHAVEN.'

"Artikins, whose villa is this?" I asked.

"This is my house, darling," Artikins said smilingly.

"If you have such a lavish villa, then why were you sleeping in that wretched one-bedroom apartment? And who's this ST?" I expressed my surprise.

"I craved sharing my nights with Sam and smelling him, so I stayed at that cozy one-bedroom flat. And don't you dare label it a wretched place; it was my haven for over four years. I want you to know that I am the proud owner of that building. The ground floor is home to two families: a watchman and my car driver; on the first floor, two maids live who diligently handle the cleaning duties for the building. All of them are early risers, often busy getting their kids off to school. Today, they must have forgotten to lock the gate when they left, allowing you to sneak in unannounced. Oh, and 'ST' stands for the initials of my beloved ex-husband and current lover's name," Artikins expressed with laughter, radiating a tone of joy.

I enjoyed a delightful lunch that Artikins mentioned came from the central kitchen, which caters to hostels, senior citizens' home, orphanage, vocational institute, hospital, and various canteens.

After our meal, she guided me through an extensive tour of the institutions, which continued for over two hours. Every institution was prefixed with 'ST': ST Secondary School, ST Hospital, ST Medical College, and so forth. The scale of the setup was immense, and by a rough estimate, I could easily approximate the investment to be plus two thousand crores. The ability to invest such a substantial amount was remarkable and almost unbelievable. She explained to me that the hospital and the school catered to the affluent, generating significant profits. The medical and engineering colleges yielded a reasonable profit, and she structured it this way so that all the profits could contribute to subsidizing the operational expenses of the nursing college and vocational institute. When necessary, she offered scholarships to bright nursing students and women who struggled even to cover that minimal cost. The orphanage and senior citizens' homes fell under her direct responsibility, and she had established a trust to fund its operational expenses.

I found the setup, her organizational skills, and her judicious spending of her wealth highly impressive. I was at a loss for words to praise her remarkable efforts, which undoubtedly would benefit thousands over time.

Following evening tea at her villa, I requested permission to head home. She responded, "No, honey, you're not going anywhere without me accompanying you as long as I'm alive."

"Are you kidding? What will you do when I return to my job in a few weeks?" I asked her with a chuckle.

"To hell with the job. If you have pricey belongings that you want to bring, we can travel to the UK together and ship them here. I made the mistake of letting you go alone once and paid a heavy price for it; I won't repeat that same mistake," she remarked with fake anger.

"Artikins, dear, I cannot quit my job without completing the projects I'm currently supervising, which could take at least six months or more. Then, I've got to receive my substantial gratuity for my twenty-plus years of service. I must go once my holiday ends, which is in six weeks," I explained.

"No, honey, you're not going anywhere without me in toe, and that's non-negotiable. Consider what your company would do if you couldn't come due to pressing domestic matters, like caring for your elderly parents or a dependent child. They could face legal consequences if they reject your resignation, even on such compelling issues that you must attend to. So, cut out the nonsense, my love. Embed in that brilliant mind of yours that you've come here for good and will remain in my sight till my last breath," I scolded him.

"Honey, you're asking me to lose half a million pounds or even more. Anyway, we've six weeks to decide on how to proceed, so relax. And I must go home now, shower, and take rest, and I'll come here in the morning," I knew she wouldn't allow me to leave, but it was giving me pleasure to tease her. Instead of responding to my comments, she rose from the sofa, came to me, took my hand, and said, let's go.

The next day, I went with her to my mother's grave. From the shop at the entrance of the graveyard, I bought a cross, crucifix, statues of Jesus and Mary, candles, and flowers. We stayed there for fifteen minutes, I prayed, and she sat with closed eyes. When we rose to leave, I noticed her cheeks had marks of tears. I had no idea why she cried, but I felt lifted with the respect she had given to my mother.

From the graveyard, Artikins took me to the Arya Samaj temple, where she briefed the priest on the events since our initial marriage, presented all the relevant documentation, and inquired about the possibility of remarrying. The priest meticulously reviewed all the papers and then left us, saying he'd be back. After around twenty minutes, he returned with a senior priest.

The senior priest addressed Artikins, saying, "We're no longer allowed to perform interfaith marriages, so I suggest you get married civilly at a Marriage Registrar's Office."

After submitting all the paperwork at the marriage registrar's office, we were given a wedding date one month later, with instructions to come with two witnesses.

On our way back home, Artikins shared the news that she had a foster daughter named Angelina Daniel. Despite being in her mid or late twenties, Angelina manages and owns a thriving construction company. She is the mastermind behind the impressive ST buildings' design and construction. I also have a son, although the formal adoption process is still in progress. He's our Caterer, managing all the food requirements of ST institutions. When you meet him, you might be surprised to see a younger version of yourself; he is a self-made individual in his mid-twenties. I'll ask both of them to attend our marriage ceremony as witnesses, and I'm confident you'll enjoy getting to know them.

Immediately after we married, we left for Switzerland for our honeymoon, which we hadn't celebrated earlier. We spent ten days shopping, sightseeing, and climbing the snow-clad mountains of Mont Blanc, Matterhorn, and Eiger. I wanted to buy everything she was looking at, but she didn't want to buy anything. Still, I bought many fancy dresses, expensive handbags, and a diamond-studded Rolex.

I wanted to return from Switzerland to India, but Artikins insisted we go to the UK. We reached Filton late at night, and the very next day, she packed my belongings, which were nothing but several cartons of books and a suitcase of clothes. She called a courier company who collected the cartons to be shipped to Hyderabad. Next, she booked a hotel suite in Bristol that was just 11 kilometers away from the Filton, and we moved into the hotel suite after handing over the apartment keys to the owner and clearing the dues. From the hotel suite, Artikins called several law firms in Bristol, and one firm agreed to meet with us, as they believed they could resolve the issue without going to a court of law.

The following morning, we met with a solicitor to seek an opinion on the consequences of my resignation. I comprehensively explained to him my employment history and the rationale behind my decision to resign. I divulged every detail, encompassing my recent journey to India, where I met and married my life's love. Unfortunately, my spouse could not relocate to the UK due to her obligations to care for her orphanage and other institutions. Consequently, the only viable recourse was for me to resign and relocate to India to be with her.

The solicitor attentively made notes of my input and offered reassurance, remarking, "You possess a strong case. Considering your over two-decade tenure, ascent to leading the scientific team, and unwavering commitment with workdays spanning twelve to sixteen hours, the likelihood of them contesting is minimal. Should they choose to adopt a confrontational stance, I'll not only pursue gratuity benefits but also assert claims for overtime compensation and compensation for mental distress caused by putting undue pressure on working long hours. Rest assured that your resignation will be accepted seamlessly. Please come back in three hours, and I will have your resignation letter ready for submission. Ensure that you submit it along with a copy of your marriage certificate. Kindly meet with the receptionist, who will inform you of my fee, which you must pay now to allow me to proceed with your work.

Expressing our gratitude, we exited the office and paid the receptionist three hundred pounds to cover the solicitor's service charges.

Two weeks later, we came back to Hyderabad, having secured a hefty gratuity and a fresh contract as a virtual consultant. The assignment was no different, except that I had to work online at UK time, supervising my team's work and participating in online meetings with the management. While the take-home salary decreased, an augmented performance bonus was added to offset the loss. Artikins was ecstatic, and my joy knew no bounds.

During a dinner conversation, Artikins mentioned that Mahendra's resemblance to my younger self makes her curious to know his parents. I didn't tell her that apart from looking like me, he bore a striking resemblance to Artikins, with his long, slender fingers, eyes, and lips mirroring hers. It seems on several occasions, she questioned him about his parents, and whenever she inquired, he adeptly deflected her inquisitiveness with a captivating smile; he never even revealed anything to his fiancée.

To unravel the mysteries of his family, I asked Artikins to invite him for dinner so that we could delicately press him for information. Artikins said it wouldn't work, and since we needed to know whether we were his biological parent, it was better to conduct his DNA test and compare it with our DNA. While the suggestion had merit, the challenge lay in collecting blood, hair, or sputum samples. Considering this difficulty, I recommended inviting Mahendra to dinner and discreetly finding a way to dampen his hair, then vigorously towel-drying it to gather a few strands for testing. Artikins agreed with my suggestion and invited him for dinner at the weekend under the pretext of discussing what we could add to the existing menu for the kids of the orphanage to help them in their physical and mental growth.

Throughout dinner, our conversation delved into the specifics of incorporating additional proteins, dairy products, fruits, and vegetables to increase babies' physical strength and intelligence. Suddenly, Artikins interrupted, requesting the maid bring a room-temperature water carafe. However, an unfortunate trip occurred as the maid approached the table, resulting in water spilling onto Mahendra's head. Reacting swiftly, Artikins rose from her chair, using a clean napkin to dry Mahendra's wet hair. Simultaneously, she reprimanded the maid for her carelessness and instructed her to fetch a fresh towel.

Mahendra spoke calmly, "Ma'am, it's fine. It wasn't her fault. Perhaps her slipper buckled, or she crossed her feet. Please allow me to go to the washroom and clean up."

"Certainly, please use the washroom; it's right behind you," Artikins guided him. As soon as he entered the comfort room, she discreetly disappeared with the napkin.

The following day, we took the napkin to a newly established genetic testing laboratory boasting cutting-edge facilities and staffed by highly skilled professionals. After thoroughly examining the napkin, they posed a series of questions to eliminate the potential for sample contamination. Once satisfied, they agreed to conduct the paternity test. They collected our hair samples to establish a genetic match and informed us that the test results would take approximately three weeks and we should wait to hear from them.

We collected the report after three weeks, which confirmed that Mahendra was our child. The accuracy of the test was over 99.9%.

Artikins exerted significant influence over Mahendra. A staggering forty percent of his business now stemmed from managing the ST Group's canteens and catering to hospital patients, orphans, and senior citizens. He divulged this information to his girlfriend Angie, who, unsurprisingly, relayed it to Artikins.

The day we received the DNA report, Artikins called Mahendra and asked him to come at five in the evening for a cup of tea, as she needed to discuss an important subject. He couldn't have said no, even if he had pressing engagements.

While sipping the tea, Artikins said, "Calling you Mahendra looks too formal. Shall I call you Maddy, like your friend Angie?"

"I would be very happy to hear Maddy from you, Auntie," Mahendra said with genuine pleasure.

"All right, Maddy. I'm going to ask you a few personal questions, and I expect you to respond honestly." Artikins tone was serious and somewhat admonishing.

"Absolutely, Auntie; feel free to inquire about whatever you'd like to know. But I kindly request that you refrain from asking about my family or upbringing, as those topics are tied to painful memories. I'd rather not revisit those chapters," Maddy conveyed in his customary subdued tone.

"Sorry, my questions are strictly focused on this topic, and I need you to answer. Were you brought up in the orphanage in Shankrapally village?" Artikins asked, his voice firm and resolute.

"I'm unwilling to answer your question, but why do you want to know where I was raised," Maddy expressed with a slight hint of irritation.

"Answer me in Yes or No, and then I'll tell you why I've asked you this question," Artikins questioned in an equally irritating tone.

"Your question is too personal, and I won't answer you unless I know the motive behind knowing my past," Maddy explained in an even tone.

"With a DNA test, we have established that you're our child, and to ensure further, we want you to confirm that you were raised in the Shankarpally orphanage." This time, Artikins kept her composure, likely with considerable effort. After finishing her statement, she handed a copy of the DNA test report to Maddy, explaining how she had collected his hair strands and submitted them to the lab along with their own samples for the paternity test.

"Yes, I was raised in that orphanage, and what difference it would make whether you or anyone fathered me. They were irresponsible people, failed to control their hormones, and when their fruit of love surfaced, they dumped me to save themselves from the social taboo or whatever the reasons they had. I particularly hate the spineless man who was my father; he was a coward who couldn't take responsibility for his irresponsible act," Maddy stated with a rage on his face.

Suddenly, Artikins rose from her seat, gave a tight slap on Maddy's face, and said, "Don't you ever dare to utter a single derogatory comment on your father. You have no idea what he's gone through and how I suffered. Sit back and hear me out why we did not raise you in the comfort of our home," before Artikins could finish her statement, Maddy rose from his seat and said, "Please excuse me; I must leave now, as I've no interest in knowing what the circumstances you were in for dumping your child to die in a cold night. If you want to cancel my catering contract, please feel free to do that, and I assure you that I'll continue to discharge my responsibilities till you get a new caterer."

"Sit down and listen to what we have to say, and if you insist on leaving, I'll call the guards to tie you up to the chair," Artikins firmly cautioned him.

"Regardless of the justifications that must be true, my stance remains resolute. The hardships I endured to break free from the upheaval of poverty and secure a place in society are beyond your grasp. Even after becoming a rich businessperson, I won't be able to marry a girl from a respectable family since I have the taboo of a love child who was raised in an orphanage. Most likely, my fate was destined for a life of bachelorhood. Consequently, your words will not sway the hardships I've endured in the past or the potential suffering in my future. I adamantly refuse to succumb to pity for your deeds. No matter the reasons that drove you to abandon me on a frigid night, I maintain that I do not need anyone to claim parentage or extend belated affection and remorse. I resolutely reject the idea of accepting you as my parents and aligning with you solely to enjoy your substantial wealth," Maddy declared, his voice unwavering, lacking anger yet unyielding and articulate.

"You think you're the only person who has suffered, and we intently created a mess in your life. Just listen to us on our side of the story, and then whatever you decide is okay with us. We'll not force you to be our child and care for us," Artikins said. Then, she slowly narrated how they met and what had transpired in their lives.

Maddy sat silently, eyes on the ground, and hopefully focused on Artikins's statement. When she finished, he rose and asked, "Can I leave now? My head is spinning, and I can't converse, so please excuse me. I'll get back to you if I decide to offer my comments on what you have mentioned. Regarding my work for the ST group, if you want to terminate the agreement, then inform me when to stop."

After Maddy left the room, I expressed in a muted voice, "Artikins, you shouldn't have slapped him. Put yourself in his shoes and think of his suffering that bounds to develop hatred toward the irresponsible couple who gave birth and dumped him to die."

"I accept I made a mistake. However, his remarks provoked such intense anger in me that I lost control. Slapping him seemed like the only way to express how strongly I felt about his wrongness. Additionally, I won't tolerate anyone speaking ill of you, not even if it's our own son," Artikins expressed with frustration, revealing the emotional pain she experienced.

"Please calm down, honey; responding intensely to every provocation isn't the answer. You must avoid resorting to a violent reaction, as it would make you no different from an immature person," I advised her.

Artikins remained silent in the face of my comments, and it seemed like my words hadn't even registered with her. She appeared lost in her own thoughts, likely grappling with the hurt caused by Maddy and struggling to emerge from the emotional pain.

I paused to contemplate how I could ease her emotional pain. Then I inquired, "Is there a romantic involvement between Angie and Maddy, or is their connection primarily rooted in friendship, forged through their interactions in a business dealing?"

After a few moments, Artikins replied, "I'm not entirely sure about the nature of their relationship. Angie mentioned to me that Maddy bought a lavish penthouse from them, and since then, they've become acquainted, occasionally having meals together or catching a movie. It's strictly a platonic connection, and he has not indicated that he wants to elevate it to a more intimate relationship."

"Let's invite Angie for dinner this weekend and try to gain more insight into Maddy and her relationship with him. If Angie could either charm him or firmly persuade him to change his viewpoint and highlight the importance of empathy and compassion in handling the matter, we should seek her assistance. While errors are a part of life, no one is at fault in this situation," I conveyed.

Artikins fell silent for a moment before speaking somberly, "Sam, that's a sound suggestion. Let's give Maddy a few days to let things settle. I hope time might allow him to see reason and accept that his misfortune isn't our personal failing but simply a cruel turn of fate that affected all of us. However, I can't shake the feeling that he's inherited my traits: stubborn and unyielding. It's unlikely he'll succumb to any pressure, even from a close friend."

I responded, "Agreed. We'll wait to hear from him, and if that doesn't happen, we can consider seeking Angie's assistance at an appropriate time."

Chapter Ten

Rukhsana Jahangir

Reclaiming a Stolen Breath

Mom died when I was pushing my thirties. Since the death of Mom, Dad has been constantly unwell, eating less and less every passing day, and not going for walks under the pretext of pain in the body or something else. Our physician confirmed that he's not suffering from any serious ailments, and we need to keep him motivated to eat well and exercise regularly. One day, while I was sitting in the living room with him, he suddenly started crying. I jumped from my seat, sat beside him, held him in my arms, and asked him, "What happened, Dad? Did I do something wrong, or are you missing mom or what? Please don't cry and tell me." I cleaned his face with a cloth napkin, and he stopped wailing after a while.

He paused for a couple of minutes and said, "I wanted to confide in you about something that deeply hurts me. However, I'll only share it if you give me your word that you will marry a person of your choosing and begin working in the company from tomorrow. Unfortunately, both of my business partners are going through some health issues, and it's causing them to take a step back from their duties. Moreover, their children residing in Western nations show little inclination to return home, as they are financially stable and content with their tranquil lifestyles.

"Engaging in the work will keep you occupied. Given your interactions with numerous customers and suppliers, I hope it will also provide an opportunity for you to meet a suitable partner. Promise me to follow what I've asked and allow me to die in peace."

"Dad, please understand I'm truly drained and lack the energy for daily commutes and actively attend to challenging business tasks. Like you, I've lost life's spark, finding no joy or motivation. You and Mom held me back while I seriously contemplated joining my husband. Marriage holds no appeal, and I doubt anything you share will significantly alter my life or bring happiness. Dad, I don't feel the need to learn your troubles, fearing they will add to my burdens rather than provide solace," I humbly conveyed.

"I know you're in a dark place right now, but I believe what I want to tell you has the power to rekindle your spirit and give you the strength to live on. Working will provide a constructive outlet for your energy and help you re-engage with life. Please allow me to pass away peacefully, knowing you've found purpose again.

"My partners are wonderful people, and they share my concern for your well-being. They encouraged me to urge you to join the company, actively participate in day-to-day running, and work on securing new ventures.

"While I don't want to pressure you into marriage, I do believe that working will offer a healthy distraction and help you gradually forget the past. Remember, countless others have suffered through similar or even greater tragedies. Please accept it as part of God's plan, something beyond our control, and move forward.

"Taking your own life would be a cowardly act, and there's no guarantee you'll find the peace you seek. This is a heartfelt plea from a loving and caring father who desperately wants to see her daughter find happiness again before I say my final farewell to this world," Dad expressed with tears rolling down his cheeks.

I hugged him and cried violently. When our tears dried, I promised to go to the office when my chamber was ready.

"My partners have already renovated my office for you, and you could go tomorrow. If you want any changes or improvements, you could ask them.

"Now, coming to what I wanted to share with you. You gave birth to a healthy, blonde baby girl with blue eyes and golden hair, which your mother gave to a barren couple but never revealed the names or contact details of the couple or whether they're in Hyderabad or some other place. Your mother went against my and your brother's wishes as she wanted you to remarry and enjoy life.

"Her reasoning was rooted in the belief that raising the girl yourself would hinder you from marrying again, and she acted with your best interests in mind. Despite our strong opposition, she remained resolute and did what we vehemently disagreed with. During her final moments, when I questioned her about the girl, she revealed that the child was in Hyderabad, being cared for and in good health. However, she declined to provide any additional details. But did mention that I should look for a golden-haired blonde girl with blue eyes; if she speaks our language and has a first name Muslim and second name Christian, then it's your granddaughter. You know your brother and I are living in a pang of guilt that won't be wiped out as long as we're alive. Your mom had no trouble dismissing your brother, but I can't forgive myself for being a weak father and husband. You would have found a purpose to live if your mom allowed you to raise your baby, and I feel so guilty that in an attempt to end my existence, I don't eat, avoid exercise, and throw away my medicine to hasten my departure. I don't expect you to forgive me; I want you to live a happy and content life, find your daughter, bring her home, and enjoy her presence in your life, and if you think what your mother did was in your interest, then forgive her," Dad expressed with tears in his eyes, showing his pain and remorse.

I needed to comfort Dad and reignite his will to survive. He's my sole motivation to keep going, and now he's thrown a lifeline to pull me out of my despair, urging me to search for Dany's daughter.

"Alright, Dad, starting tomorrow, I'll go to the office on one condition: you have to promise me that you'll take your medicine on time, walk five thousand steps daily, go with the driver to buy the groceries, attend to whatever household chores you can handle, and only watch TV when I'm around. Can you give me your word? If you do, I'll head to the office tomorrow," I stated earnestly.

"Thank you, and I assure you, I'll follow all your instructions," Dad replied with a broad grin.

The following day, I arrived at the office at ten in and observed that most of the staff had already arrived, engrossed in their work on computers or reviewing files. At the reception,

I introduced myself, and soon, a friendly, middle-aged woman appeared and greeted me warmly, stating, "I'll be your assistant until you hire one of your own." She guided me to my office, inquiring about my beverage preference. I opted for black coffee without sugar. She promptly returned with the coffee and, at my request, took a seat opposite me. She shared that one of the partners had called her early in the day, informing her of my arrival and assigning her as my assistant until a permanent replacement could be hired.

Late in the afternoon, the two partners came, and after meeting with them, I realized they were right: frail, infirm, and unfit to run the business. One had a major bypass surgery just a few months back, plus his kidneys have become weak due to diabetes. The other was walking with a metal cane because of the hip bone fracture that was fixed, but could not walk without the heavy-duty pole, and he too was suffering from Diabetes. They spent nearly two hours briefing me about projects, the current staff scenario, the banks' position, and so on.

My temporary assistant, Malti Venkat, was efficient and believed in doing a near-perfect job. Every day, she sat with me for over an hour and informed me about everything: the projects, staff, and what was happening in the company. According to her, the partners are very honest and dedicated people. Still, both were smokers and foody, which resulted in becoming a bundle of ailments in their forties. Another challenge they encountered was that each of them had only two sons, whom they sent to the USA for education and return to join the business, but they never returned. Two of them married their American colleagues, one tying the knot with an Italian-American and the other choosing a locally bred

Indian-origin girl. The remaining two sons married the Hyderabadi girls selected by their parents. All of them are well-settled and do not intend to return to be with their aging parents. The only son who married an Italian-American girl has no children, and according to his father, he's not overly concerned about not having any children.

Regarding business performance, she informed me that the company was working on multiple small and large projects when she joined. However, for the past few years, the business has been on the decline. At present, the company is working on only six projects constructing multi-story residential buildings because the two partners can no longer manage the workload of numerous ventures as they used to. Many efficient senior workers have left, and those working have become dishonest because the partners are unable to keep a tight rein on purchasing raw materials and containing labor costs per the budgeted amount. She emphasized that I must overhaul the whole operation if I wanted to run the company efficiently and make it profitable.

In the next two months, I succeeded in revamping everything on the business and home fronts.

Despite Dad agreeing to take his medicine and go for walks, I didn't observe any improvement in his condition. Consequently, I hired a professional Geriatric Nurse who requested a high salary for providing round-the-clock care, except on Sundays. I accepted her terms. Within two months, I could see the positive results of her excellent care reflected in Dad's improved health and energy levels.

On the company front, I took the purchasing into my own hands. Then, I fired most of the supervisors who oversaw projects, as they were involved in malpractice, and replaced them with young and dynamic engineers at an excellent monthly salary plus a hefty bonus on timely project completion. I replaced the entire sales executive team with younger male and female executives. Instead of traditional salaries, I offered them a modest monthly retainer along with unlimited earning potential tied to the business they would bring in.

Our company held substantial funds in the form of Fixed Deposits, as partners received a salary and a modest share of annual profits, and the rest was kept in FDs. This financial strength enabled me to go after sizable commercial and residential ventures, and our endeavors began to bear fruit. Within two years of my tenure, we were actively engaged in 17 high-end projects. Through this period, my hands-on experience and innumerable hours of dedicated study of the intricacies of costing processes and architectural details transformed me into a proficient civil engineer and architect.

Every month, twice or thrice, all the partners, including my dad, came to the office for a couple of hours to discuss what was happening and appreciate my efforts. During my tenure twice, the partners increased my earnings in the form of a raise in monthly salary and a fixed part from annual profits as a bonus, plus they changed my designation from Partner to President & CEO of the company. It wasn't the money that was keeping me dedicated and focused, but my long hours at the office and weekend visits to the sites were helping me to lessen the pain of losing my Dany. The only depressing scenario was my haunt to locate my baby, which proved futile. I spoke with many of my contacts and even hired a private eye, but all my attempts failed.

I'm now 51 years old; my company has grown considerably since I joined, yet we continue focusing on medium-sized projects. The reluctance to undertake larger ventures stems from my lack of a voracious appetite for wealth and a risk-averse nature. Dad was almost bedridden, and a few years ago, one of the partners passed away from kidney failure. The other partner was not any better and, like Dad, stopped coming to the office. I was running the company with no guidance or support, which could also be another reason for holding me back from taking up larger projects.

One day at noon, while I was busy pushing papers in my chamber, a gentle knock echoed at the door. I granted entry, and in walked the surviving partner, leaning on his iron cane; he was hunched halfway, struggling to walk with difficulty. Beside him strode a man in the prime of his middle years, whose stature matched or perhaps exceeded my own. His physique was robust, anchored by a flat abdomen that spoke of strength and discipline. A smattering of silver graced his voluminous hair, a testament to his seasoned journey through life. His features were chiseled, his gaze piercing, exuding an air of assurance and refined elegance. By any measure, his handsomeness was undeniable, a harmonious blend of character and self-assurance. The partner, Arif Ahmed, formally introduced the person as Raees Ahmed, his elder son, who had just arrived from the USA.

After exchanging pleasantries, they sat on the chairs before my desk. Arif Uncle briefly halted, appearing to compose himself by steadying his breath, which could have impeded his speech. Additionally, he seemed to be investing time in collecting his thoughts to express them in a coherent sequence. With a deep sigh, he conveyed, "I've convinced my son not to go back to the USA and to stay here permanently, as we require his support to navigate the challenges of our advancing age. To keep him occupied, I want him to take my position as a working partner of the company, which I've already discussed with your dad and obtained his consent for. However, my son has set certain conditions for working here: firstly, he must feel competent in handling the assigned tasks, and secondly, the job must be meaningful regarding his time and efforts. I suggest you assign him any task for a productive contribution to the company's growth. Raees holds a degree in computer engineering from here and an MS from the USA. Before coming here, he resigned as a technology strategy consultant for a leading US company. He had been married for more than two decades, but over six months ago, he ended his marriage with his Italian-American wife due to personal reasons. They did not have any children, primarily because his wife was unwilling to have them."

After a few moments' pause, I calmly stated, "Arif Uncle, I've no powers to say no to having Raees on board. However, I'm concerned that he wouldn't find the paycheck commensurate with his qualifications and expertise. Though he'll be getting what you used to earn as a working partner plus the annual share of profit, it would be nowhere near what he could earn in the USA."

Instead of Arif uncle, Raees replied succinctly, "Ms. Jahangir, my concern about working here doesn't revolve around the financial aspect. I'm apprehensive because I lack knowledge in the construction business. If you were to ask me about purchasing mortar and bricks or inspecting sites to ensure the work aligns with the planned roadmap, I would be at a loss. I hold a postgraduate degree in Data Structures and

Algorithms from a renowned university in the United States. This field delves into advanced data structures and algorithmic techniques crucial for creating efficient software, encompassing topics like sorting algorithms, graph theory, and dynamic programming. In my previous role, I provided specialized consulting services to clients on technology adoption, digital transformation, and IT investment decisions that could result in an increase in productivity and profitability. If your company has a position focused on computerizing your entire operation, covering everything from accounting and bidding to execution, where every penny invested and every cement bag or brick used must be accurately accounted for, then I could contribute effectively. Otherwise, I don't see a suitable avenue in your company to leverage my services."

His honest and crisp input impressed me, and I responded cordially, "I'm delighted to note that you could computerize our entire operations. We're using various off-the-shelf packages that are not even close to satisfactory. In the last one year, we've communicated with several trustworthy companies. However, some of them quoted significant sums to decline our project, while others expressed interest without firmly committing to delivery timelines. We want comprehensive software that could resolve all our concerns, from accounting and bidding and executing to handing over the venture. Nothing could be better if you could assist us in achieving our objectives. Every person's accountability and efficiency will be increased, and it also allows us to bid for large projects, where meticulous bidding and executions are critical to maintaining the project's profitability."

"It would be easy, and I hope to complete the development, installation, and commissioning within eight to ten months. For ease of use, I'll provide you with a User Manual complete with an installation guide, technical specifications, and troubleshooting. However, I would need at least one competent programmer," Raees stated confidently.

"That sounds fantastic. Once your software is installed and commissioned, we'd appreciate your support in utilizing it for bid development and keeping us updated with system-generated reports on project progress, profitability, and the like," I expressed with enthusiasm.

"No issue, Ma'am. When do you want me to join? What are the office timings, and how long would it take to effect the changes in the partnership agreement?" Raees inquired.

"Whenever you want, you're welcome to join. Our office hours are ten to six, and regarding the change of partnership agreement, I've got to check with our company lawyer, but it shouldn't take much time," I stated. I was happy that a partner would shoulder some of the critical responsibilities, and I'd be free to take a few weeks of vacation when I wanted.

"Okay, Ma'am. I'll start tomorrow, but is it possible for me to start early in the morning, say between seven and eight? Ten is too late for me, and I want to leave the office by four. So, I could spend some time in the Gym and be with my parents till they sleep," Raees inquired.

"Start whenever is convenient for you. You will receive a partner password to facilitate entry and exit at any odd hour. I usually arrive around nine in the morning and tend to stay until after seven to lessen the next day's workload. Please call me Rukhsana; addressing me Ma'am or Ms. Jahangir is overly formal, particularly if it's coming from a partner," I shared sincerely with a grin.

"Wonderful. Hopefully, I'll start tomorrow. You need to give me at least two hours tomorrow, as I want to understand the workflow and the reports that you need to see to improve efficiency and keep tight control on the costing and delivery schedules of the projects," Raees expressed.

"Sure, just give me an hour's notice so I can free myself from any pressing engagements I may have," I said smilingly.

Raees has been with us for close to a year and has kept his promise of developing software within eight months. His work was highly satisfactory in every aspect of the business. It provided perfect accounting reports and gave me excellent insight into every running project, including the profitability aligned with our projection. However, I noticed he was showing an excessive interest in me, which made our working relationship uncomfortable. I invited him to a few business lunches as I needed a senior executive's presence to impress potential clients. Unfortunately, he may have misunderstood my intentions and interpreted it as a signal to pursue a romantic connection. Undoubtedly, he displayed a multitude of admirable qualities: he was educated, intelligent, financially secure, committed to healthy habits, and diligent in his work. Initially, he stuck to his commitment of leaving the office at four, working a standard eight-hour day for a few weeks. However, he later extended his working hours to ten or twelve hours per day without expressing any discontent. Furthermore, whenever I requested him to handle tasks unrelated to his primary responsibilities, he willingly obliged without any complaints. One day, he asked me how my husband died, and I informed him of the happenings, and unintentionally, I inquired about the reasons for his divorce.

He paused briefly before responding to my question and stated, "I married a wonderful girl; she was beautiful, intelligent, ambitious, and worked as the marketing executive of our company. Our business interaction was constant; she used to hunt for potential customers and then set up a meeting with me as a consultant to secure a contract from the client for their business automation. This constant interaction led to romantic affiliation, but the initiation wasn't from me. She aggressively pursued me for over three years. In the end, I found myself reciprocating her feelings, realizing she embodied the qualities that truly mattered. She once said her parents migrated from Italy, and within a few years of her birth, they got separated; her father disappeared, and her mom passed away in a road accident when she was nine years old and was raised in a foster home of a single lady above fifty. She was a kind-hearted woman who gave up on men after two failed marriages and a son who abandoned her to live in caves with many boys and girls who subscribed to living as their prehistoric ancestors; it was an offshoot of the Back-to-the-land movement of the 1970s. Her foster mother passed away when she reached the age of twenty-five. By then, she had already graduated with a BBA degree and was employed as a marketing executive in my company.

"In the initial phases of our relationship, she shared her perspective on the world, describing it as unduly harsh. She was convinced that bringing another life into this world was an inhumane act and made it a condition for our marriage that we refrain from having children. I acquiesced to this stipulation, respecting her wishes as I was also not greatly fond of children.

"We refrained from keeping alcohol in our home and only occasionally enjoyed a couple of glasses of wine when we dined out. Nevertheless, six months prior to the disintegration of our marriage, she developed a penchant for heavy drinking. Her incessant drinking and bringing hard liquor home sparked continuous conflicts; her constant state of inebriation was getting on my nerves. One evening, a heated argument erupted as I sought to understand the reasons behind her alcoholism. Amid the confrontation, she blurted the root cause of her addiction: an involvement with a wealthy client who had promised her the position of Vice President in his company, along with a twenty percent stake. Regrettably, those pledges were nothing but falsehoods, skillfully crafted to manipulate her into a sexual relationship, to which she succumbed. He ceased responding to her calls within a few weeks of their romantic involvement. Upon visiting his office to inquire, she discovered that his wife had unearthed our furtive affair with the help of a private investigator, who provided irrefutable evidence of our physical involvement. She promptly divorced and sacked him from the company, being the actual owner of the business. Following his termination, he never reached out to her, possibly restrained by shame and humiliation.

"The following day, I initiated a divorce, a decision she couldn't dispute since I had secretly recorded her admission of adultery. In the subsequent weeks, it became apparent that maintaining even a professional relationship with her as an office colleague was unfeasible. Given the abundance of more lucrative job prospects, I chose to resign. Before joining a new company, I opted for an extended holiday to be with my ailing parents."

Listening to his statement, I observed his seamless delivery without stumbling, pausing to recollect, or weaving a fabricated narrative. This quality proclaimed him as a straightforward person, another admirable quality.

With each passing day, Raees's subtle overtures became more pronounced. He delved into discussions about my future and expressed concern about my well-being in a household overshadowed by my nearly bedridden father. I'm alone in the house; I have no one to talk to or look after my needs, which is too depressing.

One weekend, he discreetly arrived at our home, accompanied by his ailing parents, who seemed even weaker than my last encounter with them at a dinner hosted by Arif Uncle to celebrate the company's massive earnings in the past fiscal year. While their purported reason for the visit was to check on my father, a lingering suspicion hinted at motives beyond what Raees wanted me to perceive. Nonetheless, I ushered them into Dad's room, where, after a brief interval, Dad asked me to organize some refreshments. I took the hint, instructed the house help to check with the visitors about their drink preferences, and went to my room. After forty-five minutes or more, a maid came to my room and informed me that visitors had gone, and Dad wanted to see me.

Dad requested that I take a seat and draw the chair closer to the bed, a directive I promptly followed. I gazed at him with anticipation. After a brief contemplation, Dad whispered in his weak voice, "Do you know why my partner came by?" I nodded, signaling my lack of awareness. He continued, "Raees is genuinely interested in marrying you, and his parents urged me to persuade you to accept the proposal. They believe that leading a lonely life could result in both physical and mental health issues. While I was thrilled and inclined to agree on the spot, I deemed it wiser to seek your approval before confirming. My dear, grant me this final joy so I can depart for my ultimate destination, knowing that you're not alone, living with a loving partner. Raees has assured me that he will ensure your happiness and contentment as long as he lives, and I trust he is a man of his word, just like his father."

"Dad, I've been conscious of Raees's feelings for me for some time, and I've been contemplating how to address his advances. Now that the truth is out in the open, I must seriously think deeply to discern if I can move beyond my profound love for my late husband and embrace a new partner. Please understand that considering Raees for marriage is not taken lightly, but I need time to firm up my stand. Allow me to confess that he embodies all the qualities I hold in high esteem: honesty, intelligence, and a robust work ethic. He maintains a modest lifestyle despite his wealth, which resonates with my preferences," I conveyed earnestly.

"Rukhs, I'm certain that I've reached the end of the road; with each passing day, my body is giving up, and the simple act of walking to the toilet has become a formidable challenge. Nights bring a sense of fear, and despite the aid of sleeping pills, I manage only three to four hours of sleep. Throughout the day, I find myself either dozing off or contemplating how much longer I can endure this. Sometimes, I entertain the idea that finding solace in eternal peace might be preferable.

"You're an intelligent girl and know fully well what old age is all about, but still allow me to say a few words about the passing phase of life.

"With each passing day, time leaves its mark and an unyielding spirit battles against the creeping shadows of illness. Where once there was vibrancy, now resides a shell, navigating a maze of discomfort and vulnerability. Every ache and twinge whispers a quiet truth: you're at the end of the road.

"Helplessness creeps in like a thief in the night, stealing away the independence we once took for granted. Victories over illness now seem like distant dreams. Our grasp weakens, and a sense of helplessness drifts in like a murky cloud, leaving us lost without a clear path forward.

"Feelings rise and fall in this twilight stage of life. We miss the strength we used to have. But even amid this struggle, a spark of hope remains. It shines in the eyes, holding stories of all we've faced and overcome. There's a sense of mourning for the vitality that once defined the essence of the self.

"Old age is a blend of weakness and strength: accepting what we can't change while fighting for what we can. As we near the end of this demanding phase, our strength endures, displaying the imprints of both hardships and triumphs in life. The judgment of whether it was well-lived or not rests on your shoulders.

"I want to reassure you that my intent is not to engage in emotional manipulation. Instead, I am candidly sharing my daily struggles and the increasing difficulty of staying motivated in the relentless battle I face each day to see the dawn of a new day. The ultimate call hovering to come any day or moment, yet I didn't want to depart until I witnessed my daughter had a partner to face this cruel world. Please be considerate and compassionate while making your decision; your adherence to my plea will allow me to leave with peace, grace, and the satisfaction that my responsibilities have been fulfilled," Dad conveyed, his voice filled with deep anguish.

Dad's words were heart-wrenching and soul-crushing, and I had no words to say, even a few soothing words. I committed to Dad communicating my decision in the next few days and exited the room with a weighty heart and deep sorrow. Contemplating life's cyclical patterns, I found solace in the thought that someday, I, too, would experience a situation akin to my dad's today. Embracing this unavoidable aspect of life's journey, I fortified myself to confront any challenges that awaited, fully prepared to endure them with resilience and take it all on the chin.

The next day, I summoned Raees to my room for an extensive conversation, urging him to set aside any pressing matters and join me when convenient. About an hour later, he arrived, and without any preamble, I broached the main topic.

"Raees, please enlighten me on why you wish to marry someone as boring as myself. I work, and during my free time, I dedicate myself to caring for my father or reflecting on the memories of my late husband. I don't find pleasure in cooking, binge-watching, going to the movies, treating myself to dinners, or shopping. Your life would almost certainly be better without me. I strongly urge you to retract your proposal since I fear my decision may cause my sick father anguish. I'm sure there are many women who are totally on the same page as you and would be excited to say yes to your proposal. I would be grateful if you could agree to my request and save me from causing my father any distress."

Raees gazed at me, taking a moment to think of an appropriate reply. Finally, he drew a deep breath and addressed my entreaty, "Rukhs, it seems we're navigating in the same emotional waters. You're mourning the loss of your beloved husband while I'm grappling with the hurt inflicted by my wife, someone I cherished for more than twenty years. This common anguish has brought us to a juncture where both of us are devoid of the desire to pursue worldly indulgences. In this phase of our lives, the challenge lies in addressing loneliness; having children is not on the table, and there is not much drive left for physical gratification. I now crave a companion with whom I can engage in meaningful conversations and share quality moments both in and outside of the home. I don't expect you to cook for me or tend to my needs, but I promise to fulfill all your requirements. I would be your reliable companion, offering everything I have. Most importantly, our togetherness presents a chance to dissolve the toxicity that has accumulated amid hurt and profound loneliness, paving the way for a meaningful, joyful, and content coexistence. While you are under no obligation to accept my proposal, I encourage you to examine it earnestly. Consider whether it holds the potential to alleviate the pains we silently endure, even if we resist acknowledging or accepting our suffering."

It's true that there were moments when the burden of monotony and isolation became almost unbearable. Life sank into a dreary and intolerable pattern; a TV show that brought joy with a companion could lose its appeal when viewed alone.

Opting for solace in a humble homemade sandwich consistently seemed like a more appealing choice when compared to dining out alone. However, the idea of replacing Dany and filling the void with someone else seemed inconceivable. Instead of hastily dismissing the proposal, it is crucial to take the required time for careful consideration before reaching a decision.

Due to my preoccupation with my thoughts, I neglected to reply to Raees's remarks; therefore, he asked, "Do you have any comments?"

"Sure, I won't immediately dismiss your proposal. As advised, I'll take some time to soul-search before expressing my stance. However, it's essential to remember that you're here in this country to care for your ailing parents, and I also have the responsibility of looking after my dad. Even if we consider marriage, the practicalities of who relocates to whose house and how we manage the care of our folks need careful consideration," I replied succinctly.

"That's simple; you make the decision, and I'll go along with your suggestion. Moving to your house, which is much bigger than my house, won't pose a problem, and allocating a room for my parents shouldn't be an issue. Let me be upfront: whether I reside in your house or you move to mine with your dad, I'll cover all the household expenses, including the nursing care for our parents," Raees's firmness in expressing his thoughts was reassuring, affirming his admirable qualities.

It has been two months since I tied the knot with Raees, and he has proven to be an amazing life partner. While it's still too early to judge a person, thus far, no actions, deeds, or comments have made me angry or lowered his image of a well-behaved, cultured person. Yet, he misled me about his modest interest in physical pleasure; his daily crossbar exercises and jogging regimen made him incredibly fit, leading to a noticeable surge in his sexual drive. With a frequency of nearly two or three times a week, he gradually brought about moments of intimacy, often seeking permission to administer a soothing oil massage, a practice undoubtedly must have been taught by his ex-wife. It would have been foolish to decline such a comforting therapy, which inevitably led to satisfying outcomes.

During weekends, he has been thoughtful, taking me to movies or shopping, followed by dinners at exquisite restaurants where he ensures I am well-fed. His constant desire to be by my side is endearing, although, at times, I find myself yearning for a bit of personal space. Nevertheless, his unwavering love and care make it challenging for me to express that need.

During the few months following our wedding, my father passed away. A mere two weeks later, Raees's mother departed for her eternal resting place. Raees's father, deeply affected by the loss of his wife, became bedridden, and within a brief span of two months, he, too, departed to reunite with his spouse. I suspect they were all waiting for us to tie the knot, and once we did, they swiftly passed away, leaving us to brave the survival journey.

We realized that our home had suddenly become too spacious for just the two of us, requiring a team of workers to maintain it, with me having to supervise their efforts. Managing an eight-bedroom house spread over two acres of land with a large study, game room, gym, TV lounge, visitor lounge, three garages, guest house, and a storage basement became overwhelming for us. In light of this, I suggested to Raees that we consider demolishing the house and constructing a high- end luxury apartment complex in its place. I envisioned two towering, ultra-luxurious buildings, each equipped with all the upscale amenities one would expect to have when one pays a fortune to buy it.

Raees embraced the idea, and our company was awarded the construction contract. However, before the execution could begin, we needed to vacate the premises. After moving to our house, Raees sold his parents' house, which was also quite large, and according to him, it fetched him decent money. This decision was made because his brother needed funds to acquire real estate in the USA. We attempted to rent a large apartment or independent living space but couldn't find anything that fit our requirements. My farmhouse was a nice and comfortable place to stay, but getting to work would've been a real headache.

During my search for a suitable residence, I stumbled upon an advertisement from a prominent construction company offering a ready-to-move villa in an esteemed gated community. Raees agreed to purchase the villa, provided it was spacious enough to accommodate our valuable belongings.

The next day, our first stop was at the villa site to check the amenities and villa construction. The property spanned an extensive area equipped with all the essential amenities: a clubhouse featuring a gym, a swimming pool, indoor games facilities, and a spacious party hall capable of hosting 200 people. A total of forty villas were in the compound, and only two were available for sale. Each villa was constructed on five hundred square yards, a typical townhouse construction; the second floor of each villa accommodated four bedrooms with a large balcony, while the ground floor included one generous bedroom, a TV lounge, a visitor room, a library room, and a kitchen. Nestled in the backyard was two servant quarters. Every conceivable feature was in place, leaving nothing amiss. We agreed that we should buy it as long as the price wasn't inflated.

Eager not to squander time, we headed straight to the builder's office, determined to secure the villa before it was too late. Based on my solid understanding of the area's land prices and the construction cost per square foot for a luxurious residence, I had a fairly accurate estimate of the anticipated price.

When we informed the receptionist of the purpose of our visit, we were guided to a meeting room, where we had to wait for a few minutes when a young girl walked in holding a bunch of brochures and a couple of manila folders and introduced herself as Anandi, an in-house sales executive. Horse trading started, and finally, we gave our take-it-or leave-it offer with a one-hundred-percent check payment, with no bank finance or EMI. Anandi walked out, telling us to wait for a few minutes as she had to inform her superior of our offer. In a few minutes, she returned and informed us that the Boss would be with us soon.

A blonde girl in her mid or late twenties walked in and, in a muted voice, introduced herself as Angelina Daniel, CEO. She then said, "Unfortunately, we don't have room to accommodate your asking price. However, I can offer a small discount since the two vacant villas were booked by an investor who got into a financial crisis and failed to pay the remaining amount. A couple of days back, he informed us that he wouldn't be able to pay and asked us to impound his advance payment to compensate for our loss and sell the villas to any interested party. Since you're paying upfront, I would give you a discount equivalent to fifty percent of the booking amount that we had received from the investor, and that's our rock-bottom price."

I hardly heard what she said. My heart was beating so violently that I thought it would come out of my chest. She must be my baby. Her last name is Daniel, and she's blonde, just like my Dany.

While I was debating how to react to this situation, I heard Raees whisper close to my ears, "Rukhs, the offer looks good; it's better to grab it."

I nodded and asked Angelina, "Can we speak in Hindi? Feel free to let me know if you're not comfortable with the language."

"Sure, and can I call you Auntie? Your name for me is a tad tongue twister," she said in fluent Hindi.

My heart sank; now I was one hundred percent sure that this was my daughter. "Angie, I accept your offer, but before we issue the check, could you organize a hot chocolate for me? My heartbeat has increased, and I know it's not a heart attack but a lack of sleep and stress."

Raees went out, saying he would bring the drink from a nearby Starbucks. Angelina tried to stop him, but he quickly left the room. He probably got worried about my increased heartbeat.

"Angie, can you sit beside me for a while and hold my hands?" I pleaded.

"Sure, Auntie," Angie muttered.

She sat beside me, took my hands in her, and after a few moments, she checked my pulse and said, "Auntie, your pulse rate is very high, and I believe you should immediately see a doctor."

"No need to see a doctor; just give me a few minutes, and I'll be fine. Tell me, Daniel, is your father's name or husband?" I inquired.

"It was a given name; my dad's name was Rajesh Gupta, who had passed away and left this company for me to run," Angie replied.

"Angie, if I ask you a few personal questions, do you mind answering?" I queried.

"Auntie, please relax so the pulse rate can come down, and I beg you not to ask any personal questions, as I don't want to answer them," Angie said in her muted voice.

I didn't speak, but her reluctance to answer personal questions confirmed that she was my daughter. After a few minutes, I felt relaxed, and my heartbeat also came down significantly. Raees returned with the drink; I took a few sips and signaled Raees to issue the check. Within a few minutes, a sales deed agreement was in our hands, and Angie informed us that her office would call for the registration of the property in three to four days.

I hugged and thanked her and left, taking her promise that she'd attend our housewarming ceremony.

We moved in on the fourteenth day after purchasing the villa, and our house was as furnished as we wanted it to be. The days passed as before, but the nights failed to give me sound sleep as I was consumed by thoughts of the best approach to learning more about Angie's parents. Should I hire the services of a private investigator, or would a more direct approach be prudent? Perhaps inviting her to the housewarming ceremony and delicately broaching the subject could be the way. However, the pressing question remained: why should she disclose her past to me? What right did I have to inquire about such personal information, and why should she feel obligated to comply? I found myself without answers, dismissing the idea of hiring a private investigator to avoid the risk of this sensitive matter becoming known to others.

I shared my thoughts with Raees, who suggested that our approach should first involve building a connection with Angie. We must carefully gauge her comfort level and assess whether she would be willing to share the necessary information. I agreed with his suggestion and invited her to attend our housewarming ceremony on the following Saturday. She accepted the invitation and expressed her joy at attending the event.

We decided to invite the top ten executives of our company to ensure a respectable headcount for our gathering. We informed them that they should come with their families at eight sharp and leave at ten since we had other engagements.

Angie came around eight-thirty when everyone was busy sipping fresh juices and having deep conversations. She brought a bouquet of exotic flowers and a large rectangular box, which indicated it was a painting. Ladies were sitting in one group, and gents were in another group. I took Angie to the ladies' group, introduced her, and excused myself for organizing the dinner.

After dinner and coffee, everyone left one by one, and it was not even ten. Angie also sought permission to leave, but I chuckled and took her hand, saying, "You're not going anywhere, darling. Have a second cup of coffee with me, and then you could leave."

"Sure, Auntie, as I wanted to spend some time with you, I needed to ask you a few questions," Angie replied smilingly.

"I'm listening; feel free to ask any questions you have, and I'll try my best to give answers. I, too, have a topic to discuss with you," I replied with a grin.

The domestic staff promptly served us freshly brewed coffee in the TV lounge. After a few sips, Angie leaned forward, her voice maintaining its usual low decibel level, and asked, "Auntie, you never mentioned having a construction company, and from what I gathered from the ladies I spoke with, it's quite substantial. Was there a specific reason for not informing me?"

"My love, the rationale for not keeping you informed about our company was to avoid any perception that we were seeking an unwarranted discount due to our shared profession. However, our understanding of construction costs provided us with a ballpark estimate that your potential earnings in the deal would fall within the range of 20 to 30%, a standard figure for a business that requires diligent planning and hard work to deliver projects with finesse while upholding commitments to pre-construction buyers," I expressed earnestly.

"Thank you. I'm genuinely happy with your response. I always tell my sales executives who want to lower the prices to adhere to our set price range for two reasons: one, we must be able to deliver more than what we have committed, and next, we're not in a box-pushing business to settle on barebone profits that would fail us to deliver the commitments. My next question is, do you take sub-contracts from other construction companies like our company, which primarily undertakes large government or corporate contracts worth hundreds of crores?" Angie questioned.

I found it astonishing that Angie managed such a vast company entirely on her own. Even if she had partners, given her role as chief executive officer, it seemed they weren't actively engaged in the day-to-day operations.

"Angie, we've never ventured into subcontracting before, but in business, if the potential rewards outweigh the efforts, then why not consider it? After all, it's another venture, and why refuse if the 'game is worth the candle,'" I said with a chuckle.

"Okay, Auntie, I'll approach you whenever a need arises to outsource a project or part of it. Now my questions are over, please inform me of the topic that you wanted to share," Angie concluded.

"Angie, I want to share a true story and take your opinion on what you would do if you were caught up in a similar scenario," I paused in anticipation of her feedback.

"Auntie, if you believe it's important for me to hear you out, I have no objections, and I'll provide you with my impartial feedback. However, let me make it clear: I'm not a street-smart, worldly-wise individual. I've been a nerd and quite timid for most of my life. My dad pushed me to enter the business, making me a bit more outgoing and helping me overcome my shyness when dealing with business associates and colleagues," Angie explained. I felt pleased hearing her words, which reflected her sincerity and authenticity.

"I need a young person's perspective, which is why I'm turning to you. Regardless, let me share what I have to say," I said, unfolding my life story, tactfully avoiding any mention that I married a blond Yankee and my girl was a blonde. I ended the story when my baby was left on the street. Raees was with us yet remained silent throughout.

A deep, bone-chilling silence pervaded the room as I finished my narrative and paused, carefully choosing the words for my question.

"Now, inform me of the steps the woman, impacted by circumstances, should take upon rediscovering her daughter after more than twenty- five years. Additionally, should the daughter be willing to embrace her, despite the difficult upbringing she endured, potentially in someone's house or in an undesirable condition due to her irresponsible parents? Remember, the daughter is now successful and content in her current environment," I inquired in a subdued tone.

"Auntie, is this your own story? Did you find your daughter?" Angie inquired.

"It's someone very dear to me. She's hesitant to approach the girl, as she deeply desires her presence in her life, but success is uncertain. Seeking my advice, I thought of considering a young girl's perspective, and based on that, I could provide valuable guidance. Please feel at liberty to express any thought you deem a suitable response from a young girl who is well-settled and happy in her own universe," I responded smilingly.

"Auntie, I don't want to confront or upset you in any way, but I'd appreciate your honesty. I don't think this pertains to someone else; my intuition strongly suggests you're describing your own situation. If that's the case, I'd prefer to be straightforward in giving my opinion," Angie expressed in a composed tone, subtly revealing her reluctance to be involved in a situation reminiscent of her own past.

I found myself unable to grasp the reason behind the overwhelming surge of emotion, whether it was prompted by her response or my intense desire to hold her. Nonetheless, a sudden wave of emotions enveloped me, leading to continuous tears: no loud cries, just a steady flow resembling a gentle waterfall. Angie swiftly rose from her seat, approached me, and embraced me, saying, "I sincerely apologize if my thoughtless comments caused you any offense. Auntie, I'm navigating the exact situation you described. My biological parents dumped me, and before I died on the footpath where I was thrown, my dad, a kind-hearted, wonderful human, found me. However, instead of bringing me to his home, he placed me in a Christian orphanage. I don't hold any resentment towards my dad for his choice, nor do I bear any grudge against my biological parents; the path I've traveled was determined by the circumstances I encountered, without any supernatural intervention or preordained fate. I firmly believe that forgiving those who have caused you pain and moving forward is essential for a happy life."

Angie's words brought a wave of calm to my soul. Leaning in, I kissed her forehead, feeling tears welling up in my eyes.

"Yes, it's my story, and you're my daughter. Can you open your heart, just a little, to forgive your mother? The one who dreams of holding you close, of giving you everything I have? You're not just Dany's daughter, my sweet girl. You're mine, too. I know it in my bones. And I believe Daniel Theo, watching over us with his kind eyes, would want me to hold on to his precious daughter. To not let her slip away."

Angie's calm reply chilled me. "How can you be so sure, Auntie?" she inquired, her voice devoid of anger, but her facial expression reflected unbelievability. "Dates can be wrong, and resemblance can be deceptive. Maybe your daughter is out there, wondering why her parents abandoned her."

"I don't want you to believe everything that I said. Let's take a DNA test, and if it confirms I'm your mom, I'll be over the moon, or else I'll be happy with being your aunt. Is that okay with you?" I inquired.

"I'm very happy with my aunt. What purpose would it serve even if it proves that you're my mom? I'll not stay with you, and I barely find free time, even on weekends, to enjoy a movie or dinner at a fancy restaurant. Lastly, money has no meaning to me; I am not materialistic and hardly treat myself with expensive accessories. My personal wealth must be a minimum of a few hundred crores, and I own fifty-one percent of a stake in my company. Whether you're my mom or not, I love my Auntie, and whenever you want me, I'll stop all my engagements and come to meet you," Angie explained her position.

Raees, who had been quietly listening to our conversation, spoke up, "Angie, I want to share some insights with you. Your mother is a person of remarkable resilience and compassion.

She chose to marry a man who was deeply in love with her, possessed intelligence, came from a respectable family, and displayed amiable manners: a true catch. He proved his love through the ultimate sacrifice, as he laid down his life to shield your beloved mother from a barrage of bullets.

"The trauma of that event left her deeply shaken, and she contemplated taking her own life. However, driven by her compassionate nature, she chose to come here and be with her aging parents instead. She holds no grudge for her mother's actions but thwarted her dreams by refusing to marry again. Since her husband's departure, she has found little happiness. I convinced her to marry me, not out of any romantic motive, but solely to provide each other with companionship in our lonely lives. Apart from a few fleeting months of marital bliss with her beloved husband, she has known little joy. Being a person filled with love and care, you must consider offering her some solace and injecting moments of happiness into her life. Your American father wished for his first child to be a girl; wherever he is now, he would likely be happy to see you. If you join his beloved wife, his joy will know no bounds. While we may not possess the wealth you do, we are comfortable enough to offer you anything to have you in our lives, at least until you decide to marry. She has embarked on the last phase of her life. I urge you to show compassion and make this final stretch enjoyable for her. When she meets her Dany, let her proudly share the news of the wonderful daughter they have in the world. Infuse moments of joy into your mother's life, be a comforting presence, and assist her in finding a renewed sense of purpose till she passes away."

A hush fell over the room for several minutes as Raees's heartfelt comments left everyone unsettled. The person expected to respond sat quietly with her head down. After gathering herself, Angie spoke, "Uncle, I need to ensure she's my mom through a DNA test. If it confirms the relationship, I'll be a part of her life. However, I can't make any guarantees beyond that at the moment because I'm unsure how to handle this situation. When you're ready, call me to arrange the DNA test. It's time for me to go to bed, so please allow me to bid goodbye."

"Are you free anytime tomorrow? I'll make an appointment from any decent lab and call you," Raees questioned.

"Please give me time to settle, but I promise that within the next 3-4 days, I'll organize everything," Angie replied and rose from her seat to leave. I went to her, took her in my arms, and whispered in her ear, "Please hold me tight; this is the first time I'm happy after the death of my Dany." After a few minutes of holding, I let her go.

After three days, Angie phoned to ask if I could join her at a DNA lab at nine o'clock sharp the following day. She mentioned that she would provide the lab address later in the day. I replied with a definite yes.

The next day, the laboratory obtained buccal swabs from us for an Ancestry Test. We were advised to await their call for the report, which could take approximately three weeks.

After returning from the lab, I immersed myself in the boxes Bro shipped from the US, rummaging for photo albums that included my engagement, marriage, and precious moments with Dany. I found all the albums in one box and meticulously chose a few to give to Angie if the lab confirmed our relationship.

Chapter Eleven

Mahendra Reddy

Can Scars Ever Truly Heal?

I cannot recall ever being slapped. I consistently adhered to minding my own affairs; even in my childhood, I refrained from misbehaving, earning praise from my teachers for my diligent work and enthusiasm to excel academically. However, today, I succumbed to the release of long-suppressed emotions fueled by deep-seated resentment towards my parents, who abandoned me to die. Regardless of their circumstances, I endured suffering and, regrettably, uttered words I should not have. Undoubtedly, she is my mother, and her slap was aimed solely at her son, which is acceptable. I bore the consequences of my indiscreet words.

However, acknowledging them as my parents and taking pride in them is not something I can entertain. There's a risk of significant financial loss if they decide to cancel the catering contract, invoking the clause related to substandard food or poor service. Experiencing both losses and gains is inevitable in business, and I shouldn't dwell too much on it. However, the prospect of terminating the employment of close to one hundred workers is distressing and would deeply sadden me.

Even if Auntie didn't cancel the contract, working with her would not be pleasant anymore.

Upon reflecting on Auntie's account of their ordeal, I felt sympathy. Both they and I endured hardships, yet would it truly alter anything? If Auntie hadn't opted to have a child without her parents' wishes, I wouldn't have entered this world as an unwanted infant. Her impetuous and irresponsible decision became the source of my suffering. At this stage of life, Auntie has found solace in her husband and is not alone, whereas I am condemned to endure melancholy and solitude until my physical end.

Coming from a wealthy and respected family, Angie would never agree to marry me. Even if she were to agree under the condition that I adopt her faith, I would staunchly decline. I find contentment in my Hindu identity, the religion of my foster parents, who nurtured me with love, care, sustenance, and everything within their means. They were my true parents, and I am determined not to betray them by altering my faith for the sake of marriage, wealth, or anything else.

Even if I get the entire wealth of my biological parents, it will merely increase the numbers in my bank account without offering any meaningful impact on my life. I find no reason to take them on as my parents, and any attempt to utilize them for marriage purposes is bound to meet with disappointment. Auntie and I adhere to Hinduism, while the father practices Christianity; very few progressive families would be willing to accept a son-in-law with such a mix of religious backgrounds for their daughter.

Considering the perspective of compassion and empathy, there's potential for me to extend acceptance and support to them during their times of need. After all, they are the ones who brought me into this world, enduring more challenges than I can fathom. Perhaps it's time to let go of past grievances and express gratitude for the gift of life, the resilience to face difficulties. Certainly, there is room for acceptance, yet my haunting animosity towards the individuals who gave me birth was so intense that encountering them would likely ignite a surge of anger, leading to regrettable and uncharacteristic remarks.

Despite my heartfelt understanding of their struggles and sufferings, opting for a distance remains the optimal choice for a peaceful life. In the event they turn to Angie for mediation, who introduced me to them and potentially recommended me for the catering business, I must stand firm even if she implores me to set aside my sufferings and acknowledge them.

I only slept when I concluded that I should remain firm in my decision to be away from them. However, over the next few days, Auntie's slap and their struggles kept intruding into my thoughts, hindering my focus on work. To overcome this mental turmoil, I decided to consult Angie for guidance on how to get through the situation without guilt. If revealing my past to her meant losing her as a friend, then so be it.

Nevertheless, I gave myself an additional few days to determine if I could let go of the past. As each day unfolded, I increasingly contemplated whether I was failing to comprehend their sufferings rationally or if my stance was justified. However, I remained unable to ascertain who was wrong or right, and I grappled with resolving this persistent issue with the help of Angie to clear my mind and better concentrate on my work.

One evening, I confided in Angie. I sought her permission to share a lingering personal issue that was evading resolve, and I needed her perspective to firm up my stand. She agreed to listen but cautioned that she might refrain from offering feedback if she believed it could strain our friendship. I agreed to her condition and then proceeded to recount my life's journey from birth to the present, expressing my emotions regarding my biological parents. I uttered my strong loathing, which developed when I realized why I ended up in the orphanage. I can never forgive the heartless people who dumped me in the open to die on the freezing cold night.

I continued expressing the current scenario, "Unexpectedly, a few days ago, my biological parents showed up; you're familiar with them as you had introduced me to them and suggested I take up their catering business. They provided conclusive proof with a DNA test report that confirmed their parentage. They asserted their innocence in abandoning me, attributing the separation to their mother. They described her as malevolent and the cause of our collective hardships. In addition, they shared their longing for me to be with them at their place, a desire for my presence not for physical or monetary support but for the warmth and comfort of family and grandchildren.

"They possess immense wealth, affording them every conceivable facility and luxury without any impediment. I find myself caught between two contrasting sentiments: a lingering resentment towards my biological parents on one side and, on the other, the compassionate empathy that should guide one's actions in any circumstance. I pose this question to you: should I choose to distance myself from them, continuing my life as if our paths had never crossed? Alternatively, should I rise above my hardened resentment, embodying a considerate nature by caring for them, accepting their innocence in my abandonment, and attributing it to the whims of fate?"

Angie lent her full attention, refraining from any interruptions. Once I finished, she remarked, "Maddy, thank you for opening up about your life's journey. I want to avoid making impromptu remarks since it's dealing with a highly sensitive issue. From my personal perspective, practicing empathy, forgiveness, and maintaining a positive outlook are vital in all interactions. Take some time to ease out of your emotionally charged state. Give yourself at least two weeks to compose, allowing you to make logical and meticulously weighed decisions. Suppose you require my assistance in crafting a compassionate decision, considering your aversions and the hardships of your biological parents. In that case, I propose that we schedule a meeting in a week or two. During our discussion, we would attempt to hammer out a conclusive decision that resonates with your values and ensures you have no regrets when you look back. It's important to acknowledge that your parents, like anyone else, were human and subject to judgmental oversight. This realization should discourage you from adopting an overly harsh stance."

I thanked Angie for her input, and after we spoke for a while about various subjects, she hung up.

I had a hunch that she didn't like my stance, so she talked about empathy, forgiveness, and positivity. She could say that since she hadn't experienced the pain of being raised in an orphanage.

As I drifted into sleep, I consciously decided not to succumb to any pressures, whether they originated from Angie or anyone else. Considering the times when my parents were absent during my moments of need, I questioned the rationale behind being there for them now solely for their happiness. It's not a tit-for-tat scenario but a simple give-and-take calculation. I find it tough to conjure even a trace of love or sympathy for them, especially when their sufferings appear to be self-inflicted.

Chapter Twelve

Angelina Daniel

Whispers of Redemption

As I headed back home from Auntie's housewarming ceremony, I felt immense joy, realizing that both Maddy and I had found the mothers who brought us into this world. Although my connection was yet to be confirmed with a DNA test, I was confident that Auntie had told the truth. Should the test confirm it, I will wholeheartedly embrace the Muslim Auntie as my mother.

After hearing the woes of Auntie, my conviction in the absence of supernatural power was reinforced; the apparent absence of mercy from the most compassionate and benevolent left me questioning why a harmless, happily married couple had to endure such suffering. It wasn't just my personal tribulations that led me to reject the notion of God's existence; rather, a profound examination of inequality in various aspects of life and the plight of innocent, helpless individuals solidified my belief that God is nothing more than a myth. My heart clenches as I think of children withering under diseases deemed incurable while others are born burdened by physical limitations. Their tiny, innocent dreams are crushed by whom and why? And what of the stark canvas of wealth disparity, where a few bask in gilded palaces while countless souls pick at the bones? If there truly was a benevolent creator, wouldn't HIS brushstrokes paint a world of fairness, a tapestry woven with compassion, not threads of suffering?

The emergence of religion and the concept of God likely stemmed from several interwoven desires. Early humans might have struggled to explain the vastness and complexities of the natural world: phenomena like thunder, illness, and death. The invention of God offered a comforting explanation, attributing these events to a higher power or deities. Belief in a Superpower could also provide purpose and meaning, fostering a sense of security and community. Another possibility is that religion served as a social glue, uniting people under shared values and rituals. The concept of a moral code handed down by a divine entity could promote cooperation and social order within a group.

The existence of numerous religions reflects the diversity of human experience and cultures. As societies developed in different environments, their explanations for the world around them diverged. Cultural factors, historical events, and influential figures all played a role in shaping specific belief systems. This rich tapestry of religions reflects the multifaceted human search for meaning and understanding of our place in the universe.

Earthquakes rend sleeping towns, tsunamis engulf dreams under walls of water, deadly viral diseases steal the light from innocent eyes, and tornadoes violently tear apart the futures of families, leaving devastation in their wake: all testimonies to power that, if aware, seem unmoved by our tears. If an all-loving God held the reins, wouldn't these calamities be mere whispers, not deafening screams echoing through the ages?

The concept of the intricate human body as a deliberate creation presents us with a deep-seated paradox. The pervasive presence of diseases suggests an evolutionary narrative, undermining the notion of meticulous divine craftsmanship. Instead of perfection, our bodies bear witness to vulnerability and imperfection. If we are indeed shaped by a divine hand, why are these inherent flaws not rectified? The harsh realities of chronic pain, mental torment, and terminal illnesses stand as stark refutations of a benevolent creator.

Then there's the Tower of Babel of belief, religions a kaleidoscope of conflicting colors, each claiming to hold the only truth. If divinity were singular, wouldn't its message resonate with unwavering clarity and not fracture into a cacophony of interpretations that fuels wars and hatred?

Science, the unwavering tide of reason, has continuously advanced into the realms of the unknown, steadily reducing the expanses of divine explanations. The resounding thunder, once considered a celestial drumbeat, has transformed into a lively dance of electrons. Healing miracles, formerly attributed to a higher power, now celebrate the brilliance of human ingenuity. Once veiled in the supernatural, the universe now resonates with the harmonious cadence of its intricate and awe-inspiring logic.

The concept of supernatural forces can be a comforting belief, offering solace in the face of mortality. The idea of an afterlife, especially a peaceful one, can ease the fear of the unknown. However, it's important to recognize that these ideas likely stem from a human desire for continuity and a lack of complete understanding of death. No scientific evidence supports the existence of an afterlife or supernatural beings. While religion can provide comfort, it's crucial to remember that death is likely the end of our conscious experience.

When I search for proof of this grand puppeteer, my hands grasp at empty air. I've been told that faith is its own proof: a heartfelt leap across the abyss of doubt. However, burdened by the harsh realities of pain and injustice, my heart cannot find comfort in blind leaps. It yearns for the firm foundation of facts and the rationality of cause and effect.

Tiny and alone, I stand on this spinning planet, lost in the vast silence of space. The universe plays out its story around me, a breathtaking display of stars and galaxies in constant motion. Does some all-powerful being control it all? Maybe not. Maybe the real beauty lies in the messy, amazing chaos, a universe unfolding without a script. And that's okay. In this incredible show without a plan, I find peace in not knowing the answers but asking endless questions myself.

As expected, the DNA results came back with a 99.9% match. Throughout the day, my thoughts raced, making it difficult to concentrate on work. Now, I have two moms: One biological and one fostered. The fostered one, Ridhi Ma'am, being more worldly-wise and astute, must be able to give valuable suggestions, as she's dealing day in and day out with highly complex issues. I spoke to her on the phone, proposing an evening meeting, and she agreed, suggesting we share a dinner together.

During the dinner, Ridhi Ma'am smilingly said, "Shoot."

I narrated the entire story and asked her opinion on whether I should stay with Mom or ask her to come and stay with me.

After a few moments, Mom shared her thoughts, "Why consider moving in with her or inviting her to stay with you? It could become inconvenient in the long run, and potential risks might be involved. Given that you're single, your mom is married, and she's not very old, her husband is likely around her age. This situation poses a potential threat to your modesty. Instead, I suggest visiting her as needed and offering your support whenever necessary. A few months ago, I contemplated inviting you to stay with me because the nights and weekends felt exceptionally lonely and, at times, even painful to endure. However, I refrained from doing so because I was dating a widower, an industrialist with a refined and cultured personality.

Nevertheless, we haven't formalized our commitment yet, and the delay is on my part. Given his wealth, I am cautious and have asked a private eye to check whether he is prone to infidelity or as disciplined and upright as he claims or displays. Having you stay with me could potentially complicate matters if I do decide to marry him, creating a situation where things could go awry, affecting us all and jeopardizing our relationships. Honey, take your time to reflect deeply, make a thoughtful decision, and know I'll support you regardless of your choice."

"Mom, I appreciate your insights. Those were my thoughts, and your perspective helped me clarify whether my fears were unfounded or had some basis," I said.

With a warm smile, Mom reassured me, saying, "No need for thanks or gratitude, and always remember, as long as I'm alive, this is your home. Whenever you need assistance, don't hesitate to walk in without an appointment, even wake me if I'm sleeping. I don't want to face Raj, my loving, caring, honest, and down-to-earth husband, and hear him complain that I haven't looked after his daughter. I hope he's remembering me from the tranquility of this vast cosmic setting."

While on the bed in the hypnagogic state of consciousness, I decided to withhold information about my upbringing with Maddy until he settled with his parents to test his moral values. Should he be a strong believer in revenge and retaliation, I must rethink my relationship with him. Consider this scenario: during a heated argument, your careless words inflict a deep wound he can't simply forgive or forget. Later, when you are vulnerable, he might strike back, seeking to avenge the pain you caused. While admirable qualities and friendly demeanors are important, staying clear of those who harbor vengeance can bring peace of mind. After all, it's better to be safe than sorry.

Rukhs Ma'am, my biological mother has invited me to dinner every evening, a gesture I've politely declined. However, I agreed to dine with her every Saturday.

The following Saturday, after having a lavish dinner with Rukhs Ma'am, which she must have procured from an upscale restaurant, we sat in the living room with our drinks.

Rukhs Ma'am opened the conversation and expressed, "Angie, my love, I wish to impart insights about your dad's and my family, education, marriage, and other occurrences that you could convey to your children." She then calmly began informing about her husband and his family, recounting her childhood journey to the present, detailing her parents, her brother, and the ancestors who migrated from Afghanistan. Upon completing her narration, she asked if there was anything else I wanted to know.

I replied, "Mom, I want to express my heartfelt gratitude for sharing your family's journeys with me. Your openness means a lot, and I truly appreciate it. While I don't have any specific questions at the moment, please know that I value this insight."

Rukhs Ma'am then sat beside me, clutching a stack of photo albums. She showed them one by one, along with details about each photograph, occasion, approximate year, and date of capture. Watching the family photos was captivating, and the images of my father and his parents stirred tears in my eyes. My dad resembled me; he was a tall, blond man with striking features that endowed him with a debonair charm. The photo that resonated with me the most featured him seated in a boat amidst the vast ocean, a close-up shot skillfully taken by Mom. He looked exceptionally handsome, dressed in a polo neck, light blue t-shirt, and white half-pants, and he was wearing a lovely dark blue aviator.

"Mom, can I take a few photos of you and Dad?" I requested.

"Honey, please take all the albums, as I believe you should have them and show them to your children. I still have a lot of albums that I'll show you when you spend a weekend with me," Mom said with a grin.

A few days later, Artikins Auntie invited me to have dinner with her at the weekend, and I agreed to come on Sunday night as Saturday was reserved for my mom.

Following dinner, we gathered in the TV lounge with our drinks, and Auntie initiated the conversation, sharing details about Maddy and how they definitively established that he was their son. Afterward, she shared the latest developments, including her discussion with Maddy and how it concluded.

I asked slowly in my usual subdued voice, "Auntie, what do you want from me?"

"I acknowledge the purely platonic nature of your relationship with Maddy, and I'm not asking you to exert any unwarranted pressure on him that could sever your bond. Nevertheless, please tactfully convince him that he is our baby and that we want to enjoy his presence in our lives. We haven't committed any wrongdoing; whatever has transpired in his life is part of his fate. Encourage him to empathize with the situation compassionately and logically, enabling him to recognize that we have borne a significant pain compared to his relatively brief suffering. Emphasize that we sacrificed the prime years of our lives, enduring hardships beyond his comprehension. Urge him to be with us, provide the comfort of his company, grant us precious moments to savor with our grandchildren, offer the solace of his presence as we traverse the challenges of advanced age, and accompany us to our final resting places. If he remains resentful, counsel him to at least embrace the joys of life, seek a loving partner, and raise lovely children like him. Advise him against harboring bitterness, emphasizing the importance of not denying himself the rich and meaningful experience of family life. Reassure him that his financial prosperity easily makes him an appealing partner, and should he wish to fulfill any worldly desires, we stand ready to provide the means to achieve his wants," Auntie conveyed solemnly.

After thoughtfully considering Auntie's remarks, I responded with my customary composure: "Auntie, you can be certain that I will make every effort to ensure that your son understands the truth and adheres to every wish you have expressed. Notwithstanding this, it is undeniable that he exhibits persistence in his convictions; thus, my endeavors to alter his perspective might prove futile."

Auntie stressed, "Darling, we realize that we might be tasking you with breaking through an insurmountable steel barrier, yet attempting it won't harm any of us. Therefore, give it your utmost effort and entrust the outcome to the hands of our Creator."

"Auntie, rest assured that I will exert every effort to help him comprehend that life has no place for vengeance, hatred, or contempt. Especially when it concerns his biological parents, who endured more than he can imagine, he should approach them with compassion and humility," I sincerely conveyed.

"Thank you, my love. If your efforts prove successful, my eternal gratitude will be yours. I wish for our son to remain with us, giving us a chance to relish the remaining few years of our lives," Auntie implored with tear-filled eyes.

"Auntie, please wish me luck; if I succeed, my happiness will surpass anyone else's," I conveyed and took permission to leave.

Over the next three days, I thoroughly deliberated on the most effective way to address the situation. Maddy's unwavering commitment to his principles is indeed commendable. Yet, this unyielding trait makes it almost inevitable that any attempt to redirect him will likely fail, and failure could jeopardize our relationship. By the fourth day, my mind was on the brink of exhaustion from constant contemplation. I decided that my strategy needed to shift towards collaboration rather than persuasion to achieve a harmonious resolution. I envisioned a constructive dialogue akin to two climbers working in tandem to conquer a challenging peak, mutually motivating each other to reach the peak.

I called him to join me for dinner at my home around seven, expressing the need to discuss an important matter. He readily agreed and suggested sending dinner from one of his restaurants. Gratefully, I declined his offer. I was fortunate to have a remarkable female chef with outstanding culinary expertise. Her innovative approach crafts delicious, healthy meals that rival the gourmet quality of upscale restaurants. She does not rely on the usual butter, cream, or cashew paste crutches to achieve richness in her curries.

Maddy arrived promptly at seven, carrying a bouquet of red roses and a box with a variety of desserts prepared in one of his restaurants. I inquired about his dinner time, and he informed me that anytime after eight would suit him. After providing instructions to one of my domestic helpers, I escorted him to the TV lounge.

Without any formalities, I dove right in, saying, "Maddy, like you, I'm also in a fix." I then narrated about my upbringing and Rukhs Auntie, how I met with her, and what followed.

"The current situation is that the DNA test has confirmed Auntie as my biological mother. She has shared numerous photos from her marriage to my American biological father, Daniel Theo, who bears a resemblance to me with blond hair and blue eyes, evident in our facial structure and build.

"Now that it's conclusively proven that Auntie is my mom, I'm at a loss on how to proceed. As we find ourselves in a similar situation, I seek your guidance on navigating this path. Despite my previous appeal for understanding and compassion, urging you to consider your parents' pleas, I must confess that, even though I strive to embody the ideal traits of a compassionate human being, I have been unable to find even a minute trace of love for my biological mom. Moreover, I do not discern any practical need for her presence in my life. Her wealth holds little significance to me, considering I'm already among the super-rich category. The wealth I possess is merely a number devoid of any pleasure or value, so any addition to numbers is of no significance. In the absence of a love quotient, my biggest challenge is how I could treat an old lady with love and care," I stated with the intention of getting him into the net where he won't have a chance to come out without softening his stance towards his biological parents.

After a few minutes pause, Maddy spoke, "Angie Ma'am, could we have dinner now? We'll continue our discussion over a hot cup of coffee."

Following the meal, we settled in the TV lounge, where we were served steaming Ethiopian Yirgacheffe coffee. The instant Maddy took a sip, he expressed gratitude for my thoughtful gesture of remembering and serving his favorite coffee.

Following a prolonged silence, Maddy took the lead in the conversation. He expressed, "I'm wrestling with the dilemma of choosing a path forward that won't burden me with regrets in my later years. As I contemplate my final moments on my deathbed, tallying the days spent in this fleeting world, I want to avoid the haunting regret of having denied my parents the simple pleasure of my presence in their lives, questioning what I truly gained by withholding this from them.

"I should be grateful to them for bringing me into this world and giving me their traits to fight out and achieve my dreams. It wasn't their fault; they were victims of circumstances. I must acknowledge that Dad remained unmarried, proving his love for his beloved wife, and Mom was compelled into marriage but had the courage to divorce and return. Following her return, she established several institutions in her husband's name as a testament to her love. I must commend her for undertaking such an immense project. However, similar to your situation, I don't hold any affection for my parents, and I'm struggling to shake off the intense hatred I feel towards them. That's precisely why I sought your guidance in navigating this complex situation. Given the circumstances, tell me what you intend to do with your mother, and if I disagree, I'll offer my perspective on what you should do."

Maddy deftly handed me the responsibility, displaying a clever maneuver.

"Maddy, I've developed a profound sympathy for my mom. Losing her beloved husband just four months into their marriage led to years of grieving, not only for him but also for me. Despite marrying again under her father's pressure, the longing for her first husband persists, and it seems destined to stay with her until her last breath. While I acknowledge my suffering as part of my journey, and as you don't feel love for your parents, I also don't feel any love for her, nor does it seem likely to develop. The question then becomes, how can I genuinely treat her as my mom without that essential element of love? Despite lacking this affection, my intention is to wholeheartedly dedicate myself to her happiness if I can somehow overcome this love factor. An argument in her favor could be that she carried me in her womb for nine months and delivered me as a healthy baby. However, this rationale falls short, as every mother delivers their babies. The critical factor lies in raising a baby with love and care, which naturally fosters a deep-seated bond. Consequently, I find myself back at square one, grappling with how to overcome the absence of love," I calmly expressed. I threw the ball in his court as he smartly sought to comprehend my standpoint.

"Angie Ma'am, my immediate response to Mom's slap was both infuriating and hurtful. Afterward, I battled a whirlwind of feelings, holding onto resentment and unleashing curses upon her for what I interpreted as a terrible action. However, as time passed, I began to see the deeper meaning behind that slap: a symbolic assertion of her ownership and a form of correction for my irresponsible behavior. This realization led me to acknowledge a peculiar fondness for her, albeit not quite fitting into the conventional definition of love, but an appreciation for her authority to take charge and correct me when needed.

"Angie Ma'am, the source of my resentment lies in a profound aversion for not having them in my life. Even after discovering them, my animosity persists because it came too late. The void they left during my upbringing led me to curse them for what felt like abandonment. Now, in a phase of stability where I no longer depend on them, they've appeared, sharing stories of suffering. Nevertheless, it does little to ease my lasting disdain towards them. Strangely, I feel an urge to be with them, care for them, provide for them, and take them on luxurious vacations. I seek your guidance to make a decision that I won't regret now or in the future," Maddy expressed, earnestly requesting help in navigating his conflicted emotions.

I thought his stand had softened, and he needed a strong push to surrender to his parents' wishes.

"Maddy, your contemplation on the emotions we might experience on our deathbed, reflecting on the treatment we gave our parents, has certainly resonated with me. I believe avoiding such profound regret is crucial. If you assure me that my suggestion won't provoke annoyance or upset you, I'd like to share my thoughts on what we should do," I conveyed.

"Angie Ma'am, even if I don't agree with your suggestion, I want to assure you that getting annoyed or upset with you will never happen, not now and not in the future, as long as I'm alive and in my senses. Please offer any suggestions you believe will grant us peace of mind, ensuring that we can reflect on our decision without any lingering regrets," Maddy earnestly conveyed.

"Before I answer, I'd like to share my approach to tackling obstacles and maintaining a positive outlook. Focusing on the silver lining in others, even in the hardest times, is more rewarding than getting stuck in negativity or wanting to get even. Throughout my journey, whether in the orphanage, at college, or leading my company, I've always strived to approach challenges with patience, compassion, and empathy. Instead of reacting with hostility, I've chosen to ignore provocateurs and invested effort in assisting those in need within my means.

"I've always held a positive outlook on life, as I believe it preserves the best in us. My mother wasn't responsible for the hardships I faced; they were mine to overcome. However, overcoming those hurdles, with the help of a kind soul, deepened my appreciation for empathy and compassion. The woman who carried me for nine months and mourned for years for me deserves my understanding. Therefore, I've decided to fully accept her back into my life and maintain a connection with her as long as we both are alive. While living with her isn't ideal due to her husband's presence, I don't want to neglect the woman who gave me life and allowed me to encounter wonderful people like my Papa, Ridhi Ma'am, and a few others.

"I strongly urge you to embrace positivity, as it can significantly shape how you approach tribulations and maintain your wonderful personality. Similar to me, consider accepting your folks, staying with them, and enriching their lives with the pleasure of your presence. Holding them responsible for your suffering is unwarranted; instead, be grateful for inheriting their genes, which have played a crucial role in shaping you into the successful entrepreneur you are today. It's essential to recognize that they endured more hardships than you; they sacrificed their youth in dire miseries," I asserted firmly, hoping he would take my suggestion to heart.

"Angie Ma'am, I acknowledge every word you've shared. However, my profound resentment prevents me from getting close to them or establishing a bond of respect, let alone love. Like you, I consider myself a good person, a sentiment validated by my interactions with staff, suppliers, customers, and anyone who has crossed paths with me. I refrain from disrespecting or causing physical or emotional harm to anyone. I carefully choose my words and maintain a safe distance to prevent any potential hurt.

"The pain inflicted by my biological parents is so intense that, since reconnecting with them, I have been unable to sleep properly, even for a single night. While I empathize with their misfortune, it does not lessen my own suffering. I suffered and persevered, and just as my life improved, they entered it, presenting a heart-wrenching story. Angie Ma'am, I cannot overcome my pain if I see them, so I prefer to keep a distance. I don't wish to further mistreat them beyond what I've already done, and I've faced consequences for it. However, my lingering hatred is so overwhelming that I fear I may not control my frustrations and say things I never intended. Please forgive me, if you can, for not following your suggestion," Maddy expressed, his voice reflecting his profound pain.

"Maddy, I'm disappointed. Rising above feelings of vengeance, hatred, and anger is crucial. Holding onto such emotions for even one person can overshadow all your good deeds, making you less virtuous. Nonetheless, you've taken a firm stance, signaling your inflexibility, and I won't continue to persuade you any further on this matter. If you have questions or wish to discuss anything unrelated to your parents, feel free to let me know. Otherwise, it's time to rest," I conveyed in my usual calm tone, but the disappointment in my message must have been apparent to him.

"Alright, I'll take off now. Thanks for the lovely dinner. Hopefully, we'll talk in a couple of days. Good night," Maddy said, his expression indicating unhappiness.

For the following ten days, I maintained radio silence with Maddy. Whenever he messaged me, I politely declined, saying I was unavailable to talk. Then, on Sunday late afternoon, as I was preparing to head for dinner at Artikins Auntie's place, the guard at the compound gate informed me that Mr. Mahendra Reddy wished to see me. I permitted to let him in.

Maddy arrived with a large bouquet of red roses and a cake from a renowned bakery. He humbly asked me to open the box. The cake had a message inscribed on it: "Sorry if I offended you."

My gaze lingered on him, and with measured words, I responded, "Maddy, while I appreciate the gesture, I must confess your attitude deeply disturbed me. Your approach to conflict, specifically seeking vengeance and punishment, runs counter to my core values. As such, I'm afraid a relationship with you, in any capacity, is untenable."

"Angie, Ma'am, I plead with you not to put me through this. Your friendship means the world to me, and I fear I won't be able to survive without it. I am making a heartfelt effort to overcome the hatred that has deeply settled in me since the day I first realized it. Despite my efforts to leave the past behind and embrace a new chapter filled with love and care for my parents, the wounds persist, and all my attempts to remove them are failing. I won't lie; it's a real struggle, but I'm fully committed to putting the past behind me and forging ahead with nothing but love and respect for my parents. I know healing takes time, and I'm determined to put in the effort to become a better version of myself," Maddy expressed, his voice resonating with genuine anguish.

His words stirred concern within me. If he's expressing genuine feelings, the situation might be difficult. I wanted to help him overcome the challenges he was facing.

He didn't say anything, and I left him alone as I thought hard about how to help him with his problem. Taking him to a shrink might hurt his feelings and not work well.

I mulled it over for a bit. Then, after some calm thinking, I opened the conversation and expressed, "Maddy, please come with me to have dinner at Artikin Auntie's home, with one condition: that you would maintain silence, even if your parents become bothersome. If feasible, I encourage you to be affable, delve into social or business topics, or enjoy your meal without actively participating in the conversation. This approach will help us ensure the evening ends smoothly, free from any unpleasantness."

"Angie Ma'am, though I'm not eager to meet, if you insist, I won't refuse and will adhere to your dictate," Maddy acquiescently expressed.

"Okay, give me a few minutes to get ready. You could watch TV or read any magazine or newspaper," I informed him, then walked out of the lounge.

Upon entering my bedroom, I phoned Artikins Auntie and told her, "Auntie, I'll bring your son for dinner. Although he was hesitant at first, I managed to convince him. Therefore, please steer clear of any controversial subjects. Extend a warm welcome to him, and let's create a pleasant atmosphere for dinner. Your son is facing hurdles that won't be swiftly overcome or resolved in a short span of time. However, he has assured me of his commitment to instigate the necessary changes so he could treat his parents with respect and care. I'll provide my support in every way to help him overcome these difficulties sooner rather than later."

Auntie expressed gratitude for my assistance, and I disconnected the call with a "See you in a while."

Auntie and Uncle greeted us with warmth. Auntie embraced me first and then smilingly instructed her son to give her a bear hug, playfully adding that he might get another slap if he didn't comply. I burst into laughter, making it clear that it was all in good humor, and Uncle very smartly joined me and laughed aloud. Auntie then affectionately held Maddy in her arms, shedding tears and sniffling. Amidst this emotional moment, I overheard Maddy reassuring her, saying, "Please don't cry; I've come to see you." Interestingly, he didn't refer to her as 'mom.'

As we moved toward the dining table, Uncle gestured for me to join him while Auntie ushered Maddy opposite us, choosing the seat beside him. Brimming with enthusiasm, Uncle piled my plate high with food while Auntie lovingly served her son every dish on the table. With a gentle smile, Maddy politely interjected, "Thank you, but I'd prefer a lighter dinner at night, or else I won't be able to sleep with a bloated tummy."

During the bites, Uncle did most of the talking. First, he asked me about my business, which was on the rise since Ridhi Ma'am bought a 49% stake in the company and constantly pushed me to bid for government and large private sector projects. At the moment, my company is executing approximately forty thousand crores worth of projects. My staff strength has gone up to two hundred in-house professionals and hundreds of sub-contractors. However, I did not provide such specifics about my business. Instead, I informed him it's keeping me engaged for ten to twelve hours, six days a week.

Shifting the conversation to Maddy, Uncle inquired about his business. Maddy provided an equally vague response, expressing satisfaction with its operations. However, he hinted at an upcoming venture: a new fine-dining outlet set to open in a three-story building. The ground floor will feature a chat buffet, a unique concept not available anywhere else in the city. The second floor will be dedicated to pure vegetarian options, while the top floor will serve both vegetarian and non-vegetarian dishes. Additionally, every floor will have its own kitchen facilities, eliminating any potential complaints about using shared oil for frying both non-vegetarian and vegetarian dishes or utensils, plates, and so on.

After dessert and coffee, we left, and I thanked Maddy when we came out for not raising any issues that could have disturbed everyone.

My telephone conversation with Maddy resumed. In our initial discussion, he revealed that the lingering resentment situation remained unchanged. Although he acknowledged his pleasant dinner experience and recognized them as wonderful people, his mind struggled to embrace the idea of letting bygones be bygones. I suggested dedicating Saturday and Sunday evenings for dinner with both my biological mom and his parents. Despite his initial reluctance due to business obligations, I firmly rejected his excuses, and ultimately, he committed to my suggestion. I even took him for dinner at Ridhi Ma'am's house one evening. As we were leaving, she whispered in my ear, "Nice choice. Don't let him slip away, babe."

Our weekly dinners with my mom and Maddy's parents proceeded without any hitches. However, Maddy remained steadfast, repeatedly expressing his inability to overcome a deep-rooted aversion towards his parents despite acknowledging them as good humans. Handling this situation posed a challenge for me; on the one hand, I was keen on preserving our friendship and even considering taking it to the next level. On the other hand, his behavior was causing a growing sense of uneasiness within me.

One day, amid our usual conversation, I unexpectedly voiced my thoughts in a somewhat stern tone to Maddy, saying, "Maddy, over the past couple of months, I've earnestly tried to convey that harboring contempt, especially towards your parents, who brought you into this world, is not a healthy mindset. They are victims of circumstances and bear no responsibility for your misfortunes. Count yourself fortunate that you were not born into a household of illiterate parents and numerous siblings, mired in abject poverty and devoid of wealth and basic sustenance.

"Your stubborn stance is causing me to reassess our relationship. Tomorrow, an unintentional action on my part could be misinterpreted, leading to irreparable damage to our bond. I think it's best not to maintain any connection with someone who harbors unforgiving and vengeful sentiments. So, farewell, and please refrain from reaching out to me again."

"Please, don't hang up. Allow me a moment to express the internal struggles I'm facing. Every day, I battle with myself, trying to overcome these intense emotions, but I feel lost. I desperately need your guidance and any suggestions you might have to resolve this abnormal situation, which is causing more pain than you can imagine. If you think seeing a therapist would help, I am more than willing to do that, or I'm open to any other steps you believe would make you happy. Angie Ma'am, I implore you not to punish me for something that feels beyond my control. Losing your friendship would be akin to a death sentence to me. Please, don't let that happen, and help me through this," Maddy pleaded, his voice reflecting genuine pain and desperation.

I suggested, "I truly believe you should see a psychiatrist, and if you'd like, I can help you find a highly reputable professional."

"I truly appreciate your assistance, but please, I beg you, never bring up the idea of ending our friendship again," Maddy pleaded.

"Alright, I'll get back to you as soon as possible. Goodnight," I replied, disconnecting the line to conclude the conversation.

With Ridhi Ma'am's help, I obtained an appointment with a renowned psychiatrist despite being fully booked for the next six months. He graciously agreed to a few sessions at six in the morning. He has a UK MRCPsych degree and has been practicing in the city for two decades.

I accompanied Maddy to the psychiatrist for the first session, confidentially briefing the doctor on his crisis. I also instructed the psychiatrist to send me the treatment invoice and keep me informed about Maddy's progress.

After the session, while heading back, Maddy shared that he had paid the doctor's fee using his Platinum Medical Insurance Cover, which provides coverage for all medical treatments, including psychiatric care.

After three sessions, I inquired about the progress with the therapist. He shared, "I'm facing challenges in persuading him to overlook his aversion towards the individuals who brought him into the world. His stance is that, although they are wonderful people, they cannot absolve themselves of the irresponsible act. He questions why they hastily married without parental consent and argues they could have waited a few more months to go to the USA. Once there, no one would have hindered their marriage. He acknowledges that humans make mistakes and make decisions without weighing the consequences, especially when they are young. That's precisely what they did, leading to his suffering and enduring hardships for over two decades. He believes there's no merit in maintaining any relationship with such individuals. I'm working to diminish the ingrained hatred, but success is uncertain. I plan to conduct three more weekly sessions before deciding whether to continue or discontinue. It's important to note that he's young, physically and mentally robust, and affluent. Individuals with these attributes are not easily swayed."

During our subsequent nightly phone conversation, I expressed my dissatisfaction with Maddy's persistent attitude toward the psychiatrist. I questioned the purpose of continuing if he wasn't willing to follow the shrink's advice, and I suggested parting ways for our own happiness. In reply, Maddy beseeched me, assuring me that he was working hard to convince himself of the doctor's arguments. He hoped that within the next three sessions, he would succeed in changing his perspective. Reluctantly, I agreed to give him another three weeks.

After three weeks had elapsed, I received disheartening news from the doctor stating that Maddy's condition was incurable and investing more time in his treatment would be futile. Instead of directly conversing with Maddy, I opted to communicate the psychiatrist's remarks through a message. I also informed him in that message about not meeting or calling me again.

Over the following two months, he persistently tried to contact me, but I deliberately disregarded all his efforts. Despite sitting in my office for hours in hopes of a few minutes of my time, I remained steadfast in my refusal. Even when he visited my compound, I explicitly instructed the guards to deny him entry. Dealing with such a stubborn and headstrong person is nothing short of inviting trouble, and I chose to distance myself from him.

In the third month, he altered his position and sent a message assuring me that he would adhere to all my instructions without any preconditions or reservations. Despite his claim, I remained skeptical and chose to ignore his message. He persisted in sending messages, urging me to meet with him just once. However, I remained resolute, choosing not to respond to any of his messages or grant him access to see me. I don't know why, but I just never got around to blocking his number, even though I kept telling myself I should.

Toward the end of the fourth month, the receptionist informed me that Maddy was waiting in the reception area and wished to meet for a few minutes. Instructing the receptionist to have him wait, I promised to meet him when I had a free moment. Seeking to put an end to his persistent messages and visits, I decided to meet with him. After two hours, I asked the receptionist to send him to my office if he was still waiting.

The receptionist, accompanied by Maddy, knocked and entered the room. Despite wearing well-pressed formals, he appeared disheveled. He had a few days of stubble, dark circles under his eyes, and noticeable weight loss reflected in shrunken cheeks. His uncombed and brittle hair indicated the need for a haircut.

Upon the receptionist's departure, I confronted him immediately, "Why are you stalking me? I explicitly conveyed my desire not to see you. Your messages and unwelcome appearances at my workplace and home are unacceptable. If you continue to contact me or show up at my office or residence, I will report you to the police, and you can expect a lengthy stay behind bars."

"Angie Ma'am, my world feels hollow and consumed by sorrow without you. I'd do anything for you except face the pain of staying with my parents," Maddy declared passionately.

"There's no room for negotiations: it's either my way or the highway. You must accept your parents and permanently relocate to their house within ten days. Flexibility is non-negotiable, and I won't entertain any further requests for reconsideration," I firmly asserted.

"Fine, I'll agree to whatever you propose, but with a single condition. Grant me just one wish, and I'll be indebted to you for the rest of my life. I'll do anything and everything you ask for as long as I'm alive," Maddy stated in a hushed tone.

"What wish, and why should I grant it? I've made it clear that nothing is negotiable. Follow my instructions to preserve our friendship, or else it's time for you to part ways and never approach me again," I stated firmly.

"Angie Ma'am, I wouldn't ask for anything beyond your means, and neither will I endanger your well-being. I'm truly confident that my request, which I'll share upon moving into my parents house, will benefit all of us. Please, don't say no," Maddy pleaded.

"Okay, one wish, and don't seek my hand, leg, or life, as I don't consider your friendship worth that much," I firmly declared.

"Thank you very much, and sorry for taking so much of your precious time. Can we resume our weekly calls, as the lack of them has created a huge vacuum in me, causing insomnia?" Maddy expressed with teary eyes.

"No calls, just message me if you need to convey anything." I was harsh, but what should I do? The idiot left me no choice but to express my frustration.

Halfway through the week, a message from Maddy popped up on my phone. He wanted to know if he could tag along for the usual Sunday dinner at my Aunt Artkins's house. He even offered to pick me up! I sent a quick reply letting him know that picking me up wasn't necessary, but I was happy he was coming.

On Sunday, I arrived at Auntie's house around nine, a bit later than the usual time of around eight-thirty, as a brief nap unexpectedly extended to almost two hours. The quick bath and dressing-up took an additional hour, and the travel time was exceeded due to heavy traffic. Before I reached the destination, Auntie called, mentioning that dinner was cooling down, and I informed her I was in a traffic jam.

Upon arriving at Auntie's house, I noticed Ridhi Ma'am's security guards, her bulletproof Rolls-Royce, and Rukhs mom's BMW. Pondering how they came to be acquainted and what prompted their participation in the dinner, I found the situation rather perplexing.

Upon entering the house, another notable detail that caught my attention was the hall adorned with string lights, fairy lights, and color-changing lanterns, among other decorations. The festive atmosphere and the unexpected presence of my two mothers seemed peculiar. However, I opted to keep quiet until someone informed me of the occasion and the reasons behind all these people's presence.

Everyone, including Raees Uncle and Maddy, welcomed me with hugs and blessings as I entered the TV lounge. Ridhi Ma'am took my hand and seated me beside her on the two-seater sofa.

We were all served assorted fresh juices amidst sips; Aunt Artikins declared, "My son has something to say; please lend him your ears."

All eyes turned to Maddy, who stood up slowly and spoke in a composed tone, "Firstly, I'd like to express my gratitude to Ridhi Ma'am, Rukhs auntie, and Raees uncle for joining us on such short notice. Over the past few months, I've been tackling a situation that seemed insurmountable despite my best efforts.

"Embedded within me like unyielding shadows, the struggles of my impoverished upbringing in a village orphanage persisted relentlessly, holding me back from enjoying a lovely family life with my parents. Angie Ma'am, she's been my guiding star through all the rough tides, offering me support and wisdom that was worth more than any treasure. She was my rock, always reminding me that my parents were the real heroes behind my success and that getting hung up on the hardships of my childhood wouldn't do me any good. She kept urging me to be with my parents and give them the pleasure they were seeking. Nevertheless, the raw pain of past hurts throbbed with an acute intensity, hindering my complete embrace of her comforting words. In a final effort to address my troubling behavior, Angie Ma'am took me to a therapist. Even after several hourly sessions, the therapist couldn't succeed in mending the cracks in me. Desperate for healing and the ability to absorb Angie Ma'am's wisdom, I faced an arduous and elusive journey. Angie Ma'am's frustration and disillusionment led to a withdrawal from our connection. Accusing me of vengefulness and obstinacy, she deemed it wiser to distance herself from a person like me: a painful characterization, as never before had such words been used to describe me.

"Four months passed in the absence of Angie Ma'am's presence. The warmth of her counsel, once a constant in my life, had become a cherished memory, replaced by a chilling silence. I felt adrift, a castaway on an emotional island, stripped of the compass of guidance and the anchor of connection she once provided. Like a ragpicker, I scavenged through the remnants of our past conversations, desperately seeking solace in the echoes of her wisdom. The world seemed to lose its vibrancy, painted in shades of loneliness as I traversed the treacherous terrain of life without her by my side.

"I found myself constantly plagued by disruptions and discomfort, which diverted my focus from my professional endeavors. Angie Ma'am and the therapist emphasized that if I had been raised in luxury, I might have been prone to pursuing fleeting pleasures, risking my life for indulgences that have a limited shelf life.

"Unfortunately, I also forgot a piece of wisdom shared by the head of my orphanage and my foster father: never let my circumstances define my worth. Instead, I should view them as opportunities to learn and grow, like gold that is refined through intense heat and becomes truly brilliant only after constant hammering and polishing. Had I embraced the teachings imparted by my mentors, the weight of my past tribulations wouldn't have felt so devastating, and I shouldn't have permitted bitterness to infiltrate my heart like a piercing dagger.

"Shame washes over me as I remember my initial interactions with my parents, which were tainted by bitterness and fueled by my indignation. My actions, born from a warped perception, cause me immense regret. Looking back, I recognize the irony: someone who believed so deeply in compassion and empathy and strived to live a life free of ego and comparisons fell short in overcoming the hurdles of his own past.

"Blinded by my own narrative, I failed to acknowledge the complexities of my parents' roles. I held them solely responsible for the hardships I faced, labeling them as the architects of my misfortune. In my self-righteousness, I refused to acknowledge the possibility that my struggles might have been, as Angie Ma'am had tried to explain, a part of my journey, not a personal vendetta orchestrated by my own parents.

"The truth, which eluded me then, was that they, too, were human. They carried their own burdens and likely faced immense struggles in their earlier years. It's a perspective I failed to grasp, absorbed in my own self-centered world. Instead of recognizing their humanity and fallibility, I depicted them as antagonists in my personal story. Any mistakes they made, any shortcomings they exhibited, were not seen as missteps of young, imperfect humans but as calculated acts of cruelty. This distorted perception fueled resentment and animosity, leading to behavior that I now deeply regret.

"I was addicted to my friendship with Angie Ma'am so much that it became impossible for me to survive without her presence in my life. I stopped self-care, eating, or exercising, which resulted in looking like a zombie walking around.

"I made numerous attempts to reach out and connect with Angie Ma'am, all of which ended in failure. After a strenuous four-month struggle, I finally managed to meet with her in her office, sincerely persuading her that I was prepared to comply with her guidance, except for staying with my parents. However, she remained unyielding in her stance, showing no inclination to give any ground. Confronted with this deadlock, I conceded to fulfill all of her demands on the condition that she granted me one wish in return.

"She agreed, under the condition that I wouldn't request her life, or an arm or a leg, deeming such sacrifices unwarranted for someone of my stature. However, she gave me a mere ten days to diligently adhere to her instructions, with the clear implication that failure to do so would result in a permanent parting. The agreement to fulfill my wish worked so effectively that it swiftly erased all my past sufferings, instilling within me an immense love for my parents. Without the formality of an appointment from Mom and Dad, I assertively entered their home straight from Angie Ma'am's office. They welcomed me, and I asked for their forgiveness for my prior inappropriate behavior. I touched their feet and solemnly promised never to misbehave as long as I lived. Subsequently, ignoring their half-hearted protests about needing to change, I whisked them away in their comfy clothes and took them to my house so that mom could make similar arrangements for me in her house: my office, gym, bedroom, and so on.

"Angie, Ma'am, I moved into this palatial villa two days ago. I must be grateful to you as long as I'm alive for guiding me on the path of absolute happiness. Since I moved here, I've witnessed how wonderful it was to be with your parents. Thank you, Angie Ma'am, from the bottom of my heart. Now it's time to ask you to fulfill my wish, but before that, I request my mom to say a few words." The room fell into complete silence until Ridhi Ma'am broke it with applause, and soon everyone joined in.

Once the noise settled, Aunt Artikins, without standing, first cleared her throat and then slowly but firmly started expressing, "I don't want to share my journey, as it would only spoil this wonderful evening. However, allow me to tell you that my one slip created all this mess, and I paid a heavy price for that. I was insecure and didn't want my husband to go to the USA without marrying me. I was so consumed by my insecurities that I didn't see the consequences coming, which led to losing my husband and my son. I was young, intelligent, and a go-getter, and to top it all, I had built-in confidence that I could achieve whatever I wanted. But as we all know, life is full of surprises, and that's exactly what happened to me. In the US, I married a compromised person because of the pressure I was under from my mom. After the death of my mom, I decided to return to India, as my father, who invested many decades ago a few million dollars, turned into unimaginable wealth, and this piece of sixty acres of land that we failed to sell prior to going to the USA turned into a gold mine. With the help of Angie, I constructed various institutions in memory of my husband, whom I thought I had lost for good. Luckily, one day, he showed up, and we remarried. I forced him to resign from his job and stay with me.

While I was hunting for a catering company that could run our canteens and cater to hospital, senior citizens, and orphanage, Angie introduced me to my son, Mahendra Reddy.

"Maddy's initial behavior, full of scorn and rejection, was not unexpected since he was a successful businessman running a high-end and low-end chain of restaurants, earning excellent money. We thought the son we found was lost again, and there was no hope of getting him back and enjoying our last leg of the journey playing with his children.

"I must thank Angie, as she didn't give up and did what she could to make him understand that we all were victims of circumstances that were beyond our control. Thank you is a small word to say to Angie. Anyhow, we have plans to express our thanks in a different way. By the way, my husband, Samuel Thomas, has a doctorate in Aeronautics Engineering. After getting his degree, he worked in the UK for Airbus company, and he's still employed by them and working from here. Now, I'll ask my son to express his wish to Angie."

Maddy rose from his seat, holding a long stem rose in his right hand and a small jewelry box in his left hand. He came to me, bent on one knee, and said, "Angie Ma'am, please grant my wish that I nurtured from the day I saw you. I was cautious of my background and thought you were rich, educated, and wealthy, so why should you marry me? But since the day I saw you, I haven't slept without talking to your photo. I vow to care for you and stand by you through life's challenges, giving you my unwavering support and treating you with love and respect until my last breath. Angie Ma'am, please do me the honor of marrying me."

I looked at him for a couple of minutes, and then I addressed my moms, asking them to tell me, "Do you think I should marry this vengeful and obstinate man? I don't want to unless you insist and provide me with valid reasons."

First, Ridhi Ma'am said, "Try him for a couple of years, or else you could replace him with a better option. You're loaded with money, so no pressure to stay with him."

Everyone laughed aloud and chanted try him out. I then turned to Rukhs mom, and she said, "Nothing is better than a loving and caring man, and I believe he's the right person for you. I particularly admire his qualities, such as being self-taught and building his empire with hard work, diligence, and honesty. A big yes from me, and I totally agree with Ridhi Ma'am; you can ditch him if he's not up to snuff!"

Again, everyone laughed and chanted, say yes, say yes.

"Okay, I'll take a chance on you, but remember, showing me your love is a daily grind. If you can't step up to the plate, I'll be out of your life before you know it, following my mothers' advice," I remarked with a smile, eliciting laughter from everyone.

"Angie Ma'am, I guarantee you, you'll never look back on this decision. I'll forever treasure the privilege of being your husband," Maddy declared, his grin stretching from ear to ear.

I extended my hand with a smile, and he gently slipped a three-carat diamond ring embellished with smaller diamonds onto my finger.

END

www.ingramcontent.com/pod-product-compliance
Lightning Source LLC
LaVergne TN
LVHW091623070526
838199LV00044B/906